Iridescence

Speculative Fiction and Poetry Featuring Black, Indigenous, and People of Color

Edited by Monique Franz

KINSMAN AVENUE PUBLISHING, INC.
www.kinsmanquarterly.org

Registered with the U.S. Library of Congress

Printed in the United States of America

Iridescence: Speculative Fiction and Poetry Featuring Black, Indigenous, and People of Color

Cover Design by Summer Greigh

Senior Editor & Design: Monique Franz
Co-Editors: Sandhya Barlaas, Radiyah Nouman, and Sophia O. Ofuokwu

Contributing authors: (top winners) E. Doyle-Gillespie, Christina Tang-Bernas, Nicholas Samuel Stember

(finalists) Adrian Hayes, Akupue Chukwuemeka, Anna Kristo, Ann Yuan, D. M. Cross, D'Marcus Beatty, DW, Dee Mainali, Douglas Perenara Johnston, G. R. Betancourt, Gaazal Dhungana, Grace Aliyu, Ihsan Sim, Jack Wolflink, Jasmine Harrell, Joseph Marcel Ikhenoba, Klarissa Conner, Liz Johnston, Lindsey Woodward, Marcelo Moreira, Michelle Ivy Alwedo, Micah Stanton, Odette Cortés, Olugbenga Ayodeji Ayo-Daniel, Rohit Das, Sandhya Barlaas, Shantell Powell, Shenali Wijesinghe, Shilpa Kamat, Solape Adeyemi, Stephanie Chiedo, Stingray Hopper, & Victoria Sosa.

Iridescence

Speculative Fiction and Poetry Featuring Black, Indigenous, and People of Color

Edited by Monique Franz

Every story begins with a spark, and every spark needs those who fan the flame. With heartfelt gratitude, we recognize our

Honorary Supporters

Alicia Green

Allison Giordano

Anesha Grant

Beth Swallow

Cyril April Keyes

Domingo Arnaiz

Dr. Celina A. Ponce

Joyce Larkin

Kathy Bradley-Wells

L. John Swallow Jr.

Lindsey Woodward

Louis Swallow SR

Mayari A

Mildred Mills

Phil Torrejon

Simone Elizabeth

Stephanie J Maass

Stephen Swallow

Tracy Drayton

Wraithmarked Creative

Editor's Note

On October 31, 2023, Kinsman Quarterly opened the submission gates to the *Iridescence Award,* our first writing contest for speculative fiction and poetry. The name Iridescence struck us as a perfect contest name because the word iridescence is more of a phenomenon than a color. It's a spectrum of colors with a kiss of magic—the cultural essence we hoped to gain from the entries.

We expected that our call for themes of the magical, supernatural, paranormal, and science fiction would ignite excitement, and we were right. Although we were an infant literary journal, we were absolutely floored to receive 757 submissions from 75 nations around the globe. The sheer quality and diversity of the entries were nothing short of astounding, making the task of selecting winners incredibly challenging for our review team.

Choosing just three winners and twelve finalists from such an extraordinary pool of talent felt nearly impossible. Each piece we read had its own unique voice and perspective, showcasing the vibrant tapestry of stories and experiences from BIPOC communities worldwide. Our team dedicated countless hours to carefully reviewing and deliberating over each submission, striving to honor the exceptional work presented to us. Eventually, we managed to narrow it down to a list that we believe represents the best of the best. So, we are proud to present to you a book of speculative culture from the four corners of the world.

— Monique Franz, Senior Editor

Fantasy

Science Fiction

Dystopian Sci-Fi

Metaphysical Sci-Fi

Speculative Poetry

Historical Mythic Poetry

Paranormal Poetry

Magical Realism Poetry

Metaphysical Poetry

Mythic
Fantasy

JACK WOLFLINK

Ḥilda updated Word. Her laptop tried informing her of all the wonderful new features she'd just unveiled—customization! Collaboration! The Cloud! She clicked through, her mouse clacking like a roomful of geckos: *taka-taka-taka,* until she reached her draft.

The cursor blinked at her from the end of a *who...* She exhaled through her teeth. Six hours earlier, she'd collapsed into bed, having spent all evening trying to push the cursor forward. She'd written, *Pacificador said he was looking for the kid who,* and then found nothing else that fit.

Who'd smashed in the window of a police van? That had been too on-the-nose. Who had shoplifted from the Pasay City IKEA? She didn't know what Beboy would take. (She did know that the hour spent trawling their website for a candidate object had turned up some excellent new shelves.) She wanted something specific to Manila's urban poor, yet as universal as Valjean's theft of bread.

Nako, she thought, tearing small bits off the edge of her printed outline. Hilda had thought of so many possibilities, but none of them *fit* anymore. Like her clothes—too loose at the top, too tight at the waist. Too many differences to cover up with a simple patch and stitch.

Her agent, Tom, was supportive as usual. "Next year, Hil. You're on track to get *Ang Mahihirap* in front of some big distributors. The stuff you've sent me, by the way, is wonderful. Mind-blowing."

On track was the problem, she decided. *Tracks* were precisely the villain in her work, the desire to place the human mind on rails, on schedules, the character of the pursuing Lieutenant Pacificador personifying the ordering fist of the Duterte regime, of all regimes, from those generating the headlines her phone sent her to her historical source material. She intended *Ang Mahihirap* to be a rallying cry on behalf of human virtue and freedom—was it any wonder that, imprisoned by tracks, its vibrancy had disappeared?

And yet, until last week's prize announcement, she really had been on track.

Hilda had to put the loss out of her mind. She stretched back, feeling the ligaments in her shoulders pop into place. The laptop screen faded; its light blocked at this angle by her stick-on privacy filter. She felt a long sigh slip between her teeth. *More tea. More tea is the key,* she thought.

The kettle screeched. She was standing at her stove, an empty mug in her hand. She didn't remember getting up and putting the water on, though of course, she must have been the one to do it. *Exhale.* The drawer groaned as she pulled it out. That Rooibos blend she'd gotten from her cousin last Christmas seemed right for the moment. She tried looking for the steep time but couldn't focus. There was some kind of inhuman screaming going on—oh right, the kettle—and she turned off the burner.

Tea in hand, Hilda approached her wide corkboard plotter. Clusters of photos and scrawled notecards were webbed together with red yarn. A plastic takeout cup held pastel thumbtacks, two of which pinned the cup to the board. Pacificador, she imagined, would unspool thick webs of red yarn in his increasingly unhinged pursuit of Beboy. She'd thought it would be a fun touch to do the same. Now it looked like a scathing editor was suggesting she cut most of her work.

A card bearing "BEBOY," written in thick block text, sat at the center of the web. Some of the connections she understood. Others she had no idea about. Was Beboy connected to the bakery shop owner because they were fast friends, or because she wanted him to extol the virtues of *ensaymada*? The owner also linked to Pacificador, and Hilda had no idea whether she was his informant or his victim. The board was like a map that brought you to the right office tower but didn't tell you the floor.

She lifted the mug and let its warm steam fog her glasses. The blend smelled like rosewater and dark honey. She sipped, but it was too hot to taste.

It's just writer's block, she told herself. *The plan is fine. The first section is fine. The intertextuality is great. You were a nominee last time—one of five across the world! And next time, you'll be the winner.* She sucked moist, sweet air in through her nose, then out through her mouth.

She sat back down. There it was again—the blinking cursor, waiting.

Pacificador, searching for the man known to everyone but him as Beboy. Hilda, searching for the perfect inciting incident. Beyond the cursor lay empty space, like the one she'd made on her desk last week. Nothing she did could fill it.

Hilda found a package on her doorstep the next day. It was a large, heavy box, overstuffed with packing peanuts. Inside was a wooden statue, black, in the shape of a seated man. Its limbs and features were stretched, like a Modigliani sculpture, though a crossed-arm pose kept it compact. Its torso was thin and straight, and its head was oversized and impassive. Statues like it could be found at any Filipino-themed cultural store. Hilda frowned. *Who'd send me a bulul?*

She crouched down, feeling a pesky crick in her hip pop into place. It sent a rush of satisfaction through her. Her pleasant feeling faded when her fingers slid across the bulul's smooth, dark wood. *Blood,* she thought. When the Ifugao people planted each year's rice crop, they would anoint these statues with pig's blood to ensure the harvest's bounty. She'd seen this—as a tourist, of course, since the beliefs had been washed away decades ago by the influx of tractors and radio. Then, she had smiled at the weight of history she felt behind the ritual, despite knowing it was pure performance. Now, for some reason, she couldn't shake the blood.

Again, she tried to think who could have sent the statue. And why. The box lacked a return address, and she didn't recognize the toothy logo on its branded packing tape.

But the statue was beautiful. The ruddy afternoon sunlight ran over its curves like the flourish at the end of a car commercial. She almost wanted to give it a massage.

With a grunt, Hilda stood, cradling the bulul in her arms. A packing peanut slid off its lap and drifted back into the box. Most of her living room's tables and cabinets were already filled with art and tchotchkes. But her eyes fell on the blank spot on the shelf behind her desk. *I suppose I'm at the sowing stage of my writing.* Perhaps, she thought, the bulul could watch over her crop as it grew. Hilda tottered to the shelf and hoisted it up.

"Aray!" she yelped. The bulul's thick, heavy base had nipped her middle finger as she set it down. She stuck the fingertip in her mouth, tasting copper. Apparently, the corner was sharp enough to nick her. Hilda glared at it.

As the statue settled into place, the shelf creaked beneath it.

For the rest of the week, Hilda crushed her writing targets. The bulul felt like a writing partner, looking over her shoulder to keep her focused. She sliced through the plot: Beboy slipped the cops. Pacificador, enraged, attacked the kid's friends. The novel grew by nearly a hundred pages. When Hilda arrived at the chapters where Beboy throws himself at the mercy of the law, unwilling to let an innocent take the fall for his crimes, she didn't stop typing until daybreak caught on the bulul's thin, straight nose.

The morning light was almost a shock, given how little fatigue Hilda felt. It was like she was in college again—staying up all night on the adrenaline from seeing Manny Pacquiao beat the tar out of Gabriel Mira. All those screaming crowds at the Big Dome. *Oh, there's a setting to use,* she thought. A few plot threads untangled themselves. She went back to her desk, added another half-dozen pages, and smiled as the new geography restored order to her outline. When Hilda plopped into bed late that afternoon, it was almost a formality. It didn't feel healthy to stay up two nights in a row—even if the first one never seemed to hit her.

The next day, she picked up her kitchen landline and called Tom. "I've really broken through. The words are just flowing through me now! I don't think I'll need to make that research trip to Valenzuela."

Tom laughed. "Really, Hil? No more local color?"

"No, Tom—it's fine! I have my memory. Better to keep writing and skip the jet lag."

Tom took a raspy breath. "That's... actually convenient, in a lot of ways," he said.

There was a relief in his voice Hilda didn't like. She could feel her face scrunching in response, as if she'd cracked a rotten egg. Tom, of course, couldn't tell.

"The merger went through—as you know—and the word down the line is universal storytelling. They feel like their distribution's too big now. They want things that'll sell anywhere." She could almost hear him gesturing.

"Nako, Tom! Don't buzzword me. Do you have notes? Issues for me?"

A thin creak rang through the house. *Walls settling,* Hilda told herself.

"... was to stay at, like, medium geographic detail. If you're skipping that Valenzuela street survey, you're probably fine."

"Okaaay," she said. Tom always led with the smaller ask.

"The title. *Ang Mahihirap.*" Mispronounced: *Ang* like the Taiwanese director, *hirap* like syrup. She'd never drilled it out of him. She'd once considered calling him *Tohm,* like the Thai soup, but he wouldn't have noticed.

"What about the title?"

"The good news is they don't want it gone. Just, like, a subtitle. After the colon."

Tom was confounding, but Hilda had learned to accept his instincts. He'd grown up in the industry—publisher parents—and had an almost autonomic sense of audience, of trend, the way she knew when to speak Tagalog and when her native Kinaray-a. But Hilda yearned, just once, to jump the track. She felt her hand clench around the phone.

"Tom—you're great, but you tell them they keep their white hands—"

"Annnnnd," Tom said, drowning her out. "Annnd, Hil... you go on Oprah."

Oh.

"Oh."

Hilda knew that, on the other end of the line, Tom was grinning like the Cheshire Cat. She had to grant him this one. She felt buoyant, like pumice on the tides.

"Gotcha! Hah. You thought bad news, I thought best news! I just sent you the contract. Sleep on it. Talk tomorrow." The line went silent.

When she rounded the corner to check Tom's email, the bulul faced toward the kitchen, not her desk. *That's funny,* she thought. *I don't remember ever touching it since I put it there.*

She turned the statue back toward her desk. Beneath it, the shelf creaked. She tried not to realize that it was the same sound she'd heard earlier.

Tom stood in the driveway of Hil's Pacifica home, running a finger through his sandy mop of hair. His trips up from L.A. were always disorienting—the sun from his plane window shone just as bright, but the wind was cold and clammy. He'd had to get a light jacket from a store just past the train station, then spent the walk down her street tugging off the various stickers and tags that hung from it.

Usually, he could just take the steps and bang on her sky-blue door until she stopped her last-minute tidying and let him in. But the succulents in her xeriscaped garden had developed shriveled brown spots and dropped their waxy leaves as if emulating an East Coast fall. They must not have been watered in weeks. Her wicker mail basket was overflowing, and the wind had taken the top layer off, scattering it across the eastern half of her porch.

There was a check in there, he knew. Plus, a baker's dozen of letters from him, her publisher, her friends. Tom had received the full manuscript—titled *The Wretched Ones: Ang Mahihirap*—in a heavy envelope last month. Nobody had heard from Hilda since. No response to his excited voice messages, or emails from Oprah's booking agent. Nothing from the breathless blurbs he'd solicited from Jonathan Franzen and Jay Caspian Kang—"Hilda Jimenez sets *The Wretched Ones* in a Manila that could be anywhere"—or from the doubled advance Tom had negotiated.

Tom walked up onto the porch, feeling a chill penetrate his jacket. It must have been caused by stepping out of the sun. He bent over to gather up the mail, carefully negotiating a few envelopes from between the spines of the prickly pear cactus that had caught them. Credit card and PG&E billing statements—maybe Hil had gone to Valenzuela after all? But she'd already sent the manuscript.

He went back and banged on the door. "Hil? Hey, it's Tom! You home?" Nothing.

He peered through the windows, rapping periodically on them too. The last thing he wanted was to get taken for a prowler. A dog down the street began to bark. The panes of glass were cold and slightly damp. Hil's blinds were drawn haphazardly so that, through the slats, he could see lights burning in the kitchen and office. There was a large, dark silhouette in the office, but the figure was as static and lifeless as everything else on Hil's property.

Years ago, when Tom had taken Hil and her editor out for drinks after signing the contract for her first American publisher, he'd had to drive her home after she'd dropped her keys into a drain. He watched her shuffle around the side of her house, wondering if she was further gone than he thought, until she'd returned with a spare keyring, cackling with triumph. He had to do something, he decided. Something more than checking her mail. What if—he thought with a jolt—she'd had a heart attack?

White gravel crunched beneath Tom's shoes as he negotiated the edges of the cactus. He kicked over larger rocks until—there it was—he saw the dirty brass key. Another awkward squeeze, and he was sliding it into the lock. Hil's front door squeaked open.

The chill Pacific wind accompanied Tom into the house. Dust whirled in its wake. There was quite a lot of it. Tom pushed the door closed by its brass handle and found even that had been coated with a thin gray layer. He wiped his hand against his jacket.

"Hil?" he called. No answer.

The kitchen drew him first. That's where Hil usually was when she was too caught up to realize someone was at the door. Not today, though. There was just a ceramic tea infuser, filled with now-cold water, and an open box of loose-leaf standing next to it. He knew the brand—its scent should have filled the room. But it smelled just as dusty as the hall.

Tom clicked the light off and went to the office. The dark shape was a big, black, wooden statue with a long face and blank expression. It was standing at the desk, where Hil's chair would be. A similar statue, much smaller, was on a shelf above it. Between the two, he could tell the larger one was female: its elongated shape curving outward at the chest and hip. Hil had shown him statues like this before, he remembered. A kind of ancestor spirit. Maybe this was a prank?

He placed a hand against the smooth, stained wood. "Hil, it's Tom! You got me, hah! Punked, like you always said! Hil?" His voice echoed in the empty house.

There was another large shape beneath the desk—a tall cardboard box filled with packing peanuts. It was a custom size, clearly fitted to the dimensions of the larger statue. There was an unfamiliar, toothy logo printed on the sides. He tugged the box into the open.

"Huh," he said. It took him a moment to understand the label. Neither an arrival nor a return—this was a fresh box meant to send the statue to some third party. The sticker label was prepaid and already placed, with a big QR code in the center. It was addressed to an apartment in Long Beach, recipient Tony Salcón. He recognized Tony as a Filipino graphic novelist—just signed with Marvel, if he remembered correctly.

"Super weird, Hil!" he said. But it made a certain kind of sense. Maybe this was a kind of mutually supportive tradition she was starting up. He thought about the statue while wandering the rest of the house—yelling respectfully up the stairs rather than further imposing on Hil's privacy. Maybe this Tony would have some insight into where she'd gone. He certainly wasn't part of Hil's usual circles.

The dying evening light lent the statues a warm, almost threatening glow. Tom couldn't help but feel like the larger one was angry, specifically at him. "Well, off you go," he told it, and lowered it into the box. The smaller one sat impassively on its shelf.

Tom pushed Hil's mail basket inside and left the box where UPS could see it. As he closed her door, he heard a long, loud creak. It wasn't until his flight back that he realized it hadn't been the hinges.

A Day Lost in Time

DOUGLAS PERENARA JOHNSTON

Mere noticed Tama's *nguru*. It was only fair she hid the nose flute to get back at him, although it was impossible to stay angry with him for long with that winning smile. Closing her eyes, Mere listened to the ocean roar as it assaulted the land in endless waves, the hissing water sucking at the stones. She felt the energy of the Pacific. She heard the bird song nearby. The aroma of sea salt, *tarutaru* and *rimurapa* drying in the sun. A loud bird call made Mere open her eyes to catch a glimpse of the *karoro* high above. She then dropped her gaze to the beach. Where was he? She looked out to sea, then along the beach. There was no sign of him. It was unlikely he would forget his belongings if he had somehow made it past her back home.

"Tama!" she called. "Tama? Where are you?"

Tama surged through the water. He powered through the waves, but when he stopped and looked back, he was shocked at how far from shore he was. After deciding to head back, he soon realized he was getting tired. He must be caught in a strong current. There was fear then as his limbs grew weak and his breathing laboured. Eventually, he slipped under, trying desperately to hold his breath and struggle back to the surface.

Stubborn wounded pride and anger had kept Tama above the surface for a while. He knew he was a strong swimmer. How could it come to this? Then came an irrational rage coupled with desperation. Why wasn't Mere here to rescue him?

After several bouts of battling back up, he went under for the last time. Lungs burning, he finally gave in to the urge to take a breath and water flooded down his throat. A sense of detachment replaced terror, and everything went black.

Alex sat bolt upright jand, after a moment of fogginess, realized he wasn't drowning and could breathe in gasps of air. He was soaked in sweat and bit down on the scream that was trying to launch up from his chest and out of his mouth.

What the...? Why does my head feel like it's going to split open?

He lay back and checked his alarm clock. *3:01 a.m.—oh, that's just bloody brilliant!* The morning of his school cert math exam, and he was waking up from a bloody nightmare at 3 a.m. And drowning? He couldn't swim and hated water.

Alex thought back to the dream and recognized the beach. Five minutes south of Oamaru near Old Bones Lodge. He and his brother had gone fishing there for elephant fish at the weekend. It was their favourite spot.

His hand hurt, too. In his sleep, he must have been clutching that piece of agate he found on the beach. He lay there for a while and tried to go over some of his math revision in his head, but the migraine refused to go away. With a grunt of disgust, he got up and went to have Panadol and breakfast. His exam was looming ever closer.

On the ride to school, he tried to shake the last of his migraine. First came the rainbow-coloured aura around the edges of his vision, and then the intense skull-splitting pain, followed by a faint urge to spew. Migraines were nothing new, especially with the stress of exams. The disturbing dreams were newer, however.

Just put it out of your mind for three hours, damn it! Exam mode now, do this exam, then school cert is over.

Still, the sense of drowning seemed so real. The sounds of the ocean sucking against the sand and pebbles, the smell of the salt air, and the feel of the sun on his face as he ran to the water. *And Mere, those huge eyes, so pretty, so... Get a grip, boy! Dream of pretty girls later, Jesus!*

He came to his senses just in time to avoid running his bike straight into one of the poplar trees that lined the avenue to school.

"Shit! Pull it together..." he said. Missing the exam by being in the hospital wasn't what he had in mind. It shocked Alex that he had let his mind wander so much.

Daydreaming was one thing, but this was getting dangerous. So, she had nice eyes, so what? But then he wasn't remembering her eyes, was he? He suddenly felt himself blushing as he remembered how few clothes Mere had on and how curvy her tanned figure was.

Alex arrived at the bike shed and went to get off and lock up his bike.

He felt dizzy and almost fell. His heart thundered, and his breathing grew difficult. A saltwater taste formed in his mouth, and his limbs grew weak. He fell, rolling onto his back as his vision seemed to recede, then turned to black. His last thought was of drowning as a roaring in his ears dimmed to silence.

"Alex? You alright, mate?"

"What the hell? What just happened?" Alex looked up in confusion at a couple of familiar faces.

"You tell us. You just dropped like a rock. Want us to get the nurse?" Alex recognized Eden's voice, and then his red hair and freckles.

"Nah, mate, I'm fine. I just jumped off the bike too quickly and got all dizzy. Must be some exam nerves getting to me is all." Alex tried to make light.

"Bloody hell, Al, you nearly gave us the shits, bro," chimed in Wayne as he reached out and helped Alex up. "Hang on, are you sure you're, okay? You're covered in sweat. Actually, you smell like the beach... or saltwater..." Wayne narrowed his eyes.

"Yeah, and seaweed, what the hell? You can't have been for a swim already, mate, surely?" Eden added, bemused.

Saltwater? Seaweed? What the hell was going on here? He must have had another vision. If "vision" was the right word. This was not good... not good at all.

This was more like a bloody attack or seizure! So much for the harmless thoughts of pretty girls. How can a vision leave you on the ground gasping and smelling of saltwater and seaweed, for Christ's sake?

He glanced at his friends as they walked away from the bike sheds and didn't know how to respond to their puzzled looks. He didn't understand it either.

"I went to the beach last night before bed and slept in this morning, so didn't have time for a shower," he lied.

"Aw, okay. Still reckon you should go to the nurse, bro," Eden cautioned.

"Nah, I'll be right." He changed the subject. "Hey, how'd the study go, guys? I'm pretty happy with my preparation."

After the exam, Alex was free. His thoughts were troubled by the dream, the trauma of drowning, and haunted by Mere's beauty. To be honest, he wasn't sure which disturbed him more. After returning home and changing clothes, he set out on his cycle again. He couldn't shake the feelings that Mere stirred deep within him... and he needed to confront the trauma of drowning, since it felt so real.

There was only one place to go. He set out and soon arrived at the familiar beach, the scene of last night's dream. He knew his big brother Bobby would be there fishing.

"Hey, little brother. You should've brought a rod," Bobby said.

"I'm not really into it. Just wanting to relax, and..."

"... and?"

"Dreamt of this place last night. Seemed different, though, in ancient times. I think I've had similar dreams before but couldn't remember them until now."

"You mean nightmares? You used to wake up screaming. Used to give me the shits! I always thought you could see things, bro, like before Grandad died. Was it a pleasant dream?"

"There was a beautiful girl. Just thinking of her makes me feel lightheaded."

"That's always good..."

"I also drowned..."

"That's not so good."

"No shit, Sherlock."

"Smartass, I..." Bobby paused as Alex turned his head; something caught his attention.

Alex saw a flicker of movement in his peripheral vision. It startled him, a glimpse of someone hauntingly familiar, like someone from his dreams.

"Wait... we're being watched!" said Alex as he ran up the beach.

"What? Who cares bro!" Bobby shouted, running after him before he hit an invisible barrier.

Meanwhile, Alex caught up to a Māori girl dressed in strange clothes... it was Mere! When he caught up to grab her by the arm, she screamed.

"Mere?"

She hesitated and looked up at his face. "You know my name? How? And you speak strangely, but somehow, I can understand you. Who are you?"

"I have... dreamt of you and your brother Tama..."

"Wait! Your name is... Alex? I see you whenever I dream of Tama disappearing."

"Yes, I am Alex..." he managed, though he was flustered. Mere was even more attractive up close. *Those eyes.*

"Hurry, we must go back to the whare. The storm is about to hit again," Mere said, grabbing Alex's hand and leading him inland, back to a settlement unlike anything Alex had seen, except in paintings of old Māori settlements.

"Quick, there is no time!" Mere said. They headed indoors as the storm hit.

Alex entered a simple structure of wood and wetland *raupō* with a packed earth floor. A couple who seemed to be Mere's parents looked up uncertainly as they saw Alex.

An old man stated, "You don't belong here, stranger. You should go while you can, there is danger here. Tama returns, and his rage seems heightened by your presence. We may not survive his wrath."

"Tama? Tama drowned, I saw it. I don't understand. You mean the storm?"

"You saw him drown? We only know he went missing," said the old man. "Tama *is* the storm. Somehow, his panic and anger have become a storm that assails us. This day restarts in an endless cycle, with the storm returning more powerful than before. We are trapped here. Perhaps you are too."

"So, this day has been repeating for centuries?"

"Yes, we can't leave the area of our settlement, the beach, and maybe an hour's walk in any direction. Tama was young and untrained, but he was destined to be a powerful spirit singer. That potential, mixed with his terror and rage, has created a terrible force. I am now too old to meet it as his rage grows stronger. He may not wear the agate *tāhei* of a spirit singer, but he will soon overwhelm me. There is no one left to aid me. All our people must be long dead by now."

Agate? Alex thought, as he reached into his pocket and brought out the piece he had found, the agate he had clutched so tight during the dream. He listened to the growing sounds of the storm assailing the whare and closed his fist around the stone. Alex poured all his concern for this trapped family and the love he felt for his own into the agate. He pictured the polished, unbreakable stones of Mere's *tāhei* and opened his eyes. Everyone gasped as the stone glowed, perfectly polished on his now opened hand.

"Not all your people are gone," replied Alex. "That blood runs in my veins too. I now know what I must do. I have long dreamed of confronting a thing of anger and pain. This must be why I'm here." And with that, he turned to walk out into the storm.

"Wait, you'll be killed!" pleaded Mere.

"He's right, child," countered the old man. "I sense the same power in him that I and Tama shared. My name is Ra, and I'm now too old; *he's* strong, if unschooled."

Alex went outside to be greeted by gale-force winds and stinging sleet. The ocean raged and lightning lit the sky. As he reached the beach, he called out Tama's name. In response, he was blown off his feet and thrown several metres. As he struggled to rise, his eyes were blinded by a flash, and a noise beyond sound hammered into his head as the surrounding beach exploded.

Lightning struck right beside him, and he bled from the ears and other wounds from the beach gravel.

"Tama, please. Stop this. You are going to hurt your own *whanau*."

Another lightning bolt struck, and Alex was again thrown from his feet. Two huge, glowing eyes looked down at him from within the roiling clouds. Bolt after bolt struck, and Alex, in terror, was sure he would die. He lost count of the blasts he dodged, but he knew he was getting tired, and it would only take one slip-up to get badly hurt, or worse. Added to his fatigue were anger and frustration. He was trying to help but took numerous wounds from the gravel battering against his body like shrapnel. The thought of a direct hit and the damage it could do to someone as beautiful as Mere finally pushed him over the edge into rage.

He only wanted to help Mere and her *whanau* and bring some peace to Tama. Suddenly, he reached his hand to the heavens and screamed, "ENOUGH!"

A massive bolt of lightning streaked up from his hand to explode right between the eyes in the centre of the storm. The storm dissipated, and a body dropped from the clouds into the water.

Alex heard the soul-rending sound of sobbing, confusion, and utter loss. He surged into the surf and waded until he made out the figure of a young boy. Alex held forth his hand.

Tama shrunk away and cried, "Leave me alone!"

Alex hesitated, then smiled and calmly said, "Give me your hand, little brother. Mere and the others miss you and want you to come home. They love you very much."

"I can't find my way home! Mere didn't come to find me." Tama sobbed.

"She couldn't, so she asked me to find you. You want to go home, don't you?"

"More than anything. Are you Mere's friend?"

"Yes, I am."

"Can you be my friend, too?" Tama asked shyly.

"Of course, Tama."

The two walked hand in hand as the others ran towards them. Alex hung back and smiled as Tama was embraced by each member of his whanau. There was indistinct talking. Then Tama ran back and hugged Alex.

"Thank you for bringing me home, big brother. My Koro says we must go. This day is finally ending."

Alex saw it was indeed getting darker but was confused by the boys' words. Tama ran back to his parents, and they all smiled and waved, then started to vanish. Alex looked on, confused, and turned as Ra and Mere approached.

"We both have inherited power that helps us to stay a moment longer to thank you, Alex," Ra explained. "Bless you for bringing Tama to us and setting us free. We can now move on and be one with our people."

"You mean—you will die?" Alex asked, stunned, as he glanced at Mere. She was someone he had just met but it felt like so much more.

"In a way, everyone we knew is long gone. Perhaps we will be reunited with them. This day ends at last, and we have no place in your world. Look over there." Ra pointed down at the beach. "We can see someone trying to come to you. Do not mourn for us. We all feel a sense of peace and joy as dusk approaches at long last."

Alex turned to see Bobby looking at them, pushing at some barrier and calling out, though no sound came through.

"I will go now, as I know my granddaughter wishes to speak with you. I am overjoyed that one with our gifts still lives in the future to guide our descendants. Thank you, Alex, once again for setting us free. Farewell." With that, Ra turned and walked up the beach and slowly vanished.

"I will miss you, Alex." Mere looked up at him with huge brown eyes filled with gratitude and tenderness. "I wish we had more time to get to know each other."

"I..." Alex hesitated, then found himself holding and kissing Mere. "I hope you will come and visit in my dreams."

"I hope so, too. Goodbye, Alex."

And she was gone. Tears ran down his face as he desperately tried to hold on to the feel of her skin, the taste of her lips, and the smell of her hair. As he opened his eyes, he knew he was back in his world.

Dusk was replaced by the midday sun. He suddenly felt Bobby's hand on his shoulder.

"I wouldn't have believed any of that if I hadn't seen it, Alex. I thought the lightning had killed you!" Bobbly said. "I couldn't reach you and couldn't hear anything. Shit, bro, I've got so many questions. I..."

Alex turned his tear-streaked face to Bobby. "I... don't have the words, bro. I don't know if I ever will. I will never see her... them again. I feel like I lost an entire whanau in that place. I am devastated."

"There are still whanau who love and need you here, little brother," Bobby said gently. Then he playfully cuffed the back of Alex's head and ran off to his surf caster. "And anyway, I need a little brother that I can blame for stuff and pick on when I'm bored. Right, stink bum?"

"Gee, thanks for that, dickhead. I thought it was my job to blame you for stuff."

Both brothers laughed, and Alex looked back up the beach, hoping to still see her. He sighed and turned to join his brother.

The Jupilag

SHANTELL POWELL

akturalik first heard the chainsaws while studying her grimoire. She set the spell book down and turned to look out the upstairs window. Two big work trucks straddled the verge in front of her house. One was connected to a woodchipper. Nakturalik gaped when she saw the man in the tree right outside her second story window. He was close enough to spit on. He wore a dayglo orange shirt and a white hard hat. When he pressed his chainsaw into the meat of a big maple limb, the whirling teeth bit in. The leaves, still spring green and soft, shuddered and then the branch lurched before thudding onto the ground. Another man in orange with big yellow ear protectors dragged the branch over to the chipper and fed it in.

The sounds of heavy machinery drowned out the cries of baby robins. Nakturalik ran downstairs and out the door. She stood with her hands on her hips on the front step. Another severed branch slammed down, this time into her three sisters' garden. She had watered the pumpkin, corn, and pole bean seedlings just a few hours ago, before the day got too hot. Now they were collateral damage.

"What are you doing?" demanded Nakturalik.

One worker walked over, turning off the woodchipper and pulling out his earplugs. "What?"

"Why are you doing this? And why are you doing it during nesting season?"

The man looked over to the mutilated tree and then to the chipper. "Uh, I appreciate your concern—"

"I don't think you do," interrupted Nakturalik. "You are throwing baby birds into a wood chipper. These trees shouldn't be coming down, but if you must destroy them, why now? Why during nesting season?"

He scratched his neck and looked back at her. "These are the City of Kitchener's trees."

"Trees don't belong to a city. They belong to the land."

"Look," he said, "we need to cut them down right away. They're a hazard. See how close they are to the lines?" He gestured up to where insulated wires pierced through the foliage.

"Yup. And they've been like that for years, so why now?"

"We only received our orders last week."

"Why?"

He shrugged.

"Has the City of Kitchener consulted with Six Nations over this?"

"I don't have that information, ma'am."

"The Haudenosaunee have a moratorium in place on destruction and development. This should not be happening without their consent. Kitchener is part of the Haldimand Tract, and this is their territory."

"I hear what you're saying," said the man.

As he spoke, another branch crashed down, missing her sweetgrass only because it came to rest atop a naked H-stake. Nakturalik's hands shot to her mouth. A sign declaring "This is Indian Land" had been on that stake. Now the wire frame was stripped of its message. This was the third time someone had stolen the purple and white sign. At least the stake had saved the sweetgrass. She let her hands sink back down.

"You're dropping and dragging branches through my garden."

The man looked cross now. "We are doing our best not to damage it, ma'am. You don't really think we are trying to destroy your garden, do you?"

Nakturalik was shaking like the leaves. "This whole region was once a garden. These two sugar maples are the last shade trees left on the block. All the others have been cut down. Where are the birds supposed to nest now?"

He took a deep breath, then held his palms up toward Nakturalik in a placating gesture. "Hey, I'm just doing my job."

"And so am I," said Nakturalik.

She was a land defender. The trouble was, she didn't feel like a very good one. Although she took good care of her yard, the neighbourhood's ecology was in decline. Last summer, the huge silver maple with its tire swing in the neighbour's backyard had been cut down, and the crows who'd favoured the tree hadn't returned. Nakturalik's own yard, which had always been pleasantly cool on even the hottest of days, lost its shade.

Though the sun-loving plants thrived, she was having a hard time keeping the woodland herbs healthy.

The worker cleared his throat and took a half-step back. "We'll be all done and out of your hair soon," he promised, while backing away and stuffing his earplugs back in. The conversation was over.

He flipped the switch back on for the woodchipper while Nakturalik retreated to her doorstep and wrung her hands. It felt like someone was tightening a belt around her chest, and her breathing was quick and shallow. Normally, when she was upset, she'd go for a walk, but there weren't any nice places to walk anymore. Walking around the deteriorating neighbourhood only fed her anxieties.

Just around the corner, the copse of old-growth trees which hid a petroleum plant had been felled. Stripped and debarked logs lay in neat piles amongst the destruction and yellow bulldozers. Without the filtration of the leaves, a thick pall of dust covered the area, and the humus dried up and blew away. Nakturalik had no idea where the foxes, raccoons, possums, and skunks who lived there had gone.

She went back inside, closing the door behind her. If she wasn't careful, she'd have a full-blown anxiety attack. She struggled to control her breathing.

She couldn't even enjoy the park around the corner anymore. The chokecherries, high-bush cranberry, and staghorn sumac ringing it had been chopped down for no apparent reason. She used to forage there to make jelly. There'd be no more jelly for her, and no more berries for the birds. Instead of trees and meadow, there was a vast expanse of half-dead lawn. Poison had been applied to every single dandelion that dared rear its head, and the native plants she'd guerrilla gardened had been mowed down. To top it off, the local community garden with its magnificent wildflower fields had been paved over a few months prior and replaced by an equipment yard. No wonder bees and monarch butterflies were endangered. Nakturalik's tiny yard with its native flora was more important now than ever.

The chainsaws roared back to life, loud as helicopters. It jolted her from her thoughts. The maples had received their death sentence. While she watched through her front window, the tree furthest from her medicine garden was decapitated. The amputated limbs heaped around its trunk looked like a pyre intended for burning witches.

It was time to contact the city yet again.

In the years since she'd moved here, she'd written innumerable letters to the editor and local politicians, complained on social media, taken to the streets with banners and round dancers, and called up developers about the continuing destruction of habitat. It had all been for naught. Would this time be any different? Probably not, but she had to make the effort.

She stomped back up the stairs to her room and sat down at her desk. She closed the blinds as she couldn't bear to watch the continuing destruction. She fired up her computer and logged into the complaints page on the City of Kitchener's website.

"To whom it may concern," she typed. "I hear land acknowledgments all the time, but I've yet to see any good come from them. The words are empty. My neighbourhood is being destroyed. All its wooded areas have been chopped and bulldozed over the past two years, and now the beautiful sugar maples next to my garden are being cut down during the height of nesting season. Why is this being done? Where are the animals supposed to live? How does this fit in with the city's pledge of reconciliation when Indigenous communities have not been consulted?"

She clicked the send button and rolled back in her chair. The chainsaws were still going strong, and now her head ached as much as her heart.

She considered chaining herself to one of the trees but knew it would do no good. She'd only get carted off to jail or sent for a psych evaluation; she'd probably get roughed up and sexually assaulted in the process. Cops didn't take kindly to folks getting in the way of ecocide, especially when the folks weren't white. It was part of the Mounties' MO. She closed her eyes and rested her head on her desk.

With her desk cool against her brow, she thought of the land defenders in Wet'suwet'en First Nation. Wet'suwet'en was under attack by Coastal GasLink with the help of hired goons in uniform. Not too long ago, heavily armed RCMP officers violently apprehended peaceful land defenders, made them strip, and transported them to the distant courthouse in dog kennels. It was hours and hours before the injured people received medical treatment or could stretch their aching legs. They were forced to attend their trial in their underwear and forbidden to speak in their own defence.

The racism was systemic, and reconciliation was a lie.

Nakturalik peeked out through her blinds. A pair of robins perched on the power lines across the street. They looked angry. Maybe they were. It had been only a couple of months since they returned, migrating thousands of kilometres to nest. All this, just to see their children hamburgered in a woodchipper.

She let the blinds drop and checked her email. She'd already received a response. That was fast.

"We have opened a service request to rectify the tree issue you have reported. Our team will assess the situation and perform the necessary work as soon as possible."

Nakturalik scoffed. The autoresponder made promises the region would never keep. She knew bloody well city workers would not suddenly be reforesting the region because of her complaint. Neither would the city be giving stolen land back. She didn't have that kind of power. Best not to hold her breath for that.

Though the blinds were closed, she imagined the robins staring at her through them, blaming her for not stopping the machines of progress. She was hyperventilating again. She focused on slowing her breathing. She had to do something, but what?

Nakturalik flipped through her grimoire, looking for something, anything, that might help. It was filled with instructions on creating amulets and talismans, with recipes for charms and divinations, with ways of invoking supernatural powers for good or for ill.

She didn't know enough of her Inuit ancestors' teachings, so she augmented what she did know with things she'd gleaned from anthropologists who had studied the traditions. It was tricky deciphering information through a colonial lens, but she did her best, supplementing it with teachings from other Indigenous knowledge keepers. It's how she'd learned about the sacred medicines of the First Nations.

That being said, she hadn't avoided the European traditions. Those had been her gateway to studying magic in the first place.

The chainsaws kept buzzing, the chipper kept chipping, and Nakturalik couldn't tune them out. She flipped through pages of necromantic rituals, green witchcraft, and folk magic before stopping at a page of drawings. Monstrous images of *tupilait* from the eastern Inuit adorned the page. She rested her finger on one of the drawings.

A *tupilaq* was magic of last resort. It could just as easily turn upon its maker as it would its intended target. Her vision blurred as her eyes brimmed, and then a teardrop fell and splotched the ink. She closed the book and wiped at her eyes with her wrist. She had to pull herself together. Crying wouldn't stop the machinery, but a *tupilaq* might.

When the workers left to go on break, Nakturalik went back outside with tobacco in hand. Almost all the severed branches were gone now. Their chipped remains had been taken away. She laid her cheek against the maimed trees, thanking them for all they had given.

A couple of cars slowed down. She ignored the gawkers. She placed sacred tobacco beneath the trees and looked up. The top halves of the trees were gone. The robin nest was gone. She couldn't hear birdsong anymore—just an endless stream of traffic driving past on cracked asphalt patched with tar and littered with chip bags and empty plastic bottles.

She laid down in her garden amongst the sweetgrass, milkweed, and goldenrod. A mullein leaf, soft as a kitten's ear, brushed against her neck like a kiss while a fire truck wailed its way down the road. A black-and-white butterfly fluttered past.

Kitchener wasn't her ancestral land. She was far removed from that, but she considered it her duty to care for the land she occupied. It was everyone's duty, and part of the Dish With One Spoon Treaty. Nakturalik loved the land. How could she not?

When she'd first moved here seven years ago, the soil in her yard was bare and dead, so she got to work. She nursed it back to health with homemade compost and soil infusions from healthy naturalized areas. She transplanted native species and grew others from seed. Two years ago, she celebrated when fireflies lit her yard in a miniature fireworks display. That had been her greatest achievement. With the help of her non-human relations, she'd rebuilt a tiny ecosystem.

While she lay amongst the medicine plants, a fat bumblebee with pollen-thick legs buzzed overhead. The bee alighted upon a dandelion. Nakturalik reached over and gently stroked the bee's fuzzy butt. The bee didn't mind, busying itself with collecting nectar.

"I will find a way to make them stop," Nakturalik vowed.

The bee flew away.

Nakturalik got up. She picked up a short branch from her garden, overlooked by the city workers, and carried it to the front step. Then she went back indoors.

She grabbed a knife and a lighter from the kitchen, a packet of maqtaq from the deep freezer, and a hoodie from the coat tree. She put all these things, plus a bottle of water, into a backpack and peeled off a sticky note. She wrote:

I've gone to see our mother. Not sure when I'll be back. Please water the plants while I'm gone. I love you.

She stuck the note on the fridge and went back outside, locking the door behind her. She didn't know when or if she would ever come back.

"Goodbye, house," she said. "Goodbye, garden."

She picked up the branch and put it, along with her backpack, into the basket of her bicycle. She got on her bike and rode through an industrial park to a trail running alongside the Grand River.

She followed the trail for hours, passing row upon row of identical houses in identical subdivisions. It was unseasonably hot, so she kept to the shade as much as possible. She pulled over at one of the intersections when she found a roadkill squirrel. She pried the pancaked remains off the pavement and placed them into her bike basket.

By late afternoon, she was in commercial farm country. Monoculture soybean fields stretched out all around her. It was very dusty here. Nakturalik stopped to add bits of roadkill to her basket as she found them: feathers from a sparrow, quills from a porcupine, and a smear of blood from something unrecognizable. She looked up when a shadow passed over her. A turkey vulture soared high overhead, its unmoving wings held in a V.

Nakturalik biked until she found a wooded area outside the city limits next to a stream. What she planned to do called for the ocean, but she was too far inland. The stream would have to suffice. Streams lead to rivers, and rivers lead to the sea. The maqtaq would help. The ocean would call to the spirit of the narwhal.

While Sister Sun set and Brother Moon rose, Nakturalik built a little fire close to the water's edge. She fed it white bits of birch bark and orangey-brown cedar fronds, then added dead, fallen branches. There were plenty to choose from; the area had been hit by a *derecho* last spring. She kept feeding kindling to the fire until it blazed cheerily, then she started carving the maple branch with her knife.

Light pollution shrouded the stars, but the light of the strawberry moon shone through. She had just enough moonlight and firelight to see what she was doing. She carved all night, pausing every now and then to feed the fire. A monstrous figure emerged from the green wood with flaring nostrils, sharp teeth, rolling eyes, and seal flippers. When it was finally carved to her liking, she allowed herself to sleep.

She awoke in the late afternoon, staring up at the sky through a canopy of cedar and birch. Even in the shade, the day was hot. A red squirrel chittered down at her from the top of a tree.

Nakturalik sat up and investigated her handiwork. The carved figure looked even more monstrous under the light of day. One eye was a third again as large as the other—just as it should be. What few leaves were left on the branch had wilted. It looked both alive and dead at the same time.

She opened the package of defrosted maqtaq, gave thanks to the hunter and the narwhal, and sliced off a sliver. She fed it to the tupilaq. Then she cut off another sliver and chewed it slowly, savouring the oily, nutty flavour before washing it down with a swig of warm water.

There hadn't been mosquitoes last night, but there certainly were now. Flies swarmed, too, attracted by the roadkill in her bike basket. She ignored the stinging and biting as she gathered more tinder.

She had one more face to carve, and she was dizzy with heat and hunger. She spent the rest of the daylight in meditation, calling upon the mother of all breathing things, calling upon the mother of the sea. She chanted the words until her voice cracked and the sun vanished behind the horizon.

Wild-haired woman of the water,
Forced and flung from Anguta's qajaq,
Mother to the sea with ice floes for clouds,
His paddle smashes finger phalanges.

Forced and flung from Anguta's qajaq,
Bleeding broken fingers transform.
His paddle smashes finger phalanges.
Anirniliit with flippers and fins.

Bleeding broken fingers transform,
And a phalanx becomes a whale.
Anirniliit with flippers and fins,
Nuliajuk will never again be alone.

And a phalanx becomes a whale.
Her phantom fingers breathe and swim.

Nuliajuk will never again be alone.
She makes their camp in Atlivun.

Her phantom fingers breathe and swim.
Drip sweet water from your mouth to theirs.
She makes their camp in Atlivun.
We must maintain equilibrium

Drip sweet water from your mouth to theirs
I speak to you, oh Nuliajuk.
We must maintain equilibrium.
Wife to a red and white dog.

I speak to you, oh Nuliajuk,
Wild-haired woman of the water,
Wife to a red and white dog,
Mother to the sea with ice floes for clouds.

When the sun set and the fire crackled, she carved the second figure on the branch in silence. Although it was hard to work with green wood, she persevered. The land counted on her. A great horned owl hooted mournfully in the distance, and another answered further downstream. Naked branches of dead cedars clawed at the sky. Under the cover of night, she carved gills, pointed ears, and a pair of human-like hands.

She thought she saw its fingers twitch. Startled, she fumbled and cut herself, hissing in pain. Blood dripped onto her carving, and she massaged it into the wood. She wasn't sure, but she thought she saw the other figure wink. A shadow soared past—an owl, its silhouette backlit by the moon.

The maqtaq had gone bad. Flies crawled over the rancid blubber, and when she picked it up, her fingers sank into the melted fat. She pinched off a piece and placed it into the hands of the second figure. Then she brought the rest to her mouth and bit down. It tasted putrid. She forced herself to swallow but couldn't keep it down. Vomit surged up, and she retched all over the carved figures.

She wrapped the carving in the dried husk of the dead squirrel, pinning the skin shut with porcupine quills. She jammed the sparrow feathers into the edges and smeared the entire thing with blood and the remaining maqtaq. Then she put her hoodie on backward, securing her creation against her skin.

The tupilaq scratched at her like a living thing trying to escape. Its teeth dug into her flesh, but she didn't cry out. She pulled the hood up over her face, making it hard to breathe, and sang dark lullabies from deep within her throat and chest. Finally, the tupilaq grew still.

When she fell asleep, her spirit travelled to the far north and took the form of Nanook, the great white bear. As Nanook, she dove from an ice floe into Atlivun. She descended through the icy waters, far past pods of vertical-sleeping whales, past shimmering shoals of silver fish, and sleek harp seals, until she reached the underworld. Spirits swayed along the ocean floor like forests of kelp. When they sighed, butterflies fluttered from their mouths and ascended toward the surface. Crimson char darted through the current.

On the ocean floor, the mother of the sea—a woman with hair like a snarled knot of lampreys—was coupled with a red and white dog.

Even in her bear form, Nakturalik was terrified, but she pressed on. Atlivun was where weak spirits were reforged into something stronger. Nakturalik felt weak. She lacked the traditional skills expected of Inuit women her age. She bore none of the *kakiniit*—the tattoos women of her age should have earned. Her bare face marked her as one of the incomplete spirits dwelling in Atlivun, awaiting rebirth.

The dog unstraddled Nuliajuk, turning to face the opposite direction. Still connected at the genitals, the two formed a chimerical creature, half woman, half dog. Their four eyes bore into Nakturalik's soul, stripping her bare. Nuliajuk's body was covered in tattoos—her arms, chest, and thighs ringed with marks painstakingly sewn through her skin with sinew, soot, and bone.

Nuliajuk raised a hand in acknowledgment. The hand had no fingers or thumbs.

In her bear form, Nakturalik approached the mother of the sea and reached out with her massive paw, using her claws to comb through Nuliajuk's unruly hair.

When Nakturalik awoke, she was back in her body. She could feel butterflies resting across her skin. She lay in the living soil of the forest all through the next day, her monstrous poppet pressed against her chest and belly. She didn't dare lower her hood or look at the tupilaq.

She sang throughout the day, weak from hunger, thirst, and heat. When the sun went down, she listened for the sound of water and crawled to the stream. The mud squelched beneath her hands and knees, rushes and pebbles pressing into her skin, but she kept going until the cold water soaked her hood.

Only then did she pull the tupilaq out from beneath her hoodie, birthing it into the stream. She pushed it away, and the current carried it toward the distant sea.

Nakturalik rolled onto her back and lay in the water. The coolness revived her just enough to crawl out of the stream. Past the mud, she struggled to peel off her soaked hoodie, careful not to look downstream. It wasn't safe to look upon what she had made.

She pressed black cedar mud into the scratches and bites on her skin. It felt soothing, but she knew she had an infection. Who knew what runoff came from the fields? Who knew what the tupilaq had done? Even with the mud, her flesh burned with fever.

She crawled back to the ashes of her dead fire. It took a long while before she found the strength to drink the last of her water.

When the sun rose, she was too weak to get on her bike. Instead, she sang. She sang curses to the tupilaq, now swimming away to do her bidding. She sang until her voice gave out, until her heart stopped beating and her breath left her in a long, rattling sigh.

Someday, Nakturalik would live again, reborn into a new body. But now, in the moment of her death, the tupilaq followed her spirit back to Atlivun. It followed her to the mother of the sea and all breathing things.

The tupilaq, forged from so many creatures, returned to the city.

The two sugar maples had been reduced to stumps, but when the tupilaq arrived, it brought spirits with it. Shadowy maples rose from the stumps, and where living trees had been unjustly felled, phantoms of pawpaw trees filled the air with their carrion stink.

Though the summer sun burned bright, Waterloo region was swathed in shadow. Ghostly leaves rustled, and branches creaked in the wind. Emergency rooms filled with people convinced they'd been drugged. CBC, CTV, and the local papers reported mass hallucinations.

As summer turned to autumn, the visions intensified. Animals rose as shadows, too. Sluiceways filled with the spirits of trout, while ghostly cattails painted shadowy stripes along the concrete. The ghosts of roadkill and exterminated vermin repopulated the twin cities. Scampering rabbits, rats, and field mice swarmed across all of Waterloo region.

The spirits of starved pollinators moved through subdivisions, devouring pollen from flowers that weren't entirely there. Ghost moose and bears stalked the highways, causing hundred-car pile-ups on the 401. With the sound of distant rolling thunder, a million-bird flock of ghost passenger pigeons blotted out the sun for three days straight, while a herd of eastern elk grazed calmly in the parking lot of a Walmart.

A stampede of shadowy bison tore through the streets of downtown Kitchener, trampling anyone foolish enough to remain outdoors. Woolly mammoths trumpeted along the spectral wetlands of uptown Waterloo.

People were consumed with fear, unable to combat the onslaught. The region was forced into a state of emergency. The military was summoned, but they were powerless against the spirits.

By the end of summer, every settler community along the Haldimand Tract had become a ghost town, with only a handful of residents left. Only those who truly loved and cared for the land were spared.

By the time of the Harvest Moon, living animals had returned to the region, and trees and prairie grasses sprouted in the abandoned spaces.

The Six Nations reclaimed their land, and no one would ever take it from them again.

Aghnashini's Secret

SHILPA KAMAT

Konkan Coast, 1687

When Aghnashini offered to go down to the river to fetch water, everyone was grateful. The clouds were gathering, and the monsoon rains were sure to drench the ground soon. "Come back quickly," her mother told her, and Aghnashini let her mother think that the worry that likely showed on her face was a mirror: that she shared her fear that the chill from being drenched would make her ill.

In actuality, she didn't mind the rain, which soothed her on these hot summer days. In actuality, if Aghnashini decided she didn't want to get wet at all, or that she'd had enough of a downpour, she had the ability to stay dry–but what would people make of such a thing, to see a girl walking in rain without getting wet at all?

Aghnashini assured her mother that she would be fast as she picked up the large water pot. "I'll come," she said, which, in their language, was what they said instead of "goodbye": a promise to return.

As she was leaving, the neighboring family arrived, dressed in their best clothes. "Namaskar," she greeted them, and they greeted her back, quietly rebellious, because even this simple greeting was forbidden. They were coming to attend her family's quiet Ganapati celebration, though she questioned how quiet it actually was when the word had been spread to so many neighbors.

"We've done this so many times," her grandfather had pointed out when Aghnashini told him she felt uncomfortable about others joining. "They are all careful like us. It will be okay." But a queasiness nagged at her, and she couldn't shake it.

Aghnashini moved quickly—like the river, her father would say—bare feet walking straight through puddles, enjoying the sensations. She rushed down to the stream and along its banks to the place where she could easily stoop and gather some water. When she was little, she used to pretend that this was the Aghanashini River, which ran beside her grandmother's home village, far to the south beyond Goa's borders. She had been named for that river, which her grandmother had always spoken of fondly.

As Aghnashini grew older, she wondered how much her grandmother's nostalgic connection to the river was wrapped up in the freedoms of that place. In Goa, speaking their language and practicing their religion had been forbidden for as long as even Aghnashini's grandfather could remember offenses that could cost people their freedom or their lives. It hadn't been that way in her grandmother's home village.

Perhaps the freedom of her grandmother's upbringing allowed Aghnashini's family the confidence to continue their spiritual practices in secret. And perhaps being named after the river was what caused her deep affinity for water—or perhaps it was coincidental.

Whatever the reason, the older Aghnashini grew, the more constrained she felt in her life, the deeper her capacity for communication with the water seemed to grow. It wasn't just water, exactly. It was the form and flow of it: the currents of the river, the streams of rain, even the steam that rose when a large pot of rice was boiling. Aghnashini found she could somehow connect with this moving force, to harness and redirect it at will.

She reached out now with something beyond herself, the something that allowed her to brush against the river's currents and get a sense of them. The river was large with the rains that had already fallen, and its power seemed amplified.

She tried to immerse herself as she walked alongside it, to enjoy the sense of its flow and let it consume her anxiety. As the clouds thickened, however, she couldn't shake her discomfort. Aghnashini couldn't pinpoint the moments she had learned when to speak or not speak; she had been taught, since before she could remember, that some things shouldn't be said. Her parents had always hidden from her the details of the tortures of those who were arrested, although even she herself had actively tried not to hear about such depressing truths. She had absorbed over the years an awareness of the things that could happen. She remembered the hushed warnings of her friend's mother: that people who prayed in Sanskrit—or any language that the Portuguese priests didn't deem acceptable—could be burned at the stake if they were discovered.

If the Inquisitors threw Goans in jail for something as simple as growing a tulsi plant in their entryway, how would they react to seeing her family openly celebrating Ganpati? She knew without asking that her parents would be killed, that the smaller children in the family would be taken away by their oppressors and forced to practice only Christianity, to speak only Portuguese—but she didn't know how she knew such things. The knowledge had seeped into her over the years, like her awareness of the water.

Some families were too terrified to do anything other than acquiesce, to change their beliefs and language and way of life—to act like they were Portuguese. These families increased their status under the law, but they could also be targeted if they were suspected of holding onto their old ways.

Aghnashini's family feared the Inquisitors as well, of course, but they fiercely resisted the idea of renouncing their language and beliefs. They spoke Konkani behind closed doors, defying the law. They kept murtis, tiny ones, buried in a box beneath the banyan tree behind their house.

On most holidays, they didn't even bother digging them up, quietly setting up a coconut or a stone to represent the divine, quietly singing and praying in the shelter of their home, where no one would even know.

On this day, they had dug them up, of course. It was a big holiday, and two neighboring families were joining them to celebrate. The families at the gathering wanted to believe that praying to Ganapati would make their lives easier, that Ganapati would give their oppressors some wisdom and prevent them from bringing harm to their community.

But innocent people were accused and dragged off to prison all around them, and Aghnashini knew it.

As she lowered her pot toward the river, Aghnashini remembered the day when she had come to this place with her older sisters and shown them her talent. Her middle sister had just shown that she could wiggle her ears, something not even their oldest sister could manage to do. Aghnashini had thought that it would surprise and impress them she had finally discovered a skill that they didn't have. She made them both walk to the river bank with her and proudly showed them how she could convince the stream of water to move up toward her pot and fill it rather than having to bend down to collect it.

She had quickly seen from their faces that she should not be smiling about her newly honed ability. Eyes wide with distress, her sisters said it was a terrible thing, that no ordinary person could do this. "They'll think you're a witch!" her eldest sister whispered fiercely. "We'll all be unsafe!"

As Aghnashini had grown older, she understood that what she had shown her sisters was far from ear wiggling, though it had felt that way to her: natural, innate. Their Portuguese rulers could target such a difference, and so might others in their community.

She couldn't entirely give up her ability, though. It was too much a part of her. Just as her family kept their traditions going in secret, Aghnashini began quietly continuing to hone her abilities. Not even her eldest sister noticed; after a year or so of intermittent warnings never to mess around like that again, she relaxed, satisfied that Aghnashini had listened. She had wondered, sometimes, whether her sisters or other family members were suppressing such abilities themselves, but she knew better than to ask.

Now, Aghnashini timidly tilted the pot so that the river's current would quickly fill it. Even as she knew she could easily command the current to enter, that no one would even notice. She whispered a prayer to the river, the one that made her feel safe and connected. But the knot in her stomach only grew —

—and then she saw them, in the distance: hard-faced men moving urgently, deliberately, toward her family's hamlet.

Aghnashini's qualms turned to full-fledged terror, flaring through her nervous system, but she felt something else as well: determination. She couldn't let what happened to the families they had heard of happen to hers. She wouldn't!

With only moments to act as the men rode toward the hamlet, Aghnashini let something in her belly and in her hands grasp at the clouds' heaviness.

Part of her doubted she could succeed after so many years of suppression. What she needed to do now was much more forceful than anything she had ever let herself unleash. But something inside her rose to squash her doubt. She wasn't little anymore, and she wasn't playing; Aghnashini was ready for battle.

The sky burst open. Aghnashini stood still even as enormous raindrops pelted her, as the gushing rain created waterfalls along the banks. For a moment, she hesitated. She didn't really want to hurt them, just to stop them.

Then one of them looked at her with a cold sneer, and she sensed his intent: how he wanted to obliterate everyone who wasn't just like him, how comfortable he had grown with inflicting harm.

A lifetime of fear that she had pulled into herself, that had balled up in her belly, charged outward, toward her fingertips. Aghnashini squeezed her fists together. With a gentle flicking open of her fingers, she felt the full force of the rain as it knocked the men off their horses. They tumbled toward the river, grasping at plants to steady themselves.

Then Aghnashini entered the river, connecting with the water's malleability, with the current's strength.

Perhaps the soldiers saw her standing there, unaffected by the rain, controlling it all. Perhaps she only imagined so, the instant before she dipped into the currents and directed their full force toward them. The river swept unnaturally upward to meet them and washed them downstream as they screamed.

Aghnashini picked up her pot of water and ran. She was sure that she would have nightmares about this day, even though these soldiers were monsters who had tortured and killed so many innocent people. She worried that the church might send more people, that she had only delayed the inevitable.

As she approached her house, Aghnashini let herself get drenched, too careful to show up unaffected by the downpour. She could hear her family, her community, their fervent singing.

Casting a warmth, a sense of safety, her heart was beating hard as she entered, greedy for connection.

"Aghnu!" her mother shouted, alarmed, and ran to her. Aghnashini let her fuss over her, let her help her dry off and change into brightly colored clothes. She had never felt so grateful for home, for the innocence of her younger siblings, for everyone's ignorance of how close they had been to destruction.

The news spread the next day that two of the Inquisitors' soldiers had been found washed up on a riverbank in what appeared to have been a freak accident, a mudslide somewhere upstream caused by heavy rains. Aghnashini found herself more relieved that no one would be interrogated because of her than guilty for what she had done. At least one of the soldiers had been conscious and described how it seemed that the river came to life and pulled them in. He blamed the devil, but he did not blame the girl who stood on the banks of the river, unimpacted by the pelting rain. He didn't mention seeing her hands turn to fists and then release, fingers splaying open, as the water surged out toward them.

Her mother grasped her arm. "Are you okay?" she asked, brushing back a lock of her hair.

"I'm good," she assured her; Aghnashini knew how to keep secrets.

Urban Fantasy

For the Love of Death

CHRISTINA TANG-BERNAS

Sandra gasped when she turned around in her kitchen to find another woman standing in it. She hadn't heard the woman come in, not from the creaky hinges of the doors, the footsteps, or even the rustle of clothing.

The woman was not particularly tall—rather average all around, to be honest—shorter than Sandra, with plump curves clothed in a simple black wool sweater and dark jeans. Her closed-smile was soft, and her eyes were intelligent and kind. It was this gentle gaze that put a dent into Sandra's fear. No one who looked at Sandra like that was likely to be there to rob or murder her.

"Who are you?" Sandra asked. "What are you doing here?"

The smile widened, as if the woman had heard these questions in a million different ways—likely, if she made a habit of showing up in people's houses unannounced.

"Most know me as Death," the woman said.

Sandra examined the woman more closely. Her face was pretty, if a bit on the forgettable side. "You don't look like Death."

"What is Death supposed to look like?" the woman countered.

"More—" Sandra thought a bit. "More skeletal, I guess."

Death laughed. "Do I not look skeletal to you?"

"The opposite, really."

"Interesting," Death said, looking thoughtful. "Well, regardless of how I look, I'm here for a reason. It's time, Sandra." She held out her hand, her long fingers unfurling in invitation.

Sandra took a step back, her gaze swinging around to take in her kitchen: the oven warming up, the two trays of peanut butter cookies waiting on the counter, the calendar full of handwritten appointments tacked to the wall, her laptop sitting on the kitchen table playing an album she'd purchased just that morning, and the golden afternoon light glowing through the pale blue curtains.

"I—I can't. I'm not ready. I have so many things to do." Sandra flailed a hand out in the general direction of the entire kitchen.

"Don't you think everyone I come for has a lot to do? There is a never-ending stream of things to do and see."

"At least let me turn the oven off so I don't burn the house down." Her words sped up. "And my daughter, she's supposed to visit me tomorrow. I haven't seen her in so long, since she moved out of the country. These cookies—they're for her. They're her favorite. Please, just—just one more day. Please. I have to tell her goodbye."

Death cocked her head. "One more day?"

"Just one," Sandra pleaded.

Death looked around the kitchen. "Hmm, interesting" was all Death said. When next Sandra blinked, Death was gone, as if she had never been there in the first place. Sandra's breath shuddered out of her. She couldn't believe it had worked, and for a moment, she stared out the window, soaking in the sun and enjoying the moment. Her thoughts were interrupted when the oven beeped at her.

The next day, Sandra's phone rang. It was her daughter, telling her that something had come up at work and that she wouldn't be able to make it out—that she would rebook the flight as soon as she could, she promised. Sandra missed her daughter desperately, but this was not the first time her daughter had canceled on her at the last minute.

Her daughter sounded genuinely frazzled, stress tightening her usually bright voice.

"It's OK," Sandra said. "Sounds like they're overworking you, so you get some rest when you can. I'll make another batch of cookies when you make it out."

"Oh, mom, you made me peanut butter cookies? Now I'm really pissed at my manager. I'm really sorry—truly. I'll make it up to you."

"Just take care of yourself. That's what I want most of all." Sandra pushed through the shakiness threatening her own voice. "You know I love you very much, right?"

Her daughter's voice was soft and also a little shaky. "I love you too, mom. You're my favorite mom in the world."

Sandra laughed. "And you're my very favorite daughter."

When she turned around, Death was standing in her kitchen again. "Did you say your goodbyes?" she asked.

Sandra drooped. "I couldn't tell her. She'll find out soon enough, and, well, I can tell she's already at her limit. How could I say anything?"

"Then, are you ready to go?"

Sandra looked out the kitchen window, then down at the plate of cookies awaiting her daughter. "Would you like a cookie?"

"What?"

"Are you allergic to peanuts? Uh, are you allergic to anything?"

Death laughed. "Do you mean am I human enough to have medical failings like allergies?"

Sandra shrugged.

Death shook her head. "I'm not allergic to peanuts." She looked over at the plate. "Sure, I'll have a cookie."

The two sat together at the kitchen table, sharing the plate of cookies and a pot of tea, though Sandra was careful not to brush against Death in any way. Sandra had expected it to be awkward, but it turned out that Death was a decent conversationalist.

After the dregs of tea were washed out and the last crumbs were brushed into the trash, Death again stretched out her hand. "Shall we?"

Sandra reached out but hesitated again before their fingers touched. She quickly withdrew her hand and hid it behind her. "I can't."

Death raised an eyebrow.

"I—I need to write a will. I haven't gotten around to that yet."

"Wouldn't your daughter get everything anyway?"

"That's the thing. That's not guaranteed. Not without a will. I have to make sure she's taken care of. And I have to—" Sandra's gaze whirled around the kitchen. "I have to pack things up so it's not too difficult for her when she comes. I have so much stuff, you know. Please, just one more day."

There was a strange glint in Death's eyes as she scrutinized Sandra. "One more day, you say?"

"Yes, just one."

More than three months later, Death said, "I'm curious to see how long you will keep this up." She crunched through another cookie, this time chocolate chip. "How many more reasons can you come up with?"

Sandra had long since lost any remaining fear of Death. Instead, she cherished every moment spent with the woman.

She had noticed Death had stayed longer today, hours probably, though it had felt like minutes. "Don't you have work to do? Souls to harvest?"

Death laughed. "Do you know how many people die at any one moment in time?"

"More than one?" Sandra ventured.

"Definitely more than one," Death said. "If I couldn't be in more than one place at a time, I would make a poor Death, wouldn't I?"

"I suppose so," Sandra said. "What's that like? Being in multiple places at once?"

"I'm not sure how to explain it," Death said. "It's my reality. It's normal to me. I don't know what's normal to you—the way you see things, the way you exist. So, I'm not sure how to explain the difference."

"I see." Sandra tried to think about what it'd be like to be here and there at the same time. Then, she tried to think how to explain only being in one place all the time. "Well," she finally said, "would you like more cookies?"

"Yes," Death said, laughing. "Definitely."

Later on, Sandra said in a low voice, "You're welcome to stay as long as you want. I don't mind."

Death looked back at her, solemn. "Thank you."

And she did.

After six months, Death finally asked the question that Sandra had been dreading: "What are you holding on to?"

Even two weeks before, Sandra would have had an easy answer for the smiling woman in front of her: "Life," she would have said. "I love life too much to leave it. There will always be a reason for me to live life one more day." Or she would have said, "My daughter. I can't leave her. I don't want her to lose her mother."

But now?

Life would always be amazing. There would always be more she wanted to do. And deep down, she knew her daughter was grown, independent, and strong, with a great life of her own. Sandra would be lying to herself if these were the sole reasons behind her daily requests now.

She had to face the truth. Her reasons for remaining alive shifted to wanting to spend one more day with Death, eagerly anticipating the moment she turned to find the woman in her kitchen. One more, and one more, and one more. Once Sandra took Death's hand and Death led her to wherever she was meant to go, there would be no more cookie-and-tea-laden conversations. Just the thought of that lonely eternity made her ache.

A realization swept through her like the wind blowing away all the dust. She loved Death. What the hell was wrong with her? Who fell in love with the personification of mortality? Apparently she did.

She had always known she liked looking at both men and women. After marrying her husband, however, she'd quietly packed away those feelings and focused on her marriage and family. Even when their marriage had floundered and they'd found a new footing as good friends instead of lovers, even when her husband had died, she hadn't allowed any of those feelings to resurface. Too busy, she'd always told herself. And then, who would want an old lady anyway?

Instead of answering Death, Sandra responded with questions of her own. "Why are you here all the time? What do you even see in me?" Sandra grabbed a fistful of her graying brown hair, the other hand patting the burgeoning paunch bulging a bit over the waistband of her pants.

"I see you," Death said. "Your soul. The person you truly are. And I like to spend time with the person that I see."

Sandra looked down at herself. "I wish I could see myself the way you see me."

"Same here," Death said. "What do you see when you look at me?"

"What do you mean? You don't know what you look like?" Sandra laughed. "Do they not have mirrors where you come from, or are you like a vampire, without a reflection?"

"I look different to everyone," Death said. "So, I want to know how you see me."

"Certainly nothing as poetic as your soul," Sandra said. She wondered how her husband had seen Death.

"Some would say that I don't have a soul," Death said. "I couldn't very well harvest it from myself, so what would be the point of having a soul then? Ironic, isn't it, that Death can't die? How could I know how you feel if I've never experienced it for myself?"

"I don't know if you have a soul or not," Sandra said. "But you're kind and smart and funny. That's enough for me."

"But what do you see when you look at me?" Death pressed.

Sandra considered the woman in front of her. "Well, you're shorter than me, for one." She started describing all of Death's features. Death leaned forward as if fascinated.

Afterward, Death sat there for a while, deep in thought. Finally, she asked, "Do you like what you see?"

Sandra smiled. "Oh, yes." Then, hesitant, she asked Death, "Do you? Like what you see?"

"Yes," Death said. "You're beautiful."

Those three words wrapped around Sandra like a warm, comfortable, handmade quilt. "I'm afraid," Sandra blurted out in confession. "That's what I'm holding onto."

"Of death?"

Sandra shook her head. "Actually, it's the opposite. Now, at least. I'm afraid of what happens afterward." She looked into Death's eyes. "I'm afraid that once I die, you will disappear from my life—uh, afterlife. I'm afraid of losing you."

Death's eyes widened. "What are you saying?"

Sandra glanced down, feeling blood heat her cheeks. "It's what it sounds like." Feeling suddenly bold, she let go of the words that had been huddled in her chest for longer than she'd realized. "I think that I've gone and fallen in love with you."

Silence fell over the room.

"N—not that I'm expecting you to respond in any way," Sandra said. "I just wanted you to know."

"What if," Death said, "I could still come visit you in your afterlife, wherever that is? That instead of these visits—of these reasons you come up with each day—we could just have an eternity together, if you wanted."

"Is that—what you want too?" Sandra asked. Her tightly clasped hands in her lap trembled. "Would you want an eternity together?"

"Yes," Death said. "I think I do."

"And you're not just saying it to please me?" Sandra asked. "To get me to move on to the afterlife, and then you're just going to disappear afterward?"

"I can't lie to you, Sandra," Death said.

Sandra drew in a long breath, holding it deep in her lungs until they burned. Would she miss this—this sense of being alive? Maybe, but maybe it was worth it. "In that case, I'm ready," she said, standing up from the table and brushing any remaining crumbs off her clothes.

Death stood too and held out her hand, unfurling her elegant fingers to Sandra like a blooming flower. Sandra stepped close, breathing in the familiar scent. Why had she ever been afraid of this beautiful woman who smiled at her like the sun streaming in through the windows?

Carefully, she settled her own hand in Death's grasp and marveled at how well-matched their hands looked clasped together.

"Are we going now?" Sandra asked.

"We're already here," Death said.

"What?" Sandra said, her question coming out as more of a statement. "Where? We haven't gone anywhere."

"Yes," Death said.

Sandra pulled her hand away and looked around at her familiar surroundings. She blinked, and then all of a sudden, realization blossomed in her. She whirled around to face Death. "You—you never gave me those extra days, did you?"

Death shook her head. "No one gets extra time, Sandra. When it's time, it's time."

"Then, why did you pretend to do so?"

"I never said you did. You assumed it of your own accord. And didn't you find it strange that you never went to any other parts of your home?"

"You let me assume," Sandra shot back. "You knew I assumed, and you never corrected that assumption."

"I'm sorry," Death said. "I just found it so interesting that your afterlife was no different than your usual life—that nothing changed and so you never noticed that you had died already."

That stopped Sandra. "Wait, this is my afterlife?"

How boring of her. How confined. She could have imagined anything else in the entire universe, yet her soul had chosen her own kitchen?

But the more she thought about it, the more it made sense to her. This was the place she cherished the most—this place of comfort, familiarity, and warm memories. A place that had been her refuge during her darkest days. A place where her loved ones had gathered in happier days. This place where she had fallen in love with the woman standing within it, with a wry smile on her beloved face.

"This is the afterlife you've created," Death chuckled. "When you want to, when you're ready to step outside the door, you'll create new parts of your afterlife. You're not stuck in one room for eternity—unless you want to be, of course."

"How?"

"You already contain all the knowledge you need. You only need to think it, and the answer will come to you."

"I've created my own afterlife, my own idea of heaven." Sandra marveled at that, and then, just as suddenly, she frowned—a thought striking her. "Wait, if all this knowledge was already within me this whole time, does this mean that I've created you? That I've created this whole thing between us? That—" Her words trailed away.

"That your idea of heaven is to love Death and be loved in return?"

"Was none of this real?"

Death shrugged. "If it's real to you, what does it matter if it's real to anyone else?"

"No," Sandra said, throwing the word at Death. "No, I want to know if you're truly Death, or just a figment of my imagination."

"Sandra," Death said, reaching out to clasp their hands together again. "No matter what I tell you, there will always be a part of you wondering if your mind is putting words into my mouth. So, instead, let me just say that I love you too. I want to be with you. If you want to believe that I am real or that your mind created me for you, it's up to you. If you want me to stay with you or to leave and not come back, again, that's up to you. Sandra, it's your choice."

Sandra swallowed, looking at Death before her. Her heart tightened, and she knew that Death was right, but did it matter in the end?

She loved and was loved in return. It was enough.

The Last Blood Moon

ANN YUAN

The nurse said he had been ranting and kicking since lunch; the doctor ordered Xanax.

"Do you know where he is?" the nurse asked, her eyebrows raised—another way to say, *You heartless jerk, you only come now?!*

I ignored her glance and walked into 908.

Inside the room, an old man sat in a wheelchair, his head tilting to one side, his eyes half-closed.

For a moment, I wasn't sure; then I saw the name tag on the bed.

"Hi, Dad," I said.

His head wobbled a little, but he heard me. I had nothing more to say.

In the letter, he wrote down all the information: the address, the room number, the place where he must "finish the business" and the escape route.

I waited until it was quiet outside and pushed him out. We passed the empty nurse's station and moved toward the door at the end of the corridor. My palms sweated as I gripped the wheelchair, the wheels soundlessly rolling on the glittered floor. Behind the door was a flight of concrete stairs leading to the roof.

I disconnected the IV line, collected the half-filled urine bag, and put it on his lap. I lifted him in my arms.

A whiff of sour perspiration made me turn my head. He was only slightly heavier than a thick comforter. The six-foot-two man had shrunk so much that he could easily fit in a cradle.

His beard covered half of his face, and the other half was just lines and folds, hair scattered on the age-spot-mottled scalp.

A werewolf won't die, at least not like this.

"It always happens in a blood moon," he once said.

"How?" I asked.

"You'll see."

In my five-year-old head, I pictured him splitting in half or dissolving into the air—definitely not something I wanted to witness.

When he was out of drink and Mom wasn't yelling, he took me on a motorcycle ride. He swung me up to the front of his Honda XR. I sat astride the gas tank, hands gripping the handlebar, feeling the embrace of a beast's body odor. We sailed through green fields. When a crescent moon appeared in the sky, he yodeled like a hungry dog crying in the dark.

One week after my ninth birthday, he disappeared. I hadn't seen him until now. So funny that after all these years, we were still in the same awkward position—one in another's arms.

I elbowed open the roof door. All at once, we were immersed in a sea of light. Above a junkyard of rusty chairs and broken shelves, a huge red moon hung in the sky. It felt so close that I could just reach out my arm to touch it. The color was fierce, lively—a ball of liquid iron that was about to overflow.

"Leave me alone," he groaned.

"As you wish." I laid him on a crate next to the water tank.

He looked around and said, "I knew you'd come."

"What the hell do you want me to do?"

He coughed, heaving his chest like a balloon pumping and leaking at the same time. "I needed someone to take me here. It's a blood moon tonight."

"You left us! Now you just summon me to help you die?"

"We're different." He lowered his head and hissed, "You and your mother, I can only hurt you two."

We froze in a moment of silence. The air was cold and crisp. The moon was at its peak fullness.

"What're you waiting for?" he finally said. "You can go now."

I should go back to the floor, return the wheelchair to his room, and walk out of the building in front of the surveillance camera—an alibi he planned. Where did he learn this shit?

"What're you waiting for?" I jerked my head at the moon. He was not going to abandon me again, not this time. "You promised. I have to see it."

He shook his head and chuckled. "Thank you."

He stood up, stripping off the gown and ripping all the lines from his body. His skin glared under the moonlight. A layer of gray fur spread across his body. He shuffled across the roof, mouth protruding and ears enlarging. His thin figure flickered in the glowing redness. Then he howled and leapt. The ferocious whoop pierced the dark-blue sky, shook the building, and echoed on the street. It was a werewolf's shameless farewell to the human world, where he felt no remorse at all.

A moment later, a security guard and a nurse rushed onto the roof. They only saw a lump of hospital gown and me.

Some Men are Dogs

VICTORIA SOSA

I started following her a few weeks ago. I know it's been weeks because the chicken she gave me is still there. The bones have turned brown like the leaves and the color of the shoes she wears. Her concrete-flavored white sneakers have been replaced with a furry suede that sticks to my tongue. I hate how the pieces of fake fluff melt in my mouth, but it makes her laugh.

I noticed her laugh first. The sound was sharp and withering; so much like a wounded animal that I pounced from my hiding spot underneath the broken metal stairs of an abandoned store. She looked at me, mouth still open, clutching a box of chicken. She bared her teeth.

"Are you hungry, boy?" She threw her last pieces of chicken to me. I caught one midair and was satisfied by the instant crack. I ran up to her for more, licking at her feet.

"Hmm, what should I call you?"

I sniffed up her legs, up her thighs.

"Maybe I should tell you what I'm called first?"

Bitch, I yapped. She said her name was Doris.

I padded alongside her. She leaned down every few minutes to pat my head. When we arrived at a yellow brick heap with white doors and windows, she squatted. One hand aimlessly scratched a spot behind my ear while the other held up a picture of a dirty sand-colored dog. I whined as the hand moved. She rested the tip of her finger on my nose. "That's you."

Before I could decide whether to lick her finger or the screen (both smelt like chicken), she moved them away. I watched her disappear inside the mouth of that wide and windowed monster.

The next day I nipped at Doris's ankles as she squealed, "I don't have anything to give you goofy." She let out a high-pitched squeak. "That's perfect! I'll call you Goofy."

When we arrived at her heap, she met the grass again. This time poking it. "Stay."

After she disappeared, I dug at the spot she'd been poking, hoping to find whatever she might have buried. The hole was empty. A chunk of ham falling from the sky grabbed my attention. I devoured all but a single piece. This I placed into the hole and covered with dirt for her to have later.

He started following her a few days ago. I was used to the confusing smells of many people on one street, but his scent remained as we made our way through the back roads, never any closer or any further.

It smelled like the kennels. No, it smelled like the last cage in the corner of the kennels, the one that no one walked toward except the man with metal keys and metal boots. It smelt like that man, but it wasn't him. The smell just gave me the same sensation as the bottom of the man's boots crashing down on my face.

I ignored it. Men often smell like violence. But it was there the next night, and the next night, and the next, always accompanied by the rise and fall of feet, the rustle of a jacket, and the breathing. I might have imagined the breathing, a nasally huff that wouldn't mingle with the wind. Maybe I thought I felt hot breath on my scruff because of the chill down my spine.

The first night he followed, I walked closer to Doris. The second night, I stopped. She slowed down before stopping also. We all stood in silence. I turned to look at the silhouette behind us. It was darker than the empty black air, a sign of something in the nothingness that can reach out and touch you. I watched until it seemed that it may have been a pole or a strange bush. Then, the silhouette stepped out of my vision, and there was no doubt.

The third night, I stopped again. Doris paused without hesitation. I waited for the silence. Heavy footfalls continued to penetrate the quiet. The man-shaped hole in the night became clearer. The scent grew thick: I growled.

"What's wrong?" Doris asked.

I barked. *Your small ears and pale eyes make you unfit to survive in the darkness. Your big chest heaves with fear because you are prey in the wild of this city. I have seen women like you rotting. I have tasted the flesh of women like you. I stand between you and all the other dogs.*

"Goofy boy," she muttered, and we walked on.

It was getting colder, so Doris began letting me inside. Her home had warmth and gentle blue walls, but she never let me past the first square and cluttered room. I laid on a dusty but soft blanket in the corner and listened to her patter around the place, talking to no one.

"I'll see him again. He works at the office next to mine. Apparently, we get off at the same time. He offered to walk me home. Isn't that sweet?"

When her aimless chatter ended and the rooms filled with stillness, I slept.

I walked out with Doris onto the porch, my eyes tracking the large bag of dog food in her arms. She poured some into a metal bowl. GOOFY drawn on the side in big, black letters. My bowl. She walked away while I ate, disappearing into the clear day.

After licking up the chalky crumbs, I started my prowl. My hunts were no longer a scavenge but a curious walk around town as I slowly made my way back to my hiding spot. There, I escaped the beating of the afternoon sun and napped on cool, moist dirt. A streetlight flooded through the cracks in the stairway, waking me up and letting me know that Doris was on her way. But Doris hadn't come. Though the metal beasts had stopped rolling down the roads, and the moon had traveled across the sky.

I whimpered. *Alone.*

My nose perked up. Alcohol and wildflowers. I darted onto the sidewalk and sprinted toward her. A husky sour scent crawled toward me, arriving before I reached her. I froze.

"Goofy!" Doris hurried up to me, a clumsy pathetic waddle. The man strode on even feet, covering more distance. She turned toward him. "This is my dog. Well... kind of... he comes over and we hang out."

She dragged a mittened hand over my head. I didn't wag or nuzzle or stick out my tongue. I looked at him. "I guess you could say he's a friend."

The man didn't try to pet me, but I knew his rough hands would've pushed down on my skull.

"Are you sure that's a good idea? He could have fleas or a disease." His voice was skateboard wheels on pavement, scraping and erratic.

She opened her mouth wide, her pink gums showing. "I've always been the type of girl to let in strays."

The man's teeth peeked out, his lips tight. "As a stray myself, I'm happy to hear that.

Doris's face turned red. She walked on, safely to the other side of me. The man made to walk past me. I leaned forward, my legs stiff, nose wrinkling. When his foot came within biting distance, I bit. He jumped back.

"Oh my god! Did he get you?"

Rage built up in his eyes, but he caged it there. "No, I'm okay." He tried to hurry past again and I growled, forcing him to retreat. He raised an eyebrow at Doris, but she was busy casting suspicious glances from me to him. He stepped back further. "Does he hate cats? I have two. They get all over me in the mornings."

"Oh," Doris exclaimed. "That must be it. I've never seen him around cats."

They stared at each other for an awkward, silent moment.

"Another time," she finally said.

The man nodded and walked back into his shadows.

I had a dream that I was the dog in the last cage in the kennels. I was trapped with the corpse of a bitch, leaking milk and blood, but my nose was assaulted by an odor worse than death. I barked as the man approached my cage. To my surprise, he began to bark back. Everything grew long: his teeth, his spine, his face. He extended until we were snout to snout. A directionless knocking echoed through the room. The cage door swung open.

I woke up, still barking. I knew I was awake because I could feel the damp cotton fabric of my makeshift dog bed. The gray bars were now just the gray walls of Doris's mudroom. The cage door was just the entrance of her yellow heap. The man was just a man again.

"Goofy, quiet!" Doris stood over me. Her hands didn't curl into a ball or flatten into a board but hovered helplessly.

"It's the cat fur again." The man stood in front of the doorway, theatrically picking at a brown furless coat. He glared at me but his voice didn't lose its honeyed tone.

"Maybe you should put him outside."

Doris reached for me, and I bit at her fingers. She startled backward. My voice threatened to tear my throat to pieces.

Liar!

Liar!

Liar!

I screamed and screamed but was never heard, only feared, only silenced, only overtaken. The man moved forward, challenging me, so I attacked. I caught the hems of his slacks and pulled him to the ground. Doris shrieked behind us. I lunged for the throat, but something slammed into my back.

"Bad dog!"

The pain traveled along my spine, paralyzing me for a moment. I was stunned long enough for him to throw me off. The blows kept coming. I ran blindly from them, stopping when I felt the sting of cold air. The door slammed behind me.

I thrashed at the air, spit flying from my teeth. I'm not sure how long I turned in circles, frightened by even my own tail. I wanted something real to bite, something tangible to sink my teeth into, something more than silence. The quiet persists; it outlasts the howling. I fell into a stupor.

Doris's high-pitched noises of surprise shook me out of my daze. My ears perked up, my body frozen—waiting. Wind rattled naked branches while hidden creatures made their desperate conquest over the earth. Rain gathered at the edges of the night sky, preparing to fill anything unfortunate enough to be under it.

I darted to the door. I grabbed the doorknob with my jaw and pulled, pressing my paws against the door to stay on my hind legs. When that didn't work, I scratched at the panels. Once my claws had pierced through the first layers of wood without success, I ran to Doris's bedroom window.

I knew what was happening. I knew what a man was doing when he struggled with a woman. I knew what it meant when the struggle stopped. I jumped on my hind legs, yowling at the closed window. I needed a way in. I ran around the house. I ran around it again. I ran around her giant yellow box until my legs wobbled. There was no way in. I collapsed on the porch.

The man swung open the front door with confidence, but I could hear the anxious pause to check his escape route. I could smell the lingering scent of his crime. He swung keys in his hand, strolling to the gray four-wheeled beast waiting for him on the corner. I could taste those keys like blood in the mouth. I followed him.

The beast came alive as he approached it. *Now! Now, before he cowers in its impenetrable belly! Now, while he is still a dog!*

There was no more strength to gather. The man slipped the keys into the pocket near his crotch. I did what I couldn't in the cage; I aimed. He saw me coming too late. My teeth sank past polyester into a salty lump of flesh. The man howled. He struck me hard across the face. Three more strikes, nails slashing at my eyes. Something cracked beneath my teeth. He screamed, a swirl of agony and rage. His fists began to pummel my jaw, forcing my retreat. I reared up to attack again, but when I leapt, he kicked out his trembling leg. I thrashed into the grass. Whimpering, he hobbled away from my deflated body.

I would lick my wounds later. I limped back. The door was ajar, as if inviting more thieves, but it was only me squeezing my face through the small gap to pry it open. There was no light.

I sniffed my way to Doris, ignoring all but the spoiled fruit smell of a woman. There was a large lump in the bed that squirmed as I jumped on top of it.

"Goofy?" Doris whispered. She didn't move any farther. Her bare chest rattled violently, shaking her whole body. My own body tremored with each movement. With a sigh, I lay next to her. She reached out a hand to stroke my back. "I wish I would've let you kill him."

I knew she couldn't understand me, so I didn't tell her that it was all true. Dog eat dog. Dog eat anything it can overtake. Dog eat until it's full. I didn't need to tell her anymore for her to understand it. I settled for dragging myself to the end of the bed to lick her feet. She didn't laugh.

Dance With Me

D.M. CROSS

M.I.A.

nicole had awakened with those letters before her eyes every morning since she'd heard the news: WE REGRET TO INFORM YOU THAT YOUR HUSBAND...

Two years of not knowing, getting up with a headache, getting advice from those who had been through it and from those who hadn't. Getting drunk most nights and getting up with M. I. A. appearing as big as a highway sign.

Getting out of bed was slow and time-consuming, so the clock was always set an hour earlier than it had been before. Somehow, she did get up, get dressed, get food in her stomach, and get to work. Her co-workers, for the most part, were supportive—as supportive as they could be for never having experienced the ambiguity of not knowing for sure.

"One day he'll come dancing through that door," the ones who knew him would say, the ones who knew how they met.

"Pardon me, Miss. Would you care to dance with me?" was the first thing he'd ever said to her. He walked up and extended his hand to her at the check-in stand at the dance hall. He waited patiently for her answer, smiling at her as though she were the answer to his prayers; as though if she had said no, it would have crushed him. It seemed not to matter to him at all that she was Black and that he was White. To her, it had seemed more like a challenge than a request, and it wasn't in her nature to resist such a challenge.

"Yes, actually I would like to dance," she said, taking his hand.

He's brave, she thought, and not because of the difference in their skin tones. It was because she was always the one who had to ask the guy to dance. Guys always told her they weren't drunk enough, so she would end up dancing with whichever female friend she had come with that night.

But this one was already fearless enough to ask her. Not only was he obviously not drunk, but he could dance! He did not suffer from the eponymous White Man's Disease. He kept in-time and in-step, even with faster beats.

By the end of the third song, she thought he would be tired, so she was ready to thank him and leave, but she never got a chance. The next song was slow, and without skipping a beat he took her left hand, then put her right hand on his waist. Her immediate reaction: DAAAMN! What a trim waistline! He must be in the military.

The co-workers and friends who knew the story always used the word dancing instead of walking when they suggested he would come back to her someday. It made her happy and sad at the same time. They were trying to encourage her, give her hope, but after two long years, she was nearly ready to give up.

When she arrived at work Monday morning, she was greeted by the usual nods and smiles. She weakly nodded and smiled in return, sat in her cubicle and started pushing papers. Around 10 a.m. her friend and co-worker, Rosalee, popped-in, her smile seeming perkier than usual.

"Nikka, what are you doing this Friday night?" she asked. Rosalee was the only friend Nicole allowed to call her that.

"I don't know," Nicole answered without looking up. "The usual, I guess."

"You mean staying home alone," Rosalee said, punctuating the last three words.

"Yep, that's pretty much what I do," Nicole said, adding another sheet of paper to an already tall stack.

"Well, this Friday's going to be different. I need somebody to go with me to Brick's. There's a live band I love, playing there this weekend, and I don't want to be stuck waiting for a guy to be drunk enough before dancing with me."

Oh no, she's trying to help me again. Nicole looked at another paper, but instead of items on a purchase order, she saw: M. I. A.

TWO YEARS... EMPTY HOUSE... GETTING DRUNK

"OK," she finally said, her tone flat. "What should I wear?"

Rosalee clapped her hands, bouncing; her beautiful Filipina features glowing. "You will? Oh, Nikka, I'm so happy! I know, you won't regret it.

As to what to wear, it doesn't have to be fancy—just pretty. Do you want me to come over to your house and help you pick something out?"

First decision to give my well-meaning friend: do I want her to come over and see my messy place?

"No. That's ok. I'm sure I can find something that will work," she said, looking off and wondering what that might be.

"Would you like me to pick you up—or will you meet me there?"

Oy, another decision. Nicole furrowed her brow, which Rosalee picked up on.

"Never mind, I'll pick you up. That way you won't have to worry about parking, and I can make sure you get there and back."

Nicole nodded with a faint smile.

Rosalee entered the cubicle, came around the desk, and gave her a quick hug. "Really, Nikka, I'm so happy! Thanks for saying yes. I'll pick you up at 7:45. They start playing at 8:00, and we can start dancing as soon as we get there!" Rosalee almost skipped out of the office, leaving Nicole wondering what she had gotten herself into.

There were so many times between Monday and Friday that Nicole wanted to back out. There were so many decisions to make—*again. Should I shower after work?* Yes. *Eat at home or there?* Home. Who knew what was at Brick's or how much it would cost. *Should I call them and find out?* No. *Make-up?* Just the usual lipstick and cheek powder. And, of course: *what should I wear?*

Nicole had never been a clothes horse or a shoe hound, something her husband was actually more proud of than she was. She slipped on black, straight-legged pants with a loose-fitting silver shirt that revealed her collarbone. She fastened a big black belt around it, cinching her small waist, then chose silver earrings along with a silver necklace that hung below the top button of the shirt.

She had a grand total of five pairs of shoes, including flats for the office and the flip-flops she used as slippers. Her dancing shoes lay in their original box, placed apart from the others. She picked up the box and, for a moment, held it to her face. *If I wear them tonight*, she thought, *I'll be wearing them for somebody else.*

The alarm went off on her bedroom radio: 7:40 and Rosalee, always punctual, would be there in five minutes. Nicole hastily slipped the dance shoes in her bag, put on her makeup, and headed for the door.

The old folks would have said, "This joint is jumpin'!"

Once inside of Brick's, Rosalee grabbed Nicole by the wrist and ran to one side of the room, seemingly to scope out the "offerings." Nicole remembered the drill. Obviously, she was not finding anything to her immediate liking. Rosalee once again grabbed Nicole's wrist and pulled her to the wide dance floor.

Nicole knew timing was everything; the band was only 15 minutes into their first set, so the floor wasn't completely full. Some couples were dancing together, but as usual, there were more women dancing with each other. This gave ample opportunity for the non-dancing men to fulfill their role of checking out the women while getting drunk enough to dance.

After their second dance together, the band played a slow song, and Nicole followed Rosalee to the bar.

"What are you drinking? I'll treat you to the first one," Rosalee offered.

"Ginger ale for me, thanks."

"Ok, I get it—it's your first time back in a while and you want to play it safe." Rosalee got the bartender's attention after a few minutes. She imitated her favorite movie gangster. "Rum and coke for me, and a ginger ale for my pal, here, see?"

With drinks in hand, the two turned on their barstools in observation mode, Nicole more casually than Rosalee. It wasn't long before the excitement in the air made Nicole relax a little.

"See anybody you like yet?" she asked Rosalee.

"Yee-ep. I'm goin' in for the kill right now. Watch my drink for me."

"Sure."

Nicole watched as Rosalee approached a big, curly-haired blonde with a big, bushy mustache. She had always wondered what Rosalee found so attractive about that type. She spoke with the guy for a few seconds, then headed back to Nicole at the bar.

"I asked him to dance. Dork said he's not drunk enough yet. Maybe I'll ask again when he is. Hey, Nikka, you listening to me?"

She wasn't. She was focused on an old, White man with a full head of gray hair, wearing black-rimmed glasses. He danced with a woman clearly half his age, keeping up with her moves. In fact, he danced better than she. When the song was over, he bowed and mouthed the words *thank you*. Before the next song started, he extended his hand to a different woman, asking silently if she wanted to dance; she readily accepted.

"Who is *that*?" Nicole asked without taking her eyes off him.

Rosalee followed the direction of Nicole's stare. "Oh, that's Sam. At least, that's what everybody calls him. Nobody seems to know his real name. He doesn't talk much, if at all. Seems like he just arrives, dances with every woman who says yes, then leaves."

"Have you ever danced with him?"

"Who, *me*?" Rosalee's tone was a little more incredulous than it needed to be. "I'm not that desperate. I like my men big and burly."

"I know, I know."

Rosalee went back to sipping her drink and scoping out the men, while Nicole watched Sam. She had no idea why Rosalee would be so opposed to dancing with him. She thought him quite handsome, and he was trim, no doubt from all the dancing. His hair, a sparkling silver in the occasional spotlight, made him look like a mature actor from an action film. He was obviously not on the make, since he was dancing with women regardless of their age, size, or color.

"You wanna dance some more?" Rosalee asked, after finishing the last sip of her drink.

"Yeah, I do," Nicole responded, grabbing Rosalee by the wrist and bolting to the floor.

Nicole made sure she positioned herself close to Sam. She could see he was focused on his moves and current partner. Though she understood that someone so focused might not notice her, she let herself dance like she did years before, freely, yet in step.

Rosalee was immediately delighted by Nicole's performance. "Git it, girl!"

Sometimes the song would indicate a movement like stopping or getting down to the floor: Nicole followed the cues. Several people watched and cheered her on. She glanced in Sam's direction, but he was into the music and still focused on his partner. When the song was over, several people applauded her before scattering from the floor.

"Girl, you were *good*! Just like I remember you. You wanna—," Rosalee's eyes stared behind Nicole.

Nicole turned to see Sam, his hand extended toward her. He didn't say a word, but she understood.

"Yes," she said with her eyes slightly lowered.

Another fast song was fine with her. At one point she looked down at his shoes; they were professional dance footwear instead of sneakers. He looked at her shoes, then pointed at them; his pearly white smile suggested he approved. As if to thank him, she danced as hard, precisely, and as beautifully as she could.

When the music ended, the band announced they would take a break. Sam bowed and mouthed the words "thank you."

"No. Thank *you*," Nicole said out loud. She was about to ask his name, but he turned, hurried away, and entered the men's room.

Nicole shrugged. After a quick search she saw Rosalee talking to a different beefy guy. She walked over to them. As soon as she was within reach, Rosalee grabbed her.

"Excuse me, this is my friend, and I've got to talk to her for a minute," Rosalee said, hurrying them out of earshot. "THANK GOD you came when you did! I couldn't get that guy outta my hair!"

"You mean, you *do* have a limit on how big and burly a guy can be?"

"Yes, and he was it. Sooo, how'd it work out with Mr. Smooth?"

"He was wonderful," Nicole sighed.

The band's intermission lasted thirty minutes, and in that time, Sam never came out of the men's room. Nicole had kept an eye on the door, hoping to get a chance to talk to him when he came out. She hoped to find out his real name, what dance school he went to, and maybe ask his age. As the band reassembled, she sighed and turned around to finish the same ginger ale Rosalee had bought her earlier.

As she got to the last sip, the band began with a slow piece. As the music began, Nicole felt a light tap on her shoulder. She turned to see Sam with a lovely smile, and hand extended.

On the floor, Sam brought her in close. Her uneasiness lasted only a few seconds. He put her right hand on his waist, its trimness confirming what she had thought while watching him. He led her through some intricate dance moves, which she easily followed and they moved as though they had known each other for years. The dance seemed to last for hours.

When the music was over, Nicole wanted to join the others applauding the band, but instead of releasing her hand, Sam held onto it, causing her to look at his face.

Suddenly, Sam's hair changed from straight and grey to wavy and brown, his glasses were gone and he looked exactly like her husband. His lips parted before he spoke out loud, "Wait for me."

She closed her eyes and shook her head. When she looked again, Sam was smiling at her. He nodded, still holding her hand, and as he bowed, he kissed it gently and mouthed the words, "Thank you." He then turned to dance with the next woman who would say yes.

Stunned, she remained on the dance floor for moments before slowly making her way through the crowd. She sat on the barstool, staring blankly into space, just as Rosalee came up.

"I saw you two; you guys looked great together. I told you tonight would be different, didn't I?" Rosalee seemed to notice the bewildered look on Nicole's face, and on the verge of anger, she asked, "What'd he say to you?"

"I'm all right," Nicole said before smiling slightly. "Rosalee, can you take me home, now?"

"Now?"

Yes, I need to rest up for tomorrow," Nicole said, nodding with a far-off gaze.

"Well, okay," Rosalee relaxed, "but can it wait until after the next fast song? Dork says he'll be drunk enough by then."

The next morning Nicole woke up without a headache. The three huge letters that had appeared before her for so long were replaced by the three new words: Wait for me.

Before getting out of bed, she mouthed the words, "thank you for the message and the messenger."

She picked up the picture of her husband in uniform from her nightstand. She opened up the top drawer, found a sticky note and marker, and wrote the words WAIT FOR ME on it. She stuck it to the picture and returned it to its place.

Nicole started cleaning her house, staying on task until she got hungry. She drove to the grocery store for some head-clearing food and drink. In the afternoon, she called Rosalee and invited her to lunch the next day to thank her for getting her out of the house. That night, Nicole watched two of her favorite movies: one that always made her cry and one that always made her laugh.

At lunch on Sunday, she found out Dork's real name was Frank and he was a third stringer or some such, on the city's football team. They were planning on meeting later that evening at a non-dancing venue. Anytime that Rosalee asked Nicole what Sam had said, Nicole would change the subject back to Rosalee's budding relationship.

The workweek improved; there were still a lot of issues, but things started to get under control. When Nicole felt pressured, she looked at the picture of her husband on her desk, comforting herself with those three words.

On the one-week anniversary of going to Brick's, Rosalee popped in to ask Nicole if she wanted to go and see her "boyfriend" again.

"No thanks. I'm good."

"Well, OK. I won't push it this time." Rosalee waited for a response, but when Nicole didn't seem to bite, she added, "And do you wanna know why?"

"You have a date with Frank."

"How did you know?"

"Just a lucky guess," Nicole said, then winked. "Have fun."

After work, Nicole stopped by the store to pick up some groceries for the weekend. She grabbed the mail from the box without looking at it and placed it with the grocery bags on the kitchen counter. After putting the food away, she went through the mail. She started opening a packet of ads when she noticed an official-looking envelope from the government. The ads fell to the floor. She nervously opened the envelope:

WE ARE PLEASED TO INFORM YOU THAT YOUR HUSBAND...

Nicole didn't tell anyone, not even Rosalee. She wanted no fanfare, no congratulations, no one saying, "told you so" until after she held him in her arms.

It wasn't long before Nicole watched him come up the walk through the window, and the years of waiting melted away.

Silently, she opened the door and stepped back to let him enter the room and put down his bags. He locked the door behind him, and only then did she leap into his arms. They kissed long and hard. He looked down at her and brushed away her tears without wiping away his own.

His lips parted, "Dance with me," was all he said.

Gothic Fantasy

Harvest of the Blood Moon

LINDSEY WOODWARD

Claudia stared at her outstretched hand as she fingered the ring with her thumb. Despite the clinging gloom in the barn, the diamond winked at her. A smile pulled at the corners of her mouth. Then she frowned, dropping her hand and turning her gaze to the trailer attached to the Athens Municipal golf cart. The assortment of stuffed animals, framed pictures, trophies, jewelry, and other things looked like a collection for a yard sale. Her hand balled into a fist, and she walked to the barn door.

The first day of autumn shined bright and clear across the manicured acres of the golf course. The morning's chill had burned away in summer's relentless grip, yet Claudia tugged her green hoodie closer. The afternoon heat couldn't warm the barn. Not today.

Her heart broke all over again, remembering the tears on cheeks, young and old, as each citizen gave their tribute. And now it was her turn, she reminded herself. Her phone buzzed in her pocket, giving her a moment of reprieve. The text made her smile.

Got her. Be there soon. ;)

As if there had been any doubt. Isaac was the best hunter in the county. Her smile faded as she looked at the ring again.

It's a small price to pay, her brain suggested. *Too high,* said her heart.

But that's why she had to let it go. Odren demanded that which was most precious. And for their sacrifices, he would favor them with uninterrupted electricity and internet, good harvests for the local farms, relative safety from predators, and peace with the surrounding towns. The rhyme every citizen in Limestone County knew by heart played across her lips.

The heart has currency greater than gold,
The loss of which can wound the soul.
Wrapped in sorrow and soaked in tears,
The tribute is made for seven years
Of life and love and peace and joy
And the happy smiles of every girl and boy.
His due, He takes, not a penny less,
And with His smile, we shall be bless'd.

Her ears twitched at the faint rumble of an engine. Dread squeezed her heart, and she turned away from the bright day. Too fast. Everything was happening too fast. She crossed a few feet to the trailer and stared at its contents with her balled fists tucked under her arms.

Before she could think about it, Claudia pulled the ring from her finger, put it in a black velvet box, and dropped it into the trailer. Her hands returned to their balled state, digging nails into her palms as her eyes stung. She sucked air down her throat, squeezing back the tears.

"I said I'd get you another one." A pair of arms went around her waist. Isaac pressed his face against her hair.

"I don't want another one," she said, her voice cracking. "I want that one."

"You're so cute when you pout."

Claudia jabbed him with her elbow. At his groan, she turned and gasped. Smudges of red streaked across his face in his effort to clean himself up. She found a tear in his shirt stained with more blood. "You need to see the doctor!"

"I'm fine. You can't hunt a griffin without getting a bruise or two."

"This is more than a bruise—"

He put his hand over her mouth.

"I'm fine," he said. "Odren's waiting."

She pulled his hand away with a teasing smile. "You sound concerned."

He didn't return her smile.

"C'mon," she said. "You're not afraid of Odren, are you?"

He shook his head. "I hate Him. He feeds off the tears of others. He's cruel."

Claudia's shock gave way to a frown. "You didn't think He was cruel last cycle."

"You weren't taking the offering to Him last cycle."

Odren required "unknown" women, eighteen years or older, to deliver His offerings. The town council chose the eldest of those who met the requirements. Being twenty-two and unmarried put Claudia at the top of the attendant's list.

"What if He demands the last sacrifice?" Isaac asked.

Claudia stifled a laugh. "Are you serious?"

"Don't," he said and pulled away.

She caught him by the hand, bringing his gaze back to her face.

"Hey—have you ever met someone who even heard of anyone who made the last sacrifice?"

He looked away in answer. She couldn't believe he was giving any credence to that urban legend. And even though she'd heard the rumors of other lord protectors turning down the Blood Path, she considered Limestone County lucky.

"Look at me," she said. "Even if it were true, He can't take what I don't have to give." She squeezed his hand. "I am yours, Isaac Haberth. Body and soul."

"I am yours, Claudia Wraak—heart, body, and soul."

She shook her head. "Do you always have to one-up me?"

He gave a playful tug on her hand but didn't smile.

"C'mon. Odren's waiting," she said, but he wouldn't release her. She followed his gaze to the pale strip of skin across her ring finger. "C'mon," she said, pulling out of his grip.

She sent him out of the barn with a push and climbed behind the wheel of the cart. A last-minute check for her phone in her left pocket and her pistol on her right hip. Better safe than torn to shreds by wargs. As she pulled out of the barn, Isaac took the lead on his ATV, his trailer loaded with the slain griffin.

The griffin queen was the largest Claudia had ever seen. She frowned as a pang of loss bored into her chest. It was the greatest trophy Isaac would likely ever bag. With a shake of her head, Claudia popped in her earbuds and selected an upbeat playlist on her phone. They'd need to hurry if they were going to make it in time for the eclipse.

By the time Claudia and Isaac arrived at their destination, dusk had dwindled into twilight. They pulled up to the gates of Odren's estate, and for a moment, she wished the eight-foot iron gates would have stayed closed. But they swung open just as the council had said they would. Her heart pounded as they drove down the pea gravel drive toward the massive dwelling.

She'd only seen Odren's mansion from behind the gates. It had always reminded her of a hunched beast keeping watch over them, and that had comforted her in the past. Now the house stalked as if on the hunt.

"It's just a house," she said. "Just give Him the offering, get His blessing, and leave. Simple."

She and Isaac parked at the front of the house. The building loomed over them, inspecting them with dozens of dark, empty eyes.

"Should we knock?" Isaac asked, making her jump.

In answer, the double doors opened. Claudia shuddered, staring at the darkness beyond the threshold. She forced herself to take slow, even breaths. Then she pushed herself out of the cart, threw a smile at Isaac, and ascended the stairs.

Before she could think about it, she crossed the threshold and jumped as the foyer awoke with electric candlelight. Piles of what looked like garbage covered the floor and inched up the walls. Clothes, toys, pictures. Just like the offerings she'd brought. A narrow footpath snaked along the floor and branched off into several dark hallways. The flickering bulbs blinked and illuminated a hall to the right, but Claudia didn't move.

"S'okay," Isaac said, taking her hand and pulling her behind him.

They toed their way through the heaps of past offerings, down the lighted hallway straight through the house, and out the backdoor. The offerings spilled out of the house and rolled across the grounds. A fat, yellow harvest moon hung over the trees. But it wasn't completely full. A shadow had begun to inch across the lunar surface, turning yellow to red. Rows of toy trucks marked pathways all leading to a ring of thirteen stones. Each stone stood taller than a house and as wide as a barn door. At the ring's center, a bonfire clawed at the sky.

Claudia stared in astonishment at the griffin queen lying on a stone altar behind the fire while the offerings of the town sat in a modest pile on the ground. She looked to Isaac, who shook his head. His attention snapped past her, and she turned. Her stomach clenched as she caught movement in the shadows. Then something sailed into the flames.

"You two!" the voice snapped like a whip from the darkness. "Come here!"

Claudia and Isaac exchanged uncertain glances and hurried to the stone circle but stopped when they reached the perimeter. Claudia watched a dark figure crouched over the offerings. Agitated swipes scattered items across the ground with a grumble. Then another object went flying into the fire.

"I haven't lapsed into Greek again, have I?" the figure muttered. "Doesn't sound like Greek to me."

The figure stood and faced the pair. The dancing, orange light of the fire revealed a tall, slender male figure in a dark suit and tie. He pointed at Claudia.

"Am I speaking Greek?" he asked in a gentle tone.

Claudia shook her head. "No."

"Then what the hell are you still doing over there!"

Isaac and Claudia hurried toward the altar.

"You," the man said, now pointing at Isaac, "this... thing is yours?" He motioned toward the altar and the griffin.

"Yes," Isaac said, "it's my off—"

"No. It's a pile of shit. You brought me a pile of shit."

Claudia and Isaac fell to their knees, realizing who was addressing them.

"We mean no offense, Odren, Lord Protector of Limestone County," Claudia said. "The griffin is our most sacred animal—"

"But it's not sacred to this asshole," Odren hissed, stabbing a finger at Isaac.

Claudia looked up in shock. Odren approached, squatted before her, and huffed in frustration.

"Am I asking for too much, Claudia?" he asked.

Her mouth moved, but no words came out. He knew her name?

In a stammering voice, she managed to say, "Of course not. Nothing's too much—"

"That's the problem!" he said in a high whine.

"I don't understand," she said. "We did as you have instructed."

"It's not enough." He shrugged. "It's not enough that I give you greedy bastards peace and prosperity." He snatched a football trophy from the ground. "This one wants to get laid before he turns eighteen." He threw the trophy into the fire and picked up a pair of red pumps. "She wants a promotion." The pumps disappeared in a frenzy of sparks. "So, go back and tell those stingy hicks to either put out or get out. I am not a charity."

He began to rise, and Claudia grabbed his arm.

"I beg—"

He wrenched free and hit her across the face.

"This suit costs more than all the souls in your town!"

She fell back as her head rang with the blow.

"Claudia!" Isaac helped her to stand and, using the firelight, examined her face. "You okay?"

She tried to smile, but the cut on her lip stung.

"You still here?" Odren asked.

Isaac's hand curled into a fist.

"Isaac—don't," she whispered. "We need to inform the council."

His anger gave way to fear. She knew what he was thinking. Everyone would blame them, but they had a duty to prepare the town. With a nod, he kissed the top of her head and pressed his face into her hair.

"I love you," he whispered.

They turned to leave.

"Hold on a sec, Ozzie and Harriet," Odren said. "I've got an itch I think you can scratch—if you're game."

Claudia and Isaac faced him. Before they could respond, he pushed Isaac aside and took Claudia by the chin, turning her face toward the fire.

"Tell me the truth," he said with a smirk. "Exactly what would you give to help your hick town, Claudia?"

"Anything."

Glee split his face. "You sure about that?"

His thumb ran along Claudia's lip. A cold, burning sensation flashed across her skin, and the cut was gone. Claudia wanted to pull away, but she couldn't turn her back on this opportunity. Everyone was counting on her. She nodded.

Odren turned his gaze to Isaac and asked, "What about you, Shit-pile?"

Isaac bristled but answered, "Anything."

"Deal," Odren said, taking Claudia by the arm and leading her to the pile of offerings. "Find yours."

Kneeling on the ground, she reached into the pile and found the velvet box.

"Great," he said, holding up a finger. "One sec." He turned to the altar and shoved the griffin off with one hand. "Won't be needing that." He beckoned to Claudia and patted a spot on the stone. "Show me what you got."

She set the box down, glancing at Isaac. Odren brought it to his nose and inhaled. His body shuddered, and a moan of pleasure escaped him.

"So close, Claudia." His eyes turned to her. "But so proud. Your pride cheated me."

She opened her mouth to apologize, but he raised a silencing finger. He opened the box and examined the ring.

"Wouldn't have made you for a romantic, Shit-pile." He popped the ring out, and to Claudia's confusion, slipped it onto her finger. "It's useless to me without your tears," he said.

"Then what do you want?" she asked.

"Your hair."

Her mouth opened, then closed, as she touched her head. "My hair?"

"Yep." Odren twitched his head toward Isaac. "It'll be his offering."

Claudia looked to Isaac. The pain in his face stabbed at her chest, but she took hold of the braid.

"No," he said. "Shit-pile's gotta cut it off and offer it to me."

Claudia closed her eyes as she called out, "Isaac."

Isaac's voice rumbled in the air. "I won't defile you for his amusement."

"Defile." Odren laughed. "You don't know the meaning of the word, boy."

Odren hooked Claudia around the neck and mashed his mouth against hers. She gagged on the taste of rancid butter. She had the sensation of dozens of hands touching her. Her body felt unwashed and used. Humiliation rose up her throat like bile.

Isaac's roar echoed in the stone circle. "Let her go!"

Odren pushed Claudia aside. She yelped, seeing Isaac on his knees with his hunting knife in hand while Odren held him by the throat.

"There it is," Odren said. "It's your virginity he prizes." He leered at Claudia.

Isaac struck with his weapon, but Odren caught the blade with a snort. His mouth puckered in disgust.

"Too spicy. Anger won't do." He pried the knife from Isaac's hand. "You said anything. You a liar, Shit-pile?"

He released Isaac, who collapsed to the ground gasping and choking. Claudia was at his side, but he wouldn't look at her.

"It's all right," she said.

"It's not your hair he wants," Isaac whispered.

"I know." She tried to smile. "It's okay."

A tap on her shoulder made her look up where Odren stood over them, holding the knife out to her. She took it and pressed it into Isaac's hand.

"I'll help you," she said.

She turned away from him, fixing her gaze on Odren, and guided Isaac's shaking fingers to her braid. With her other hand, she brought the blade toward her, tugging as Isaac's arm stiffened in resistance.

"Please stop, Claudia."

Odren nodded as his eyes glazed with hunger. The blade sliced through her hair in a sawing motion up her scalp. In less than a minute, the braid came free, and what was left of Claudia's hair fell around her face.

Isaac pressed his face against her head. "I'm so sorry."

She touched his face and squeezed her eyes shut as his tears trickled across her fingers.

"Hmm. I don't remember asking for a bad reenactment of *Romeo and Juliet*," Odren said.

Isaac stood and approached Odren with the braid in one hand and his knife in the other.

"My offering to you, Odren," Isaac said, his words cracked and hard, "Lord Protector of Limestone County."

"So let me have it, Shit-pile," Odren said with a smile.

Isaac plunged the blade into Odren's chest.

Claudia clapped her hands over her mouth. Odren's smile didn't move as he took hold of Isaac's throat and wrist.

"So predictable."

Odren pulled the knife from his chest and sank it into Isaac's stomach. Claudia screamed and pulled her gun. Odren ignored her as he lifted Isaac onto the altar. Isaac's skull cracked against the stone, but he didn't notice as he clawed at the hand on his throat. Claudia squeezed off two rounds into Odren's back, but he didn't acknowledge them. She rushed the altar and hit him on the back of the head with the flat of her gun.

"Let him go!"

Odren grabbed her by the wrist. She squealed as his grip crushed her wrist and her gun fell to the altar.

"It's time for your sacrifice, Claudia."

She looked at the knife in Isaac's gut.

"All right," she said, "but first, please take out the knife and heal him."

"No can do. We need it where it is. Your offering is in his chest right now."

She gaped at Odren. "You can't ask me to do that."

"I believe I just did."

"I won't."

"You don't seem to understand, Claudia."

She whimpered as his grip tightened on her wrist.

"We had a deal. You agreed to give me anything. Shit-pile's given his tribute." His manicured nails broke her skin. "It's your turn, Claudia. You don't get to puss out of this just because the terms of the agreement upset you." His fingers bored into her flesh. "There are no loopholes. No escape clauses."

Her voice was a barely audible croak. "Why?"

"I am yours, Isaac Haberth—body and soul," he said in a perfect imitation of her voice.

"No."

His voice changed to Isaac's. "I am yours, Claudia Wraak—heart, body, and soul."

"Please—"

Her knees buckled as her wrist snapped in his grip.

"I will have what is mine, Claudia." He smiled. "I'll even give you a hand."

Horror made her mute as his hand and arm melted into hers until they shared one arm between them. Even though she could feel the appendage, her arm flexed and her fingers wriggled without a thought.

"Now we can begin," Odren said.

"No! Please!"

Claudia dug her heels into the earth and backed away from the altar. Her own hand grabbed her by the throat.

"You're pissing me off, Claudia," Odren said. "We don't have much time. Shit-pile's bleeding to death, and if he dies before I have my offering, your Podunk town will be a blight in this county. I'll give burritos and Ex-Lax to harpies and direct them to your fields. Your children will be carried off in the night to be raped by goblins. Every other Podunk town will turn on you in fear. Is that what you want, Claudia? For everyone to suffer with you?"

She turned away from him, but her hand forced her to look at him.

"Think of it this way—he's gonna die. This will give his death meaning."

"But—"

He caught the word on her lips, pressing her against the table. This time he tasted like sweet wine.

"That's it, Claudia," he whispered. "That's what I need." His tongue flicked across her cheek, scooping up a tear. "But I need more."

He turned back to the altar where Isaac had passed out. He tapped the man on the face, receiving no response.

"See?" Odren said. "He won't feel a thing—mostly."

Claudia groaned as she fought for control of her hand as it reached for the knife. With her free hand, she grabbed her wrist, but the possessed hand gripped the knife handle.

"No."

She tore into flesh as the knife pulled free, releasing a steady flow of blood.

"No."

She tried to wrestle the knife from her own grip, but it pierced Isaac's gut a second time.

Claudia watched in numb detachment as she cut Isaac open just as she'd seen Isaac do hundreds of times to his prey after his hunting trips. His body jerked while Odren held him down. The knife clattered onto the altar, and she reached into the wet, hot cavity. Her fingers wormed past slick, firm muscle, nudged aside soft organs, and took hold of a pulsing bit of meat, squeezing a gasp out of Isaac. It came free with a jerk, and she retreated with Isaac's heart squirming in her grasp.

Odren brought it to his mouth and tore into the organ. Claudia closed her eyes, but the hot, metallic tang of blood filled her mouth. Her jaw strained to shred phantom meat. Her throat worked to swallow the chunks, taking more than just flesh. Isaac's gasps for breath weakened and faded while the tearing of meat continued without pause. Then Odren made a long moan of satisfaction.

"It really doesn't look so bad," Odren said, licking his fingers.

But Claudia wouldn't look. He patted her on the shoulder.

His free arm went around her, and his voice whispered in her ear. "I need you to open your eyes, Claudia."

Claudia obeyed.

For a moment, she thought Isaac might be breathing but realized it was a trick as firelight danced over his ruined form. A remote part of her brain wanted to wail at the sky and tear at her hair, but she tightened her hold on her emotions. Then, the offering would be worthless.

"First, you hold back my tears for pride," Odren said. "Now for spite. You are the worst cock tease I've ever encountered."

The back of her hand caressed her cheek.

"I can wait," he said. "They'll come eventually."

Claudia knew he was right. With her free hand, she picked up her gun, put the barrel to her head, and squeezed the trigger.

Claudia's eyes snapped open to a blood-red moon above her and a warm glow to her right. Her head lolled to the left, and she jumped as she came face to face with Isaac. Confusion. Hope. Then, disgust. She turned away only to meet Odren's grinning face.

"Miss me?" he asked.

The stone circle filled with Claudia's pain, anger, horror, and despair. Isaac was dead. She'd cut him open and torn out his heart. The metallic sting of blood echoed on her tongue. Odren's eyes rolled back into his head with a groan as he collapsed to his knees, gasping and shuddering.

"This suit is ruined," he said, taking a shaky breath. "Thank you, Claudia."

Claudia turned away and stared at Isaac. He almost looked like he was sleeping. If she didn't look down, she could make herself believe that. Instead, she took her gaze to the dark, wet spot on his stomach. Her hand clenched as it remembered the feel of his warm insides and pulsing heart.

Odren's hungry voice slithered into her ear. "I can go again if you can."

With a roar, she hit him in the face, but she couldn't stop at one. He never flinched as she beat her fists against his head and shoulders. Her knuckles tore, smearing blood on his face and jacket. Her voice broke with animal wails. After several minutes, Odren snatched her hands out of the air and twisted them behind her. She writhed and strained against his grip until she exhausted herself and collapsed against his shoulder, sobbing.

"Why couldn't you just let me die?" she whimpered.

Odren released her hands and wrapped his arms around her in a tight embrace. Her chest felt as if it had split open. She held him as she wept on his shoulder.

"Oh yes, Claudia. More." His body stiffened against her. "I knew you could give me what I needed, Claudia," he gasped in her ear. "My dear, sweet Claudia."

His lips caressed her cheek as he pulled away with an adoring smile.

"He was right," she said, looking at Odren. "You're cruel."

He smiled, tweaking her chin. "Newsflash. We're all cruel." He brought her closer and sipped the tears from her cheeks. "So, don't think you can bug out and find someone warm and fuzzy who only wants milk and cookies. Believe me," he said, giving her a light kiss. "Compared to most of the others, I am warm and fuzzy." He took her left hand and fingered the ring. "Besides, you can't go." He kissed the ring. "You're mine. So, your legs stay closed."

"Except for you?"

He waved off her question and stepped away from the altar. "I was just messing with Shit-pile." He helped her off the table. "Bumpin' uglies with lesser beings is not my thing." He took her by the chin. "But I don't share. Understand?" His hand went between her legs. "This mine's closed for excavation, and I expect to see you at the next offering. Make sure they give 'til it hurts."

"As you wish."

"Cheer up. You'll love being my herald—eventually." He put his hand to her chest. "I can already feel your soul growing cold and hard." He leaned toward her, then took a step away with a chuckle. "Well... it's been a stimulating evening, but you better get home. Folks'll start to wonder what we're doing." He winked at her and tapped her on the ass.

Claudia turned and headed toward the house.

"Oh—Claudia..."

She turned, and he pointed to Isaac.

"Do you want to deal with this, or should I..." He made a tossing motion toward the fire.

"I'll take him," she said.

"Great!"

He turned and bent over the pile of offerings from the town. A moment later, a doll sailed through the air with a mechanical wail and landed in the fire.

Claudia followed her path back through the house, guided by the candles, and exited the front door to find Odren standing by her cart. A large bundle lay in the trailer.

"I know how you mortals are big on death ceremonies," he said, "so I made him presentable for you."

"I'm sure his family will appreciate the gesture."

She climbed into the cart and started the engine.

"Claudia."

She turned to look at him.

"I know you've been through a lot," he said, putting his hand on her leg and leaning toward her. "If you ever need anything or if you get lonely, just know you've got a friend in me."

Her eyes burned as he grinned with anticipation. Then she blinked the feeling away.

"Worth a shot," he said with a shrug. "Safe travels."

The five-member panel of the Athens City Council sat in silence following Claudia's report. After several minutes, the Mayor turned to Claudia with a nod.

"Thank you, Miss Wraak," he said with a sympathetic smile. "Athens won't forget your sacrifice."

"That's it?" Claudia asked. "Odren murders Isaac, and you're just going to send me home?"

His smile faded. "I'm sorry. I didn't mean to make light—"

"What are you going to do?"

The Mayor raised his hands in a helpless gesture. "What can we do? Odren…"

"… Has turned onto the Blood Path!"

The council fidgeted in their seats. The Mayor gave the room his campaign smile.

His voice became soothing, as if he were calming a hysterical child. "You don't know that. We just need to be more moderate with our prayers from now on."

"You can't—"

"Thank you, Miss Wraak." He motioned to someone behind her. "Get some rest."

None of the council members looked at her. A hand took hold of her elbow to lead her out.

She spat on the floor. "You deserve everything he does to you."

Claudia stood in the Rouwen Funeral Home viewing area. If the funeral director noticed her inebriated state, he didn't say anything. He just let her in to see Isaac tucked away in the coffin in a posture of sleep. The suit looked ridiculous. Isaac would have hated it.

She knew she should be feeling something other than anger, but Odren had taken her sorrow, grief, and love. Only her anger remained.

Anger at the council's complacency. Anger that everyone else would remember Isaac in this farcical pose of serenity. Had they noticed his missing heart? Or had they simply sewn him up in their hurry to bury the truth?

She reached into her hoodie pocket and pulled out a bundle wrapped in paper towels. Her stomach churned, and for a second, a recall of pain shot through her body, nearly taking her to the floor. She pulled a flask from her back pocket and fumbled with the lid. The slim metal container went bottom-up, draining its contents down her throat. She shuddered at the bitter taste, then made a satisfied noise as the blissful fog of drunkenness rolled through her brain. She tried to put the lid on again, but her bandaged left hand refused to work.

For a moment, she stared at the empty space where her ring finger used to be. She'd tried pulling the ring off for two hours before succumbing to the call of desperation and Jose Cuervo. Now, she stood next to Isaac with ring and finger. She tucked the bundle beneath Isaac's folded hands. As she staggered to her house, a smile stumbled across her face as she thought of Odren's rage.

The next morning, Claudia woke with a headache. She dragged herself to the bathroom, turned on the faucet in her sink, and froze. Her hand trembled as she stared at the small notecard dangling from a white ribbon tied to the ring adorning the unblemished finger on her left hand.

> You dropped this.
> Odren, Lord Protector
> Limestone County

Light in the Dark

ADRIAN HAYES

Stars had trailed off long ago; the deep inkiness of night faded into cosmic periwinkle. Svelte, moss covered pine trunks. Rotted, fallen trees in jutted unison caused agile movements as Liø and Biėl kept course.

The young warlocks had been traveling in shifts for days. Liø slept the first half of the night, while Biėl kept watch. They traded off, so Biėl snored against a suitcase. Vėktøv soared above them, keeping watch for oncoming danger. It'd been weeks since they'd seen a witch hunter. Yet they remained vigilant, lest one came plowing through the woods in search of them.

The wheels of the cart moved smoothly; blades of grass imbued with life rolled them along. Liø barely had to do anything. He hadn't admitted it to Biėl; there'd be claims it wasn't fair. Most of their life was unfair. Liø didn't see any point in thinking a turnaround was in store. The two of them needed sensibility if they were to get out of this godforsaken country. He was tired of sleeping in old barns on bales of hay. He made a solemn promise to never again let the taste of nettle soup run across his taste buds.

Biėl, thankfully, continued to rest soundly. Liø tried to let his sleep last. Each night his brother awakened him with soul shattering screeches. Ïr was to blame for those. She plagued his dreams, which began to take its toll during the day. Deep circles formed under Biėl's eyes; his tawny skin dulled. Liø concocted an elixir to help him keep the terrors at bay and took the second shift.

Dawn crept across the horizon, bleaching the sky with pinks and oranges. Peaks and hills illuminated before him. Liø watched a robin hop along the edge of its nest, beak bobbing as it mended. These were woods he knew well, land he'd played on during the long days of summer hills they'd rolled down countless times. How different they seemed under the guise of exodus.

"Kra." Vėktøv glided in a circle, leading the way.

Ahead of them a field of wildflowers with yellow buds spawned across a dale. A wooden cottage with no doors or windows sat abandoned.

Vigorously, Liø had the plants escort the wagon to the threshold. As they got closer, he saw the top of the roof was caved in the middle, as if some giant squashed it; ragged planks covered its siding.

Inside the home, the natural elements had gotten the best of the furnishings. That mattered not to Liø who'd give anything for the comfort of his mattress which was now charred to bits by the helicopter that crashed into his house. Heedfully, he slid a suitcase from beneath Biėl's legs, propping it beside the base of a moth-eaten sofa. He made a rudimentary bed by spreading out a few packed shirts.

In a few waves of his hands, he found furniture to block the entrances. They didn't need any daytime surprises. When it felt secure, Liø lay down. Vėktøv kept guard, perched at the hole in the ceiling.

Dawn came quicker than anticipated. Crisped herring awoke Liø's famished stomach. Biėl had cooked the herring in its can. Most meals were eaten in the same container they arrived in, and table manners were secondary to the boy's survival.

"Did we happen to pass a stream? We may need to get more water soon," Biėl said, reaching for a plant with white tips; he ground it over the fish.

"I didn't see a stream or hear one, but I bet Vėktøv can help us find water. We can go look while you finish breakfast." Liø stretched his stiff neck.

"Don't bother. Vėktøv can search while we eat. Better for the two of us to stick together," Biėl said.

Vėktøv picked at his decayed right side, and he extruded a fattened beetle, which he promptly devoured. As a zombie bird, he normally wasn't hungry, but in his frequent *wakenings*, his hunger had grown.

"Find water," Biėl ordered. "Then come straight back."

Vėktøv had been midswallow and gave a side eye.

"Sorry. Please find the water, then come straight back."

Seeming to approve, the bird spread his wings and, within a few flaps, exited the hole in the ceiling.

The fish was served on a bed of dandelion leaves, colored with bits of violet. The boys ate the scanty portions slowly, savoring every bite.
It wasn't long before Vėktøv returned, hopping on the leg of an upturned table.

"Seems he's found water." Biėl said, storing the remaining scraps in a jar.

The three of them took to the woods behind the house's clearing which was more arid than the marshes and bogs they'd traversed through. With no trail, they weaved along weathered trunks until a sandy bank appeared along the stream.

Armed with jars, they balanced along the smooth rocks. While bending down, Liø stared into the water. His tawny skin and dollop nose were a perfect reflection, even the top of his curls could be seen. Biėl passed, creating his own double image.

Liø filled another empty jar as a little girl with blonde hair stared back at him. He pointed across the stream; his lips trembled, rendering him barely able to speak. "Did you see her?" he asked.

"See what?" Biėl looked around.

"There was a girl there." Liø's voice turned shrill. "She was at the other bank, looking at me while I grabbed water."

"There's yet to be someone around us. If a girl was that close to you, wouldn't we have heard her?" Biėl proposed. "What about Vėktøv? If something was amiss, he'd be the first to tell us."

Perched along the edge of the stream near them, Vėktøv cocked his head at Liø questionably. "Kra?" He then flew towards the woods, scanning the area, before he returned, unfruitful of anything to report.

"See? Nothing. I'm sure it was just a trick of the light." Biėl assured him. "Grab your jars and let's head back. We've got to boil these."

They spent the afternoon boiling water, collecting kindle, and gathering wild greens. When finished, Biėl collapsed in a heap, on one of the suitcases.

After a quick dinner, the boys sat around the fire, delighting themselves with terrifying tales until night came upon them. Biėl would take the first shift to stand watch.

The stars were completely visible in this part of the world. Liø found himself staring at them before his slumber. A shadow moved across the skylight. From the motion, Liø could tell it was humanoid in form. Not wanting to look for Biėl or Vėktøv, he lay motionless; eyes forced closed. Beneath slitted lids, he peered at nothing. When his fear subsided, Liø attempted to drift off again. He dreaded not getting rest before his shift.

A breeze of warm air swept across his face. He leaned into its comfort before a befouled odor emerged. Within moments, the stench grew unbearable. Liø's eyes shot open.

He saw her stretched face and open jaw that drooped to the chest; skin appeared where eyes had been. From the mouth came whiffs of that horrendous odor—rot mixed with fish, along with the salty stench of an unwashed body. Liø screamed, and so did the woman. Her wail increased in volume until Liø thought his ears would bleed.

A force kept his limbs from moving. "Help, Biėl!" Liø convulsed violently.

Within moments his brother was there. "Liø! Liø… wake up." Biėl shook him, but Liø wouldn't respond.

The hag above him had a hold on his very being. "She's got me! Biėl, you have to get her off." Liø squirmed. Water doused his face, he sputtered upward. "Where is she?" Liø searched. Through soaked eyelids he saw Biėl. "Did she go through the roof?"

Vėktøv stared down at the two of them from an opening in the ceiling. Biėl asked. "Where is who, brother?"

"The *Woman*. She pinned me to the ground, and her breath…" Liø's nostrils creased as though still filled with that horrid scent.

"Liø, there is no one here," Bièl said.

"Yes, there was, Bièl. We have to search!"

Liø frantically went about the cabin when he saw his brother's eyes in the dim of the firelight.

"It was a dream brother, nothing more. Perhaps Ïr has bewitched you as well. We don't know the full extent of them yet." Bièl patted Liø's shoulder.

"Now, it is my turn to drift off, and your turn to stand guard." Bièl lay in his spot; his weary eyes closed. "I'm certain Vèktøv will help you keep watch."

After some time, when he was confident Bièl would not wake, Liø grabbed more kindling until every crevice of the cabin was alit. He kept lookout, using Vèktøv. He feared he'd see something the raven had missed.

Dawn rushed across the valley. When Liø knew for certain day had risen, and that the fire he'd built wouldn't consume them all, he went to sleep.

Breakfast consisted of nuts and berries, the latter of which caused frequent visits to multiple latrines. When certain digestive issues weren't of the utmost, the boys began their self-tutelage. They flung open the notebooks, kept since toddling, where they committed to memory the spells they'd invented.

"*Yach dirn*," Liø recited before a pillar of fire spiraled, engulfing a fallen tree. "*Ai gon*," he commanded before the flames ceased.

"*Itorig*—no warmth." A wave of his hand left shards of ice.

"*Giorti*." Liø made a sweeping motion, then closed his hand. At this, the ice melted. Bièl attempted to invigorate Vèktøv, but the raven sat like a statue.

"Still nothing huh?" Liø asked him.

"Yea, still nothing."

Liø made a gesture with his hand, and Vėktøv flapped his wings.

"It'll come back Bi, don't worry. For now, we'll use our strengths."

"Another one of Ïr's gifts." Biėl kicked a rotted log. "I'm glad that forest burnt down. One small comfort to know, they can only do so much." A long sigh. "Let's start foraging before dusk. Maybe we can find something better than nettles."

Relief swept over Liø as he considered *not* having nettles for the umpteenth time. They found mushrooms on a tree and Biėl found wild garlic. The two of them ate a feast of wild mushroom and garlic stew, paired with a side of roasted chestnuts—courtesy of Vėktøv.

"I believe we should take our leave of this place soon, lest we be surrounded once more. This time, we're alone. We haven't troops to march for us."

The fire flickered across Biėl's face. "This was the first time we rested in almost three weeks. Who knows where we are. We haven't gone near a village since Hÿlā, and we can't stay in the wilderness. They'll find us eventually. Tomorrow, we take our leave and find out which direction leads to Īmėrykän—America."

"Now that we've gotten time under our belts, perhaps the roads may be safer. We'll have to sweet talk folks, won't we? To get money?" Liø pinned his arms across his stomach and bit his lip.

"We'll do what we must, just as always, in order to get by. More discretion will be needed, of course. We can't leave breadcrumbs like we did last time," said Biėl.

"We were careful enough. It's those hunters we got tangled with. The village didn't get out of hand until they came," Liø said.

"Those days are long gone—at least for the moment. When we get to Īmėrykän, there'll be no more sleeping outside unless we want to." Biėl looked up. Rich purple chased away the pink of twilight; stars began to dot the sky.

"Have you been troubled in your sleep?" Liø asked.

"No. Not since before we got here. A small blessing to be thankful for," Biėl said. The rings under his eyes had shrunk.

"Have you?" Biėl asked.

"If you're talking about the other night, I think it was sort of a dream." Liø hadn't given the incident much thought.

"You mean, it was a nightmare," Biėl said.

"I guess so."

"Hopefully, there's no more left. I'm sure Ïr used up what they can." Biėl chuckled.

"Yea." Liø looked to the side.

"Where do you think we are?"

"We left the Ümbra going straight through the clearing. Maybe we're near the Ïtħř Mountains."

"You might be right on that, brother. I'd almost forgotten about them. Aren't those the mountains the dwarves mined?"

"That's what the old stories say. The dwarves are the ones who carved the tunnel to the other side. Don't you remember? Trolls drove them out."

"If you recall the story so well, why don't you regale Vėktøv and I?" Biėl asked.

"That's exactly what I'll do." Liø propped up on a crumbled cushion. They fell asleep during the building of the tunnel and the war of the trolls. Liø wasn't sure what stirred him between the dream and the wake, and on the rarest of occasions, he saw Biėl for once sound asleep on the other side of the campfire.

Click-click. Click-click. Swift and short taps across a slotted fence. In pace, it increased along the side of the cabin. The noise became a thud, thumping across the roof. Liø was certain it would be at the hole of the ceiling, but nothing emerged above.

All at once the pounding came; voices overlapped, crying in agony.

"Ēiä *erto kömtna. Vünehał näsňa wølomė*. She is coming. Let us in." The words multiplied until they were no longer intelligible.

Sounds crawled from their throats, distorted screeches like the howls of a rabbit.

Liø trembled at the thought of what made the children seek shelter.

"Bam!" A loud pound at the door.

The frame gave way; splintered wood sprayed wildly. Liø held up his hand to uphold the door, but he was powerless. Chills shot up his spine. He turned to wake Biėl and found himself inside a kitchen.

At the stove, he saw a woman, hunched and haggard. Beside her, an enormous mortar and pestle. On a counter, she pounded a substance that squelched as it was mashed. She picked up a severed hand from the basket. With a cleaver, she chopped the digits off, brushing them into the bowl like fresh carrots. With a sharp crunch, the hand was split, then diced into bits.

"Break the bones to bake the bread…" she hummed merrily.

She reached inside, spreading the contents across her skin. She rubbed her withered neck and saggy jowls. Fingers ran through wiry hair. She spread bits of bone and flesh atop the reddened paste. The scent of fresh iron was repugnant. Liø held his hand over his nose, never blocking view of the woman.

The dizzying aroma near the fireplace caused him to tumble. When he looked up, she was gone, but the little blonde girl was face to face with him, blue eyes wide with wonder.

"Can we play?" she asked.

Liø's skull suddenly buzzed with images of children running from a creature through rows of barren trees. The background then faded into obscurity.

"I know the best games to play." Behind the girl, children in tattered clothes clustered together. "They aren't fun anymore; they have learned how the game ends."

Tilting her head, the girl revealed whetted teeth, then launched at Liø, and bit his arm. The children around her held him down. He screamed in writhing pain as a chant emerged from the others.

> *"Baba Yaga*
> *Baba Yaga*
> *In her ancient hut*
> *Baba Yaga*
> *Baba Yaga*
> *Rips out your guts*
> *Baba Yaga*
> *Baba Yaga*
> *Takes off your head*
> *Baba Yaga*
> *Baba Yaga*
> *Break bones*
> *To bake the bread*
> *Baba Yaga*
> *Baba Yaga*
> *Once she is through*
> *Baba Yaga*
> *Baba Yaga*
> *Eats YOU stew"*

One child's face came into view. Their skin had been scalded, the left eye was gone, and the remaining eye stared into Liø's soul. The next child was missing part of their scalp. Another was severed from the waist down; entrails swept as they went around in a circle.

"No. Enough!" Liø woke up. The slow light of the fire glimmered.

Morning came and the brothers went about their rituals. A quick breakfast of chestnuts from the night before. Once they were full, they set off.

By noon, they made it back to where they had been before.

"It feels like we've been walking in circles," Bièl complained.

In the misdirection, they hadn't been able to locate the clearing with the cabin again. The boys made a quick camp that night, with Vėktøv keeping a watchful eye. The next morning, they ventured off again, in hopes of getting through the forest.

"What do you think of yesterday?" Liø asked Bièl.

"You mean the directions? It isn't like Vėktøv to lead us astray." Bièl's face was bewildered.

"Perhaps today will be better," Liø said.

"Perhaps," Bièl agreed.

Proving no different than the day before, the boys found themselves turned aimlessly. In desperation, they camped once again. Provisions were low; they ate very little. "Are we lost?" Liø asked Bièl.

"We're something. I don't know if it's lost, but we're not found." Bièl drew across the ground.

"Moreover, there's no one really looking for us. Not anyone we'd care to look for us, at least," Liø remarked.

"Kra." Vėktøv landed on Bièl's shoulder.

Liø strolled around the fire. Upon the ground was a large square with three dots and a few lines inside of it. Directly beside it, another square with the same structure, only the lines went opposite ways.

"What is that?" Liø asked.

"A map," Bièl answered.

Vėktøv had been gone for longer than they anticipated—so long that they'd begun to worry. They didn't call his name for fear of someone lurking, and they wouldn't move for fear of losing him. Lines formed on Liø's forehead when he looked up and didn't see the bird soaring.

"He's never taken this long," Liø told Bièl.

"He will come back. He always does," Biėl said.

"Perhaps he found something to eat. We've never had him awake for so long." This was true. The last few weeks, Vėktøv had been active, seemingly unbothered, never asking for scraps when the boys had finished their meals. The thought never occurred to either of them that he might feel hunger. He never digested the beetles eaten from his side.

"There's no sense in staring up at the sky until he comes back. We should practice our spells. We already missed yesterday," Biėl said.

When Liø didn't move, he felt his brother grip his forearm.

"Come on, Li. He'll be safe. I promise."

Twilight arose on the horizon. The fire had just begun to blaze when they heard him.

"Kra!" Vėktøv called through the canopy, frantically hopping along the hearth when he reached them.

"It seems he's found something," Biėl said.

"It's too late now to go searching through the woods with night so close," Liø said to the raven.

Vėktøv fluttered above Liø, picking his hair.

"What is the matter with you? Stop it." Liø swatted at him.

Vėktøv dodged his hands and snatched a grimoire between his beaks. Off he went; the boys gave chase.

"Vėktøv, come down. We aren't mad at you," Liø said as he blinked to transport across the forest.

"Be a good bird and give our notebook back," Biėl said

"Vėktøv!" Liø called.

Dark heavy clouds gathered above them. In this part of the forest, they could not see the canopy. Rain sprinkled in slow drops about them. From the sky, nothing could be deciphered.

"That damned raven will be the death of us," Biėl said.

Lightning flashed across the sky, followed by thunder. Worry filled

Liø's head. If they hadn't found him and a storm came... He shuddered at the thought of Vèktøv blown away by storm winds. Successive strikes flashed, making the forest bright as mid-day.

"I see him!" Liø raced through the trunks of the trees.

Bièl could barely keep pace. "Did you snag him?" he said, catching up to his brother.

"No. I lost him again."

Kraak! Thunder rumbled. The sky illuminated, divulging a small black spot above.

Deeper into the forest, the boys ventured until they came to a thick part of the woods; the trees still bare above them. Hours had been spent chasing their flying familiar. The boys could feel him slightly, like a game of hot and cold. The rain picked up, although the two did not mind.

Ka-ka boom! A violent sky eruption gave a glimpse of Vèktøv perched along a fence. "There he is!" Liø cried, rushing to him.

"Wait, please," Biel cried.

At the fence, Liø snuck up on Vèktøv.

"*Dus*." A wave of his hand turned Vèktøv stiff as a garden statue. The notebook fell from his beak. "You're not flying off this time. Sorry, old friend. We need you on your best behavior."

Bièl drew near. "Did he take off?"

"No, I've got him. I just had to put him to sleep for a bit." Liø opened the suitcase, placing Vèktøv in gently. "When he wakes up, hopefully he'll feel better."

Liø turned, anticipating Bièl's response, but only the wagon and luggage were there. Liø grabbed the handle and took off to find him.

Beyond the lines of the fence, he saw his brother. Something was in his palm.

"Bièl, what are you doing?"

Bièl held a plump, red strawberry. "Look at this, brother. Have you seen a more delicious-looking fruit?" He salivated as he spoke.

"We can't be here. There's a light on in the house. We've got to go." Liø urged his brother.

"I've already eaten a few. Let's get what we can from the garden." Bièl grabbed more strawberries as the rain poured.

"We have to find somewhere safe," Liø said, heading to the fence line.

Kr-kracck boom! Thunder exploded and a bolt of lightning made the trees fully visible.

Liø saw her beside the tree—the blonde girl. She seemed dry, although everything around her was soaked. Her cerulean eyes and serrated teeth were discernible from a distance. She let out a voracious howl, then charged on all fours. Another bolt of lightning and the vision was gone; rain poured in its stead.

As they came upon the cabins, there were lanterns that lit at once, illuminating the fence posts around the shack. Lightning struck a tree not far from them. Bièl kept his head down, hands feverishly picking at the strawberries.

"There's enough to make sure we don't go hungry for a few weeks." He wore a maddened smile, waltzing to the wagon. He tossed in the horde of berries.

Lighting cracked the sky, illuminating a hut behind them—an ominous and foreboding structure.

"I don't care, Bièl. We can't stay out here in a storm like this—even being witches." Liø was terrified by the girl. He wanted to get as far away from the hut as they could.

"What are you doing out here?" a voice called from a corner of the yard before a yellowed light appeared in the air. It was accompanied by a figure. She wore a hood over her face, and they couldn't make out her features.

"You'll catch your death of cold, the two of you will. Come here so I can see you better." As if by some force, Bièl trotted obediently.

"Liø, come on." Bièl signaled.

Hesitation clung to Liø's feet, steeling him to the ground. *How in the hell was there a hut in the middle of the woods? And why was Bièl going along like a wanton puppy?*

Looking to the gate, Liø had every inkling to blink himself and Bièl back to the forest.

"I don't bite. I promise," the woman said. "I only want to help you stay out of the storm. You'll be able to leave as you please when the rain clears." Her voice seemed like a song of kindness.

"Liø, don't be rude," Bièl said.

"Why, look at you. You're just babes. No—that won't do, not at all. Get inside this instant, we'll get you all warmed up." The woman held the lantern over the trail.

"What are your names? I think I heard yours was Liø?" The woman nodded left where Liø held the wagon close to him.

"And what's yours?" She brightened when she asked Bièl. Something Liø found odd.

"My name is Bièl. You were right about Liø. I don't know why he's suddenly shy." Bièl shot his brother a look, which Liø disregarded.

"Nice to meet you both. My name is Inånna." The lamp brightened the woman's velvet brown face; a sinister smile coiled at her lips.

The Legend of Kuri

KLARISSA CONNER

ear Chris,

Read this and know for certain I had no choice. I won't go—not without telling my side. That wretched creature cannot silence me before I tell my truth. They all think of me as crazy, as if I have gone mad. Perhaps I have—who is to say? I do not know whether it is my own voice in my head or the voice of that thing. Are my thoughts my own? Do I deserve this? These questions—I can't bring myself to a conclusion. It crawls at my scalp, you see? It began like everything does: simple yet unforeseen. Similar to a small waft before a storm or a quiet cough that leads to something malignant.

"Dear, come look, won't you? It is a cloudy day. The sun is gone," a voice echoed down the extended hallway. I was in the master bedroom, packing my things for the day I had planned. Sunny or not, I had gained the courage I thought I had lost. I packed my notebook, Chase's baby book, *Night Moon,* and my wallet. Traveling light is best these days. Without zipping up the backpack, I marched my black combat boots toward the kitchen through the hallway. Passing the living room archways, I felt his presence already on my tail. His feet slapped the hardwood floor as he picked up the pace. "Dear, don't go today. Another day, perhaps? I could accompany you then?"

I stopped walking when my boot hit the kitchen counter. "Today is the day, Christopher. I must go alone. Why must you try and stop me?" I pleaded with him. This meant so much to me now.

"It is just so hard to take, seein' em like that. For your first time, I should be there. Wait until my conference is over. Perhaps then?"

I scoffed, placing the bag down before pivoting for the handle of the fridge door. I retrieved the sandwich I had made the evening prior, then returned to stare at my sorrowful husband. It used to kill me to see him so torn—cut me right to the core when he cried for nights and nights. I couldn't shed a tear. This guilt that had been freezing over me, making me stiff, had finally begun to melt. I was ready to face Chase. It had to be on my own; I wished I could make it clearer as to why.

"Oh, Christopher." I frowned at him.

"Chris, please—you know I wish it were different. I told you; I must go alone. Please understand."

He gave a sad nod. I watched as his shoulders fell, just as I slid my ham and cheddar sandwich into my bag. I zipped it up and gave him a smile.

"Do know I love you, Chris." I walked over to him in the same motion that I threw my bag over my shoulder. I kissed him goodbye. He held on so tight that morning.

With that, I was off for the day. I drove on through town until I reached the Little Rock Cemetery. I had only been there once, during the burial. I had a vague memory of where he was placed. I followed my feet as my intuition took the lead.

I found my darling baby's grave. I broke down once I stood face to face with my 22-month-old's gravestone—far too young of an age to go. I crumbled to the ground. I needed to be closer.

"I'm so sorry. I am so, so sorry, God!" I cried into the air, to the earth. The dirt that held my darling son spat at me as my hands smacked against it. All I remember were tears and wheezes. I must have sat there for hours. The cold was fit for the likes of me.

Afterward, I wrote in my journal to my Chase. I tore out the page and dug up a tiny spot in the ground to bury my goodbyes.

"I failed you." That was the last thing I could muster before heading home for the day.

All seemed well until one night, I had been relaxing on the couch with Christopher. It had been a week since I visited Chase's gravestone. We had just finished a rather spooky film, so I was shaken. I felt a need to tinkle, so I made my way from the living room, out of my sleeping husband's grasp, down the hall towards the bathroom. That's when I heard it first.

"Rebecaaahhh..." came a chilling voice.

I had been washing my hands, but upon hearing this, I turned the knob shut. The rushing water dwindled into a shallow pool sinking down the drain.

"Chris?" I called out the door.

Nothing. I checked the hall, but Chris was not there, despite the whisper seemingly being right next to me. I returned to the sink to splash some water on my face, seeking to calm my nerves. But then, a touch cold as ice traveled up my arm, then fell to my elbow as though it were a finger sliding. I shot up and forced the faucet off again.

The room fell quiet. The house was also silent but for the faint sounds from the television. A shiver ran through me. The house felt colder than normal. If it had always been crisp, I certainly never became aware of it until that moment. Chris had to be playing some cruel joke on me, although it was not like him.

I slammed the bathroom door shut and headed back down the hall. I stood, astounded, at the sight of Christopher sleeping peacefully. It seemed he hadn't moved from when I left him.

The phenomenon happened again when Christopher was at the office late. I was alone during the night, cleaning the kitchen when I felt something grasp my neck. It lasted only a minute, but the moment felt endless. It was the same icy touch, but fuller. I dropped a dish, and of course, that was when Christopher arrived home. One look at the broken glass on the floor and my frightened demeanor, and he thought the worst. He said I had to catch up on my sleeping. Rest could cure my pain. He had prescribed the same remedy for my grief, and his "rest cure" had me in bed with depression for months after the accident.

But none of these occurrences were as bad as when the voice spoke to me as clear as day. On that day, I was left to my own devices as usual while Chris was at the office. I had been lounging on the couch for the better part of the morning when a voice whispered aloud, "So nice of you to visit me. Won't you come again?"

The voice pierced my ears and my sanity. I could no longer chalk it up to lingering fears from spooky films or drafts of the wind. There was not a cloud in sight, the day was sizzling, and the air was still. Besides, I was inside with the windows shut.

I spoke to it. I wish I hadn't.

"Who's there?" I called, as threatening as I could be.

I waited a moment or two before I rushed to the front door. I felt the urge to run or get fresh air.

"You are the evil," the voice called as my hand landed on the doorknob. I halted. Then, I felt heat on my left ear and icy claws on my neck. I paused in fear. I waited for the sensation to stop.

"Rebecaaahh," I heard to the left of me.

Since that day, the presence has remained. It lurks at every corner. These whispers accompany me around the house whenever Christopher vanishes to work or goes out with his friends, or wherever else he scampers off to during his days.

I had my lonesome days before, but after the accident, my woe worsened. The days had been endurable, but now... the voices. I cannot escape the icy prods. I spent weeks in this state, waiting for better. The voices remained, even amplifying. I presume the demon thought his torment unimaginative because one night, he adjusted the routine.

Vividly, I dreamt of a hideous face that bent over me. Its frame towered over me in my crouched position. I had been cradling something wrapped in blankets in my arms. For reasons unbeknownst to me, I could not bring myself to look below. I had my theory, though. A goblin-like creature began to dart toward me. I tried as best I could, shielding the innocence in my unbalanced arms from the snarling beast. I screamed as it struck me in the back, scratching long claws down my spine as I hunched on the floor. Then the smell came—rotten eggs? Garlic? Cabbage... flesh?! I dropped the blanket-made cradle and cried as I scampered away.

I heard the deep, low voice speak to me as I screamed.

"You're the true monster, Rebecah."

I remember the dreams as if they happened in waking life. The reality was that their consequences were highly impactful. The morning after, I woke before my husband to find that my spot in the bed smelled of sweat and seemed to be damp. Rushing to the attached bathroom, I witnessed myself. It seemed I had been dragged through the mud. My appearance sickened me to my core. My nails had dirt packed under them, and my hands were filled with blisters that had popped, leaving dried blood behind. I gagged until I vomited the night's dinner into the toilet.

"Dear, is everything alrig—Oh heavens!" I turned to find Christopher in the doorway, his horrified face staring down at me.

"What? Honey, I do not feel so—"

"Becks! My God, your back!" Chris shouted. He moved closer to help me stand properly.

I turned in the mirror to find three long, bloody marks running down my back.

I tore my shirt off, wincing. There were what looked like three claw marks with fresh blood.

Christopher sent me to see a doctor.

"I am going to prescribe you imipramine for your rising levels of anxiety and depression, sound good?" the white-coated man said as he typed away on his computer.

"What can that do for the pain?" I asked, fidgeting. Hospitals make me uncomfortable these days. The rooms, bare and white, remind me of padded cells.

"I would advise an over-the-counter medication for that. As for your sleepwalking, your husband should watch you more carefully at night."

"You think this happened while I was sleepwalking? I haven't done that since I was nine!"

To say the visit was unsuccessful would be an understatement. In the days following, I popped Tylenol like candy. Sleeping became my newest source of dread. I tried to confide in Christopher about this—about all of it. He wouldn't hear it. He figured I was stressed, that it was getting to me. He suggested I get more rest, though he offered to stay home more from work. I couldn't ask that of him; how would we make ends meet? The arrangement we agreed upon—before the accident—was that I would stay home with Chase until he was older.

"It happened again?" Chris came into the bathroom to lean over the sink counter. He inspected me while I glanced at the claw marks on my legs and arms before my shower.

"Reb... is there any chance you're doing this?"

"What?" I countered.

"The scratches? Are you doing them? Perhaps a therapist could help. You refused to go after... well, you never did go."

I sighed, turning my body completely out of his watchful eyes. "I do not wish to go now just as I did not wish to go then."

"But maybe it can help; it helped me—" Chris's voice cracked.

"No," I mandated.

About a week into the torture, I began to forget myself. Countless days I woke up drenched in sweat. I refrained from sleeping at night, developing a coffee addiction. It was my decisive blow against the grotesque goblin. I followed a routine: staying up until dawn but sneaking back into bed before Christopher woke. Thank God he was a deep sleeper.

It was that face that frightened me during the day. I loathed the creature's protruding teeth as it grinned at me. It told me of my sins as if it were Jesus himself. Even if I didn't sleep, the memory alone stirred me while I was awake. I knew better—that evil was vindictive. It would sneak into my snooze when I dozed off at the television. The creature liked this the most, you see? Then, it would creatively depict film-like dreams of women doing horrible, heinous things to their babies. Only when their faces were revealed, the faces were mine. The demon would laugh, crackling at my screams.

Another week passed. Days began to blend with nights. Caffeine helped, but I was drowsy, you see?

I killed a bird two days ago. Christopher said I must have placed it in the car. He smelt it all the way to work and back. He screamed at me. Oh, how that disturbed me! His face was red, thick with anger. I felt like he knew what I did. Did I do it? Was it me? Or that thing? I worried the creature had taken control of me—or perhaps it was me? Again, I wasn't sure.

"Chase baby, oh Chase!" I shrieked when Chris began to shout; the dead bird moved ever so slightly in his gloved hand. In a clear mind, I'd think it alive, but it only moved with Chris's hand. He couldn't get me to stop wailing. I remember it, but it didn't register what was happening. I saw Chris, I saw the car, and oh—the smell!

Chris had to slap me out of it. He didn't tell me to sleep, though. I think he knows I haven't been sleeping. I'm not as clever at hiding it from him. In fact, we've barely spoken since that night I danced in the flames.

"Becks, Becks!" I jolted awake—or more so, alert. I had been in a daze, staring at the flames on the stove. I watched Chris frantically turn the knobs off.

"What... you could have killed yourself! You could have burnt down the house!" he yelled.

I was too busy taking long blinks, assessing my surroundings.

"I—I tried."

Chris grabbed me in his arms and placed me in our bed. He left shortly after that. Not another word. I think I spooked him. He mentioned that I should up my medication. He doesn't enjoy it when I talk to the creature either.

"I didn't do it, I didn't do it," I yelled aloud at the voices in my head. "I wouldn't hurt 'em!"

"Dear, who are you talking to?"

I stiffened and slowly turned to face my petrified husband. He looked as though he'd just seen a ghost, frozen in fear.

"I am singing, dear—that is all. A song."

He didn't believe me, but he dropped the matter and hurried off to work.

I had to be louder than the voices without Chris learning of my condition. I'm tired. The competition was between me and the goblin. At night, we stepped onto the battlefield of my mind. Only one could triumph. I won last, I think. I am still alive. I think?

I spent most of my days in the corner of the living room. I waited and waited for Chris's return. The creature would reach for me or speak to me during those times.

I stay awake. Chris is here—he cooks now, since the stove incident. I am so tired. We eat together—all is well. My head aches. Once we've eaten, I return to my corner, and he goes about his nightly routine.

He used to try to pull me to bed, but he has learned better. I no longer participate; I no longer take pills. In my corner, I am truthful. In my torment, I am seen. I cry in the corners of the rooms. My eyes bleed— or so it feels. I am tired.

"You killed him. Do you feel no regret?" The demon whispers to me as I fight the drowsiness. I am grieving in corners.

"Rebecah?" Chris calls from the end of the hall.

I smell steak and greens.

"Come on, please eat."

I shuffle to him, following the smell into the kitchen. He hands me a plate before heading to the dining area. I follow his lead, listening to the creaks of the floorboards and the faint cracks of his toes. I ignore the voices whispering to me as I step. Then, I reach my chair and pull it out for myself. All is quiet for a moment.

The voice speaks to me again. My heartbeat quickens in my chest. The voice doesn't sound like it's beside me; it's in front of me. Coming from my husband's side of the table. I slowly raise my head to meet his eyes.

The plate of food falls at my feet—greens and steak sauce splatter on my toes with diverse juices. My husband is not mine. It is that thing, that face in place of his.

"Ahhh..." I scream, unable to do anything else.

"What's the matter?" The concerned words seem to come from

Chris, but they are coming from a demon's mouth. The voice returns. I hear both my husband's and its voice.

"Rebecah, what's the matter? Talk to me."

"It is me and you for all eternity. You'll die with me," it cackled loudly throughout the room.

I believe I fainted because the next thing I knew, I was in our king-sized bed. Chris was fast asleep next to me. I knew better, but I tried to sleep. Exhaustion painted me, and a small dose of sleep wasn't enough.

Regret pooled once I woke up in the forest. I winced at the shovel near my hand; mud was all over my pants. I was lying in the mud. Then, it returned.

"You cannot get rid of me, you fool," the voice snarled behind me. "Try to ignore me, and I'll find a way to you."

I began to cry as the low voice spoke. I shuffled back, but my bum hit a patch of dirt. It felt hard to the touch.

"Oh, look at that." The thing came from behind me and put its hideous face in mine—that nightmarish grin.

"What have you done, Becks?"

I recoiled as it said Chris's favorite pet name for me.

I turned to face what I did. I moved to stand far away from the demon just above the scene. A shallow grave was dug right next to the shovel. I stared at the grave, feeling the familiar guilt that I had since I buried my darling Chase.

"You think me a demon, but look here before you. You are truly wicked," the snarling creature called at my deepest wounds.

I fell to my knees, crying and begging my Chase for forgiveness.

"I'm sorry, baby! I'm so sorry, baby."

"If forgiveness is what you seek, I can offer it with one even trade."

I ceased crying at that. "How is it that I can be forgiven? How?" I cruelly spit at the creature, who cackled yet again.

"Return to your son's shallow grave in your waking life, and you shall see."

"Return? No, that, that... I couldn't possibly..." That place was the crime scene. The police have only recently determined it a murder—a kidnapping, they told us. How would that look? The town already suspects something.

"I'll even sweeten the deal; all your torment will end the minute you step foot on wilderness soil." The creature's tongue slipped out of its mouth to lap at its own chin as it spoke.

I wished to sink into the mud. With that, I woke up in the bed. The familiar beads of sweat on my forehead. My place in bed was dirty with mud this time.

Think me crazy or not, I do not care. I am going to meet the demon in the woods. Chris, I leave this for you. Do not worry, dear; soon all will be well again. I'll be as normal as a peach. Ripe even! Ha! Don't I make jokes? You see, dear—all is okay. Wait for me at home. I have taken the car. I will be back soon.

I ditched the car, and now I am walking the rest of the way. My feet are bare—I forgot my shoes. They feel blistered. Driving had been risky; the road wasn't as clear tonight. My eyes are beginning to fail me. The lights are too blurry. I think I've been walking for miles. I flash the light this way, then that, but it's no use.

"All I see is treeeesss..." my voice trails off. The ground feels heavy. No, my feet are what's heavy. My muscles ache with each step. The dark green of the trees and the dirt meld together in a beautiful swirl.

"I must..." my throat hurts. My head aches. I am tired. I feel myself go down. I reach my arms out, but they wobble loosely. I try to catch my fall, but instead, I land straight on my face. I spit out dirt.

"You're too weak." I hear that familiar snarling voice above me. Then, a cackle.

"I–I..." my muscles burn. Every part of me is sore.

"Don't worry now, you made it. You're on wilderness soil." The creature's icy touch lands on my back. I twitch on the cold dirt. However, it is no use. I cannot bring my body to move. I struggle to keep my eyes open. My breathing feels short.

"I'll enjoy carrying your body to hell." I hear the creature cackle again as exhaustion washes over me.

At that moment, I glimpse the creature's nightmarish grin before everything goes dark.

Dystopian Sci-Fi

Residual Effects

NICHOLAS SAMUEL STEMBER

A low, persistent roll of thunder announced the predicted storm had arrived. The office windows reverberated, warning John to save the computer file he had worked on.

He mouthed a curse as he watched blackened clouds roll in from the south. His iPhone showed the time—a quarter of five. John quietly cursed again, rubbing his cropped beard in frustration.

With a crash, twin peaks of lightning arched across the darkened sky, exploding sounds of thunder. This time, John didn't hesitate as he saved his document once more and shut down his computer.

"Did you hear that?" Mara asked as she stuck her head into his office. "Boy, that was a loud one. Did you shut off your PC?"

"Yeah," John said in a sullen tone. "And I still have a lot of work to do. That McPhearson project still isn't calibrated, and the client wants the data tomorrow."

"How much more do you have to do?"

"Ten minutes at the most," he grumbled. His eyes drifted back toward the outside sky, which grew almost dark as night; already, the rain had fallen. With a sigh, he turned back on his computer.

"Not smart," Mara warned with a concerned smile. "If your PC blows up, the IT department will never forgive you. None of our surge protectors here are worth shit."

"What they don't know won't hurt them," John said with a grin. "It'll only take ten minutes."

"Good luck," she said, flashing a smile before she returned to her office.

John's computer came to life as data flashed across the luminous screen. Then, a sudden bright spark shot before the lights went out; all power in the building died. John sat silently in the darkness for a moment, listening to his monitor crackle. His nose filled with whiffs of ozone as the room briefly lit with another lightning flash that caused eerie images to shift across the walls.

"Crap," he hissed.

The emergency lights came on, bathing the room in a soft glow coming from the open doorway and hall. John turned his back to the window and listened to the steady rain striking the glass behind him.

"Well, I guess that calls it a day," Mara said as she poked her head back into his office, blocking what little light remained.

"I guess so," John admitted.

"Oh, don't be so sad," she laughed. "You can finish up tomorrow morning. The McPhearson rep never comes here before eleven."

John nodded his head thoughtfully. His concentration faded to the noise of the rain and thunder.

"Can you believe that?" Mara asked, looking past him.

John turned around toward the window, astonished by a sheen of water drifting across the large pane.

"The rain's really coming down out there now," he said. "It's going to be hell driving home today."

"I hate it when it gets dark like that," Mara said. "It's unnatural to be dark at five during August."

John thought about the early morning weather forecasts. They reported on the hurricane that hit the south coast of Florida but predicted the northeast would get minor residual effects.

"I'm sure it'll blow over soon," he reassured Mara. "The weather report only predicted a few thunderstorms."

"True," Mara said, letting out a short laugh, "but they also forecasted this as one of those 'stay-at-home' days. Don't you just love it when the pollution gets bad enough, they warn you not to go out?" She shook her head, annoyed. "What are people with asthma supposed to do, not go to work?"

John sighed. "Hey, and we live in the suburbs; imagine what it's like in the city."

The window rattled as the wind picked up a gale force. John's eyes were drawn to the seal along the edges of the pane. He walked to the glass, bringing his hand up to the edge. He pulled his fingers back sharply, being in pain. For a moment, he stared at the water on his hand, then quickly wiped it off.

"What is it?" she asked.

"The window's leaking at the seal." He glared back at the window, then glanced at his hand, which had become a little red.

They both turned their heads as a growing noise began to build down the hall. Giving each other a brief glance, they walked down the dimly lit hallway to the large lobby by the reception desk. A crowd of people gathered by the vast glass doors as they stared out at the flooded parking lot.

"What's going on?" Mara asked the receptionist, Bethany.

"No one's leaving," she answered. "News is calling for over half a foot of rain, and the whole state is on a flood alert."

"I'm going for it," one of the computer programmers suddenly declared. "The roads can't be that bad yet, and I have to get home to my kids."

John was also worried about his wife. He knew she would have left for home at four-thirty, but she still wouldn't be home yet. Pushing down his concern, he opened the inner set of two pairs of glass doors leading to the outside.

"How far is it to your car, Alex?" he asked the programmer, being wary of the rain for no good reason he could think of.

"Around the corner," the programmer said, stepping into the buffer zone between the vast sets of doors. "You going too?"

"I'll wait and see if you make it first," John chuckled.

Alex returned the laugh. "Thanks a lot. You're a real comfort."

The lanky programmer momentarily glanced up at the sky as he pulled his suit jacket over his head. He opened the glass door and made a break for his car.

John watched as each footfall caused eruptions of water around Alex's feet. The programmer hadn't gone a dozen feet before he was soaked to the bone.

John shook his head with a grimaced smile, realizing he would soon face the downpour, but his face changed to one of puzzlement. Alex, instead of running faster to cut down his time in the rain, seemed to slow down, stumbling blindly into the shallow lake that was once the parking lot.

"What's wrong with him?" Mara asked, watching the programmer stagger back and forth.

John recalled his honeymoon in Mexico last summer. He and his wife were caught in a terrible storm, touring the Mayan temples in the

Yucatan rainforest. He was amazed at the rain's ferocity, as if the sacred forest tried to cleanse itself of the touch of man.

"Do you think he needs help?" Bethany asked. Her anxious voice shook John back to the present.

He peered through the deluge toward the swaying programmer, who hadn't moved from his last spot in thirty seconds. John glanced at Mara, reading the worry in her eyes, then nodded. He moved to the outer glass door and opened it halfway, feeling a light spray of water across his face. He glanced upward, grateful for the awning protecting the doorway. Taking a deep breath to prepare himself for the soaking, John stepped out of the doorway. He stopped when he saw Alex move again, reaching his hand out toward the building as if asking for help.

John sought out the programmer's face but could only make out a wash of red. Alex suddenly fell forward onto the parking lot, sending a spray of water around his body. The programmer pushed himself up onto his arms once, as if trying to crawl back, then sank back into the water and stopped moving altogether.

John and his coworkers stared in blank horror, unsure what to make of the absurd situation. Just then, Tony burst out of the elevator, his face twisted with anxiety. Oblivious to the recent occurrences, the stout accountant pushed his way through the crowd.

"Hey, everyone," he blurted, momentarily diverting attention from the travesty in the parking lot. "I just heard the news on the radio. They said that all contact has been lost with the southern states. No answers south of Virginia, no police, no fire department... no one!" He took a breath, almost hyperventilating. "That's not all," he rambled on. "There was a lot of static, but they said something about acid rain before I lost reception. Now I can't get any stations at all."

John touched his face, where the water spray had hit, and inhaled sharply. The skin was already sensitive to the touch, as if he had gotten too much sun. A sudden pang of fear chilled his heart as he thought of his wife and her long ride home in the storm.

"What about Alex?" Mara whispered, her face ashen.

John turned back to his friend who lay face down in the water. "I need something to cover myself with."

Responding right away, Tony offered his thick raincoat and rubber galoshes, while Bethany handed John her umbrella.

"He's all right, isn't he?" she asked.

John gave the receptionist a stern look before donning the rain gear. He stepped toward the outer doorway.

Suddenly, Mara grabbed his arm, frightened. "You be careful."

"I'll be fine," John said, mostly to calm his own nerves. He glanced at the expectant eyes. "I guess I'm the designated hero," he whispered into Mara's ear, which made her smile.

"I'm sure it's all some sick joke," she reassured him.

"I hope so," he nodded.

John opened the umbrella above him, like a knight's shield against a hail of arrows. Tentatively, he stepped into the parking lot, careful not to splash the water.

Being assaulted by the storm, John made his way to Alex's still body. Rain beat against the umbrella as the wind sent sprays of water across his raincoat and threatened to tear his protection from his grip. For a moment, he stopped walking, almost ashamed of his newfound fear of the rain. He glanced back at the vast glass door, where Mara was waiting—the rest had retreated to the lobby. John couldn't blame them. He fought the impulse to run back, but he needed to know if Alex was all right. If he was, then everything would be fine. With renewed strength, John trudged forward until he stood over the motionless figure.

"Alex," John called, barely hearing himself against the rain and the constant thunder. He reached out to the programmer but stopped, realizing that he had no gloves. He finally settled for digging his foot under Alex's torso to flip him over. He rolled over as if he suddenly had no weight, like a log in a river.

John blinked twice to accept what he saw—Alex's eyeless skull stared sightlessly up at him. John thought he'd be sick, staring at the remains of his friend. Barely anything remained of Alex's front—only slick, white bone jutting from a pulpy mess, a blend of tattered skin and shredded clothes.

John tore his gaze away from the horror and looked to the horizon. The sky was nearly black, periodically lit by lightning. Around the parking lot, trees bent and swayed like angry gods in the tremendous winds; water streamed from their limbs, forming tiny waterfalls. His gaze drifted back to the building. The paint seemed to melt off the cement walls while the corporate logo bleached white.

A drop of rain fell through the umbrella and struck his jacket. At first, he thought it came from the sides, but he looked up to see the umbrella sagging in many spots where pools of rain had gathered. In those areas seeped thin wisps of steam.

"Crap," John cursed, breaking into a run toward the doorway, careful to avoid splashing as he sped along. He passed the bushes outside the walkway, which were in full bloom with brilliant colors—flowers the company groundskeeper had unsuccessfully spent all summer coaxing.

Mara frantically waved at him. *What was she so worried about?*

A loud bang from behind. John peered back into the tempest when another shot rang out, drawing his attention to a small car that seemed to be sagging to one side.

"The tires..." he muttered, denying an impulse to race to his car. "We're running out of time."

A splash of water struck his left arm and hand as the side of the umbrella finally gave way. Not waiting for the pain, he ran back to the doorway, protecting his head with what was left of the umbrella.

The first wave of agony struck his hand as he entered the buffer zone, where Mara began to rip the coat off his body.

The coat hit the tiled floor like a dead fish being tossed into a bucket. John was riveted to the bright yellow rain slicker as wisps of steam rose from it; the plastic bubbled on the left arm, audibly sizzling, smelling of burnt rubber.

"Didn't you hear us calling to you?" Mara yelled as a second wave of pain throbbed in his hand.

She led him to the reception desk as blood began to break through the weakened skin of his left hand. Mara opened the first aid kit and began to wrap it.

John watched as she covered the raw wound with white bandages, his pain beginning to fade to numbness.

"We got the news on Bethany's radio for a moment," Mara continued, putting an extra layer of gauze to staunch the blood already seeping through the first. "They mentioned the acid rain again, and how it's eating everything in its path."

John's gaze drifted back to the doorway and the flowered bush near the entrance. A confused frown spread across his face. "Alex is dead," he said flatly as his eyes stayed fixed on the blooming flowers. There were more blooms now than just a moment ago.

"Are you sure?" Mara asked quietly as the others hovered around the two of them.

John nodded grimly. "If you saw what was left of him..."

A series of sharp retorts rang outside like gunfire, turning everyone toward the doors.

"What was that?" Tony asked, forcing his way to them.

"It's the tires blowing out as the rain eats through the rubber," John said before turning to Mara. "We have to get out of here before it's too late."

"We can't go out there," Bethany squealed. "We'll end up like Alex."

The crowd murmured in agreement.

"Soon, all the tires will be blown," John desperately tried to reason with them. "Then we'll be stranded here."

"Better in here than out there," Tony argued, backed by half a dozen others.

John's eyes swept the crowd in frustration, sensing his coworkers' growing panic. He needed them to realize the danger they were in, but he knew his words would carry little weight unless they saw Alex's skinless face.

"You people don't realize what's going on out there," he pleaded, locking in on Mara's frightened eyes. "This isn't just some storm that'll pass by. The rain is destroying everything."

"That's just not possible," Tony cut in defiantly.

"What about Alex?" Mara defended. "Look at what's left of him out there—if there's anything left at all." She grabbed John's left wrist and held it up for the crowd. "Look at the blood here. This was caused by the water out there."

Silence settled on the group, which was disturbed only by the roaring tempest outside and the occasional bursts of tires. Suddenly, the stairwell door opened with four more members of the accounting department rushing into the darkened lobby.

"Tony," one of the newcomers called.

The accountant ran over. "What's going on?"

"The third floor is leaking all over the place," she exclaimed through heavy breaths. "It's coming down in buckets... and that's not all." She paused. "The carpet is... I don't know, melting, I guess. But only where the water is hitting it."

"Is anyone else up there?" John asked her.

"I don't think so," she told him. "We were the only ones left."

John glared at Tony for a long moment, then scanned the rest of the faces. "The roof has begun to give from the acid rain. How long do you think it will take the water to eat its way down to us? Half an hour? An hour?"

"Or it could stop any moment," Tony insisted.

"Out there, at least we have a chance."

"Out there is death," Tony badgered. "You said so yourself."

"Out there is a chance for life," John persisted.

"How do you figure that?" Bethany asked, her body trembling.

John let out a sigh and walked toward the door, gazing through the glass for a moment in relative silence.

"The storm came from the south," he began, his voice barely audible above the deluge outside. "It didn't hit us that long ago. If we can get into our cars and head north, we'll outrun it. Maybe the storm weakens as it moves north, or maybe it will blow out to sea before it gets to us again."

"How far will we have to go?" Mara asked.

"I don't know," John admitted. "As far as we have to, I guess."

"Count me in," she said with a smile.

"Count me out," Tony blurted. "You're asking us to commit suicide. If the storm is moving as you say, then it'll blow past us eventually."

"True," John conceded, "but what will be left when it does?"

Tony's reply was cut short by a deafening crash above them. Everyone fell to their knees in terror, some screaming in panic.

John crawled over to the accountant and grabbed his arm in anger. "That was the roof giving in, Tony. How much longer do you think you have here?"

"We're not going out there," he responded sternly, his face scrunched in determination.

Frustrated, John released Tony's arm and got up. "Fools," he whispered, scanning the crowd. All eyes were upon him as he stood above them—a scorned and deserted messiah. "Won't anyone please listen to me? This is our last chance."

Many shook their heads; some eyes laced with fear as they huddled closer to Tony, their chosen protector. John glanced over at Bethany biting her lip in indecision before she rose to her feet.

"Come with us and live, Bethany," John persuaded, sensing the torment within her. "Tony's wrong."

"And John's a suicidal fool," the accountant interjected.

Bethany glanced back and forth between the two men as a tear trickled down her flushed cheek. Finally, she found her voice and sank back to her knees. "I c-can't go out there," she cried softly. "I'm sorry."

John sadly lowered his eyes, suddenly feeling a great loss. "So am I." He turned to Mara and grabbed her hand. "Let's get out of here."

"What about the rain?" she asked.

John looked around and ran inside the door labeled *Shipping and Receiving.* He reemerged with a large sheet of thick bundling plastic.

"That won't last long out there," Mara pointed out.

"It doesn't have to."

John took Mara's hand again, pulled her to the doorway, opened the inner glass door, and stepped through. He pulled the heavy plastic over their heads, preparing to open the outer doorway. He glanced back at all the expectant faces huddled like trapped mice.

"We're going to make a run for my car," John said as he turned back to Mara. "It's a four-wheel drive and has really thick tires. Maybe they're still good."

Mara gazed out at the parking lot, her eyes shimmering in the flashes of lightning. "Most of the car roofs are caved in," she said.

"I figured that," John told her. "My car has a canvas cover over it."

She looked at him. "You think that would stop rain that can eat through a steel roof?"

John glanced outside at the bush, which was now fully covered in brilliant flowers, then at the trees that were still standing, despite the pounding storm.

"Yes," he said quietly. "I'm not sure why, but right now, I think a cotton or wood covering is safer than steel or plastic."

Mara shrugged as she pulled the plastic tarp closer around them. "I hope you're right."

"Let's find out," John said as he opened the outer doorway.

The wind and rain struck their tarp instantly, hissing as it sizzled. He pulled Mara out onto the sidewalk that surrounded the parking lot, keeping them above the water. They ran along the path to his car, seemingly untouched by the devastating downpour.

A grin formed on both of their faces as they saw the thick tires standing tall in the bubbling liquid. John wrapped some of the plastic around his hand and pulled off the car cover, allowing the rain to strike the vehicle for the first time. Immediately, the bright red paint started to run down the hood of his SUV like a crimson waterfall. He quickly opened the passenger door and shoved Mara inside, not removing the protective tarp until the door closed.

Looking up at the plastic, he saw water condensing on the underside as the rain began to eat its way through. He crossed over to the driver's side when he spotted a blackish lump in the center of the parking lot like a pile of dirty laundry. It took him a moment to realize that it was Alex, or what was left of him.

John opened the door and jumped inside, discarding the plastic tarp as he closed himself in. For a moment they sat in silence, both grateful they had made it, when Mara began to squirm uncomfortably.

"Get wet?" John asked as he felt a few burning patches over his body as well.

Mara nodded. "It's all right. Let's get out of here before the tires give out."

John agreed and started the car. They both sighed in relief when the engine came to life. Through the windshield, they saw that their office building had lost another floor. The roof's center sagged in further, morphing the building into a U-shape.

John concentrated on his wife instead of the friends he left behind. With a determined grunt, he floored it out of the parking space, sending arcs of water spraying from both sides of the vehicle.

Neither of them spoke as they merged onto Route One, accelerating down the highway, which was littered with hollowed-out hulks that were once cars.

They passed phone poles stripped bare of wiring, yet standing like tall alien trees. Wooden billboards were washed bare, suddenly leaving a more powerful message than before.

As they passed an upturned commuter bus, John's eyes started to water. Mara turned to face her friend, placing a soft hand on his arm.

"My wife..." he began, tears reflecting the skeletal images of the destroyed cars. "There's no way she could still be alive."

Mara squeezed his arm gently. "We'll make it," she tried to reassure him. "We'll outrun the storm like you said; go north until it blows over."

John shook his head, considering the tropical rainforest in the Yucatan. It was as if the forest was sacred, he thought, and it was trying to cleanse itself of the touch of man.

"Don't you understand what's really happening?" he said, motioning to the trees along the side of the highway. "Look at the melted concrete, the crumpled buildings and cars, then look at the grass, the bushes, the trees."

Mara gazed through the storm at the massive destruction, yet the trees looked healthier, taller, and prouder than ever before.

"This isn't some storm that's just passing by, or leftovers from the hurricane, or even an event just in our area. We're being cleaned off this place—nature has finally said enough."

"You're serious?" Mara asked, seeming more concerned for him than what was going on outside.

John let out a low groan. "I really don't know what I believe anymore," he confessed. "But I do know that nature is resilient, and I also know we've been poisoning this planet with our pollution for a long time. Maybe this is nature's way of cleansing itself."

Mara let out a nervous laugh. "Then what happens to us?"

John shook his head and turned his attention back to the road. "I'm sorry," he whispered sorrowfully. "I wish I knew..."

He felt her hand squeeze his arm tighter as though afraid and confused.

"We'll keep on driving," he tried to reassure her. "Who knows, maybe it'll let up soon."

Mara's grip relaxed as she turned again to watch the storm.

For a moment, he was happy that she didn't seem as scared as before. He watched the windshield wipers beat against the downpour, working to keep the view clear, but his heart grew cold as he spotted the dissolving rubber. *Everything affects everything*, he thought as he struggled to stay on the washed-out highway, seeing the remains of an auto dealership.

"This is just a residual effect, you know," he muttered.

Mara ignored his words as she continued to stare at the tempest around them.

"You put enough junk into any system and it shuts down—or spews out the junk."

They both fell quiet. The SUV continued north, struggling to stay on the highway as it was losing its war against nature.

Interbreed

G. R. BETANCOURT

aya had just gotten home from work and was changing out of her navy-blue suit when the news on the TV caught her attention.

"Authorities are urging everyone to stay indoors. If you have an emergency bunker, seek shelter now," the news reporter said urgently. "Reports are coming in worldwide of creatures attacking unsuspecting people. They appear out of nowhere, targeting mostly children and the elderly, leaving them disintegrated in piles of ash."

Naya sat at the edge of her white upholstered bed, stunned. The footage showed large, shapeless beings roaming the streets while people ran, screaming and stumbling. The gray creatures flickered in and out of sight as they floated through the air. Some people locked themselves in their cars, but the phantom figures teleported inside the vehicles, where screaming victims cowered in their seats.

Is this even real?

Naya changed the channel to confirm she was watching the news and not just a bad movie. Every station showed similar scenes.

"We'll be reporting live from the studio for the time being, but..." The reporter stopped mid-sentence. Lights flickered overhead, and screams erupted from the newsroom. Her eyes darted sideways before locking onto the camera. Her jaw trembled with fear.

"Help me," she pleaded.

A dark gray apparition hovered beside her, morphing into a humanoid shape. Its body, a mix of liquid and gas, caused the camera to blur. It drifted forward and seeped into the reporter's chest, spreading through her arms, neck, and head until it disappeared inside her. She froze, her eyes and mouth hanging open.

Naya's body stiffened as if she too had been possessed.

What the hell is it doing?

She stared at the television, unblinking. Fifteen seconds later, the alien emerged from the reporter's body, glitched, and vanished. The reporter gasped, closed her eyes, and began to sob.

Then the screen went blank.

Naya jolted out of her trance and tried calling her best friend, Chloe, but got a busy tone. She grabbed the semiautomatic pistol from her nightstand, tucked it into the waistband of her black sweatpants, and crawled into the back corner of her closet.

What had she just seen on the news? The shadowy beings—could they be ghosts or some kind of alien? Naya had never believed in either before. She was a logical thinker—an accountant—who dealt in numbers and facts. With all the technology and cameras in the world, there would've been concrete proof by now.

Naya hid for so long, lying on a pile of clothes in the cozy, dark stillness of the closet, that she dozed off. Hours later, when she awoke and realized where she was, the scene on the news flashed in her mind. Panic enveloped her, and she tried her phone again. The line was dead.

Naya wondered what the state of the world was as she emerged from her closet. Were Chloe and her husband okay?

The TV in the living room displayed an emergency broadcast message, casting an eerie blue glow in the room.

"EMERGENCY ALERT: ALIEN INVASION! SEEK SHELTER IMMEDIATELY!"

Alien invasion? Invasion means they're taking over. Could this really be happening?

Naya tiptoed into the kitchen, desperate for a sandwich. It was just past 9 p.m. and she hadn't eaten anything since noon. She went to turn off the water faucet when two figures appeared beyond the bar over the sink. Their forms loomed so large, they spread from ceiling to floor. She froze, the faucet still running.

Maybe if I don't move, they won't notice me.

The creatures were almost beautiful and ethereal, their dusky gray bodies billowing softly.

What do they want?

They had no eyes—so, how could they see? Naya held her breath. Did they know she was there?

Her bedroom and closet were to the left, and the front door was to the right. Could she try to sneak out?

The aliens started floating slowly toward Naya. Her heartbeat thrummed in her ears, and she was getting lightheaded from holding her breath. She wanted to scream but instead expelled the breath she'd been holding. Her left hand crept behind her, reaching for her gun. When they were almost at arm's length, she pulled it out and shot the blob to the right. The bullet traveled straight through, and a hole materialized at its center. The blob to the left lurched forward—and into Naya.

An iciness raged through her body, so cold it burned. Her insides throbbed and ached, especially her lower abdomen. Her bones rattled, but she couldn't move. Naya thought of the reporter's face on the TV hours ago. The reporter hadn't died—at least not on screen. Where was she now?

The tremors within her body intensified, then abruptly stopped.

The alien that had invaded her now hovered in front of her. The one she had shot had regenerated back to normal. They lingered for a moment, then flickered and disappeared.

Naya was left feeling numb. She stood alone in the kitchen, her hand still tightly clenching the gun. A stabbing pain shot through her stomach, along with the overwhelming urge to eat. She doubled over, clutching her abdomen.

She tucked the gun back into her waistband, although it proved to be useless. Through her discomfort, she made a quick sandwich of mustard, ham, and cheese and scarfed it down in minutes. But the pain intensified.

What did it do to me?

Naya assessed the condition of her body, wondering if part of the alien was still inside her or if she had been infected. Her head felt clear, her legs and arms fine, but her stomach throbbed and squeezed. Her mouth was dry, and she realized she was thirsty.

She grabbed a bottle of water from the fridge and chugged half of it. Naya's stomach settled instantly. She drank the rest and tried her phone again. No luck.

A knock at her door broke the silence. Her hand instinctively went for the gun. Peering through the peephole, she saw Chloe and her husband, Alex, standing outside the door.

"Oh my God," Naya said as she swung the door open to hug Chloe, both crying in each other's arms. "How'd you get here?" Naya asked, sniffling back tears.

"We tried calling but couldn't get through. So, we drove out to check on you," Alex said, squeezing her arm.

"Drove? Those things let you drive?"

"Yeah. You got any water? I'm parched," Chloe, usually bright and cheery, looked exhausted and ten years older. Her skin was pale and clammy.

Naya handed her a bottle and watched as she downed it all. *Why was she so thirsty, too?*

"The roads were empty. Have those things been here?" Alex asked, his hand resting on the police-issued gun holstered at his waist.

Naya was surprised he wasn't out fighting the aliens. She lowered her head, her stomach still aching. "Yeah, about twenty minutes ago. You just missed 'em."

Chloe wrapped Naya in a hug again.

"When they get what they want, they seem to leave you alone," Alex explained, an edge to his voice.

That's when Naya noticed Chloe's bulging stomach. She pulled back, staring.

"What's this?" Naya asked.

Chloe started crying again.

"I think they're using us to reproduce," Alex answered when Chloe couldn't.

"Us?" Naya asked.

"Yes. Chloe, me... you." He hesitated on 'you,' as if trying to soften the news for Naya. "The whole world, I imagine."

Naya looked down at her own stomach, still small and flat, but burning on the inside.

"You too?" she asked, her eyes drifting to Alex's stomach.

Alex patted his junior beer-belly. "I don't think I'm pregnant, but two of them entered my body—one after the other. Damn near broke my balls off." Alex squeezed his groin, as if checking they were still there. "I think they took whatever sperm I had inside me."

Naya's head reeled. Her body wobbled to the side, and she caught herself against the wall.

"Woah, hey." Alex and Chloe guided her to the couch to lay down.

Did the aliens really assault us?

Chloe retrieved a bottle of water and gave it to Naya. "Drink."

Naya took a sip. "You think it needs the water?"

"Probably. But so does your body. Don't go thinking you can starve it out." Chloe pressed the bottle back to Naya's lips, encouraging her to drink.

"Where do you think they go? You know, after they're done with us?" Naya asked.

"Hell, if I know," Alex said. "Probably to find more mommies and daddies."

Naya stared at Chloe's tummy. It looked like a five-month baby bump. "When did they...?" She couldn't finish the sentence.

"Four hours ago," Chloe responded, sitting next to her.

"You said less than half an hour ago for you?" Alex asked.

Naya nodded. "What's gonna happen when it comes out?"

The question hung in the air.

The adult aliens hadn't killed them, but Naya wondered if the baby aliens growing inside them would be harmful. She tried to picture what a human-alien hybrid would look like. *How do you even care for an alien baby?*

She quickly dismissed the thought. She would kill the alien baby as soon as it came out. The bullet hadn't done much damage to the adult alien, but if the baby was part human, maybe it could be wounded or killed.

"Are the police or government doing anything about this?" Naya asked.

"I can't get a hold of anyone. I was planning on going to the station to see if someone's there. You and Chloe can wait here."

"Shouldn't we stick together?" Naya motioned toward Chloe, who had switched places with her on the couch. "At four hours, she looks like she's five months pregnant. She probably only has three hours—max—before the baby comes. You shouldn't risk being caught out there. I might need reinforcement."

Alex agreed and stayed.

Instead of three hours, the mutant baby came in one.

Chloe's thirst was insatiable. When the bottled water ran out, she started drinking nonstop from the faucet. Her stomach swelled to a massive size, moving about wildly. Chloe's body convulsed, fevered and drenched with sweat. She cried and screamed out in pain until she passed out.

"We have to get her to a hospital," Naya said, pouring water into Chloe's mouth and over her body, attempting to cool her down.

"There won't be any doctors," Alex explained, clutching his wife's listless hand. "We drove past one on our way here." His voice caught in his throat. "But it was deserted."

Chloe's stomach started to gurgle.

"Chloe. Chloe, wake up!" Naya yelled, shaking her friend's lifeless body.

Her stomach sizzled, and the skin at her belly button began to separate and rip open. A pink blob with arms, legs, and a face with black button eyes emerged. Its mouth widened into an eerie smile, showing little nubs of gray teeth. Naya grabbed her gun and fired, but the creature glitched and disappeared. The bullet entered the gaping hole in Chloe's stiff body instead, oozing blood.

"Chloe!" Naya shrieked at the sight of her best friend.

"She's gone," Alex seized Naya, gripping her in his arms. "She's gone."

Their sobs blended into one grievous howl until Naya's body screamed for water. "Is this what they have in mind?" Naya's mouth was dry and desiccated, barely able to form the words. "To create a new hybrid species and kill us off?"

Her body was no longer hers, but a vessel for the thing growing inside her. She wouldn't wait for it to drain her life and rip through her body like it had Chloe's. She grabbed her gun and pointed it at her own stomach. "Well, not me."

"Naya, no!" Alex lunged for the gun in her hand.

But it was too late.

Naya pulled the trigger. Her stomach exploded with a splatter of blood and a new burning emanated through her body. This time it was hot.

As she fell to the ground, two adult aliens materialized above her. Their fluid appendages reached into her stomach and pulled out a smaller version of a pink blob baby—half the size of the first. Alex tore off his shirt and tried to stop the bleeding from Naya's stomach. The aliens wrapped their bodies around the misshapen blob, glowing a radiant white light. The small mutant expanded, sprouting arms, legs, eyes, and teeth.

It survived.

Naya's eyes rolled to the back of her head as the blood seeped from her stomach. Little gray teeth and black button eyes were the last thing Naya saw as she drew her last breath.

Alex squeezed Naya's hand as one of the aliens plunged into his body, draining the last of his semen. As it left, he disintegrated into a pile of ash on the floor.

Tales of True Love and Madness

Brought to You from
Leo and Gali's Antechamber

SANDHYA BARLAAS

S ounds, like fireworks going off in daylight. Two bodies drop—on a bed of ashes. Red blooms on grey. It's wet, but there is no rain.

Two hands reach toward each other, grey, like the ground beneath. Two hearts hover, between one world and the next; a click, and they're locked, mid-beat. Something has come in.

Somethings. They will stay.

We will stay.

Welcome to the antechamber.

THE BEGINNING

"She must've swallowed ash. I'm telling you, Headmaster, it's a fine illusionist, sends you tripping, fast. My sister ate her man's ashes and went raving mad..."

"The girl's delusional, all women are, really. Hysterical. They make up stories in their heads and think them real. What's a man to do?"

"By God," said the headmaster, "womankind will be the death of—"

"Uncle, why don't you return to Mount Ujil?" the boy said, cutting into the men's conversation. "You need to make sure the students get home safely. I'll deal with... this."

The crowd left, one by one, until only silence remained, silence, and the two of them—she, slumped on the floor in a yellow dress stained with mud, wrists bound behind her, and he, standing above her with the brass key.

She yelled a single word after the receding figures—*Bastards!*—as if she could hear them still, see them through the closed door, sliding into the headmaster's blindcar: a Vool 900 that came out last year—3020—and was so expensive only a handful of people owned it. Not hard to procure, though, if you ran the most expensive private school in the city and sat at the Lawmaking Council, a gun glinting at your hip in silent authority.

The girl had seen the gun, and much more. To the boy she said, He knows it's real, they all do. That's why they tied me up. Because I remember everything.

"There is no portal," the boy assured her once again. "What you saw was a glance of the broken sun. It smolders somewhere behind the clouds, in a thousand fragments. That's what you saw. No magic, no portal."

Leo—

"Unless you want to go to the madhouse, I'd counsel you against perpetuating your childish story. It is all well and entertaining when you're seven, but a seventeen-year-old girl... a woman..." He shook his head, pacing the room like a rat in a glass tank thinking itself a king.

Leo, she said. Have you ever been asked for CAPTCHA before?

"What's that supposed to mean?"

That your uncle has programmed you well! Do I need a screwdriver to dismantle you?

"He should've taped up your mouth. I will do that."

If you want my mouth shut, you'll have to open my wrists.

"My uncle restrained you for a reason."

She saw his jaw tighten, saw that he would not be unscrewed with mechanical instruments. Reason would be needed. So, she reminded him, I will have to eat at some point. Your uncle won't be back for a while. As inconvenient as he finds me, don't you think he'll find me even more so dead than alive?

ANTECHAMBER

In spring, trees rise from the grey earth, color returns. Instead of flowers and leaves, what grows is sickly-looking worms, thorny reptiles, insects in the shape of branches, their sound fatal.

And bloated fruit. At the height of summer, it begins to leak a sugary syrup that can kill if swallowed. In autumn, the trees catch fire and burn away in flashes of bright reds and oranges, a mockery of the season.

In summer, it smells of rot. In autumn, death.

In winter, there is nothing left but ashes.

The tale we tell takes place in winter.

The moment the boy unlocked her hands, there came the sharp whistling of a blindcar, and he panicked. He went to the window to make sure it was not his uncle's Vool 900 rumbling back into the ash-strewn driveway to take away the mad girl in case a spot had opened up at the asylum. A second later, when he turned back around, he found her gone.

He should not have freed her. That is what he was thinking when he walked into the only bedroom and found her on the floor, stark naked, covered in swirls and smudges of ink, scribbling something onto a notebook, her hand shaking.

She didn't notice him at first—she was craning her neck to look behind herself—but then she saw him, standing there, one second, with a horrified face, and turning right back around the next.

She sprang up and pushed him down onto the floor. He swore, a knot of colorful words aimed at the female species—the telltale sign, she thought, that under his chiseled air of chivalry, he was his uncle's robot, programmed to perfection. She asked him, do you see now the message from the portal? It's all over me.

"*You...*" He shoved her off him. "... are all over me."

She knocked him back down, then threw herself at the door. Not so fast, prude! You will help me transcribe what I can't see

He had his back to her. Pinching the bridge of his nose, in a tired, restrained voice, he said, "Do you have no shame?"

Not since I saw the portal, no.

"This is why he tied you up."

Your saintly uncle, you mean? She laughed. The headmaster had discovered her shedding her sweater in the freezing air of Mount Ujil. He had descended on her in a blind rage, armed with curses and an alcohol-smelling beard, and hit her with the back of his gun in a way only a practiced man could—a man practiced in patriarchy, having learned it from the cradle. Whether his nephew was as skilled, that was yet to be seen.

The pen she had dropped, she kicked toward him with her bare foot. You will not escape, she said, till the message is written down.

She thought he was taking too much time to transcribe what was on her back, but she kept still and let him ogle, if that was the price of his transcription services. Pig.

Once the puzzle was peeled away from her body, it spelled a code— but he would not let her see it till she had, according to him, become decent again. Meanwhile, he flipped through the pages, shaking his head, muttering.

All day afterward, she flew around the house like a captive bird, scrutinizing the windows and the doors, whipping around at random, patting the air in search of the tear in the world's fabric through which someone had poured onto her skin the strange code she must now crack.

The boy's assessment of her was quick, more robotic than human. Alt-left, he thought, one of those social warrior types who shake the world like it's their cage: her words, ridden with emotion; cheeks, flushed; eyes, a window into a mind surely unstable, crumbling with disuse and rust.

Alt-right, was what the girl thought of him as she stared at him. One of those people to whom the status quo has been nothing but kind, who therefore protect it zealously, like an animal defending its own territory. Something about their eyes, she thought. Close, guarded, predatory, they made you think of sharp teeth, doors slammed in faces, cold-heartedness and cold steel. Under their every look, word, move lurked the threat of violence.

But she noticed the boy was bare of weapons. The only metal she could see on him was the brass key and the handcuffs. And was he really stone-cold? Hadn't he untied her? Transcribed the message from the portal? Yes, only his eyes...

The thousandth time she went through the notebook, she said to him, Something's missing. Are you sure you got down everything, every damn thing?

His eyes were glued to the floor, his hands clasped tight like gears meshed.

Alt-right, alt-right to the core, the girl thought. But what she said was, You lying asshole!

ANTECHAMBER

Two recalcitrant individuals refuse, for the time being, to take any part in the exercise of treading the stairs. They have no use for it at all, but no doubt, sooner or later they will be brought to see the error of their non-conformity.
— *M. C. Escher*

Square windows and archways and sloping roofs, a mismatched quadrangle of stairs. Was it going up—or down? Was it going anywhere at all? Figures kept running around the quadrangle but were they making any progress?

It's—

"It was on your back."

The sketch lay in her hands as if dropped from above. She realized that was what he had been staring at. Not her inked body, but something more horrific.

Escher's staircase, she whispered. It's a code.

"I knew you would read all sorts of riddles into it. I'm aware of the exact mechanics of your madness."

Oh, no, you have no idea, and you never will. I promise I'll become your Hamlet, and you'll spend your last breaths wondering if it's my madness at work or my antic disposition.

"What does a hamlet have to do with it?"

Oh Leo, oh Leo! she said, forgetting that just because her memory had returned, and she had seen the portal, not everyone had. Look, she said, look how they've flushed our finest literature down memory holes! You don't remember anything, you don't remember! It's tucked into our DNA, all there, but you don't remember!

"What literature? What holes? Do you know how delusional you sound?"

I'm not delusional, just desperate. But a dreaming eye can never tell the difference. Your eyes are like that. You don't see—yet. A fish doesn't see water, Leo.

"You *are* mad. My uncle was right."

Do you see this? She held up the sketch. Look how they go in circles, thinking they're going up, or down, but they're neither ascending, nor descending, and they're far from transcending. *This*, she said—and with the sketch lying on her outstretched hands she turned to him like one lost—is madness.

In the evening, the girl saw the moon come up, the jagged half of it that was left, an arc of badly broken teeth. This was the last relic of humanity's skeleton, this our future—a reminder of the tragedy from long ago, the one they were still trying to cover up. After the sun was wrecked, they sent teams to fix a perpetual lighting system into the sky's skin. But on that awful mission, somebody sawed off the other half of the moon. Later, when asked, they said an asteroid had hit the moon. But she knew better. Humans hit the moon. It was always humans that struck heavenly bodies and destroyed them.

"Is that..." The boy followed her to the window, where she stood crooning. "A song?"

The girl stopped. So what? I can sing all I like. Mad people are lucky that way. Much like old white men, they get to do whatever they like and get away with it. This is why we need to find the portal, she added, pointing to the window. Look at our skins, faded to the same white as the stars.

"What does it matter what color we are?" he asked, annoyed. It was as if she spoke another language. Mad-speak.

Diversity is no joke, she said. Evolution is simple. Someday, all that's left will be white, and male, and straight, and that will be the end of the world. The sun is already dead. All morning long their SkyLights rove the sky and spy on us. One half of the moon is bitten off. Our world is sick, dying!

And here she clutched her head as if someone had struck her. The boy did not like it, all this ranting and groaning. It was as if she had no skin. Whatever emotion bubbled up, it oozed out, spread around. Like radiation, he thought, unsettled. Like a broken nuclear plant, he thought, remembering pictures of a disaster he had once seen in one of his uncle's books. Then he looked back at her and shuddered.

Did I mention what we did to the sun, because we couldn't stand it anymore? she asked.

"It was an accident," he said, defending national pride, scientific honor, male ego. "Science is an experiment. Sometimes we get our calculations wrong."

You love your science, don't you? And your numbers? she asked softly, seeing how he sat: hunched, motionless, cold sweat gathering on his forehead.

"These are the only certainties. Even in chaos."

She pulled him up by his hands. Come on, I'll teach you, she said, and at his quizzical expression, even more softly she said, the mathematics of madness.

They take away our will, our words, our music, our simple desire to roam in nature, our choice to love or not to love, to make babies, make money, make art... They tell us to be happy, they blot out flowers like sin, they paint everything in white and black, they tell us to sit at home and travel blind in vehicles we don't drive, can't control, don't know where they lead us—to the real world or a grotesque dream or straight to hell. That's what troubles me, Leo. Does it not trouble you?

After last night, she had been droning on incessantly. He could no longer take it. When he left her alone in the bedroom and came out to breathe clean air outside her orbit, he felt broken, like a toy mangled in a child's hand. She followed him out, still ranting, and he, still annoyed, said:

Gali, listen—

That isn't how you speak, she pointed out. You don't drop your quotation marks.

"Gali," he corrected himself, "stop it. He'll toss you into a madhouse. Start practicing now how to act sane."

Sanity? Surely you mean conformity. Because they want us to dress alike and talk alike and love alike and stay in our lanes—the lines drawn by them, the dress code theirs, the rules theirs, the punishments theirs, the destinations picked and plucked and programmed by who? Them! And we go on dumbly, tokens led by our players. This is not a game played on a board. This is our life, Leo. We act like puppets, but we have scissors. We could cut the strings. Couldn't I? Couldn't you?

Her lips trembled as if the words had cut her tongue, left it bleeding.

Definitely mad, the boy decided. A step back he took, and then another; because that's what you did when you stared madness in the eyes. A match struck in the air then, an old shine from human history. Something rippled behind the girl, a silver lining. As she shook and sobbed, she seemed to sparkle, like a portal opening. Everything looked different, sharper. He wondered if that was how she saw the world.

Shouldn't he have asked her last night, before he let her do this to him, whatever *this* was?

He found himself wondering, too late, if madness was an STD.

ANTECHAMBER

How can you not dream of the sky once you know you're in the gutter? How can you forget once the lid has lifted, and you've seen stars? Once you know there's a portal... the only thing left to do is fall.

What we did, no one can blame us for it. What happened to us, no one can—or should—forget.

MIDDLE

He would have to whisk her away before his uncle's return.

So he did, moving her from one deserted building to another, in a blindcar whose circuits he had taken apart carefully, so he could drive it himself, and he could actually *see*, too, for he had made a hole for a windshield, a portal almost, and they drove through ashen streets, down grey, tree-lined avenues, past fields of swaying grass that crumbled into powder as the unblind car whizzed away on ash-smeared wheels, deeper into winter and always at night, when the SkyLights behind the clouds— filling in for the sun, watching—had turned themselves off.

It was a rickety journey: the getting and the losing of bearings; starts and stops and driving in reverse; no GPS to hold your hand, no blind- engine to cart you around. How do you navigate a world you've only seen in glimpses?

How does a child learn to walk?

ANTECHAMBER

[He waves his hand in front of her] *Gali? Aren't we supposed to be telling a story?*

I was thinking.

What about?

Your uncle. He had a really good aim.

That is the nicest thing you've said about him, considering what a [long beep] he was.

[She laughs, the sound bitter] That's the nastiest thing you've ever said about him!

She jumped out so fast that ash flew from where her shoes struck the ground. Look! We found it!

He said, It's opened wide!

It had. Out of it spilled silent fireworks of light. Around it, the air trembled, jelly-like. As they ran, the wind licked their faces, ash swirled and stuck to their skin and made them look like stone statues brought to life. They laughed, they cried, they flew toward the portal, feeling like they weighed nothing more than dust.

ANTECHAMBER

We are the residents of the antechamber, and these are the tales of true love—

And madness!

And madness—*of course*—brought to you from Leo and Gali's antechamber. Our mistake?

We discovered the invisible world and were banished for the error of our non-conformity. We refused to tread the staircase that led nowhere, we wanted to be somewhere. And if it could not be the other world, the world beyond the world, then it had to be here

The antechamber.

That's why we're smuggling you this tale. Someone did it for us, slipped us the truth through a portal, but we failed.

We're doing it for you now.

Don't fail. Open the portal again, because now you know, you know how.

Because we're telling you this story so you can live it when the time comes.

And die for it... if need be.

THE END

Is already written, a crumpled piece of paper one might find in someone's trash:

Sounds, like fireworks going off in daylight. Two bodies drop—on a bed of ashes. Red blooms on grey. It's wet, but there is no rain...

Metaphysical Sci-Fi

Dan and the Continuum

Program Update

STINGRAY HOPPER

E m's eyes darted from side to side, capturing the details of the room she was in. The walls were Santorini-white, including the floor, giving her the feeling of either being in an asylum or on a cloud. She was sitting in a generic blue chair with wooden armrests, characteristic of the seats provided to customers in a bank. In front of her was a black card table with paper airplanes and small black drones sitting atop it. One drone rose from the table and floated listlessly in the air. Em watched it, wondering without care why she was here in this room and what significance the drones had. Did she make them? Em turned her head to her left. Her best friend, Dan, was sitting beside her.

He's here, she thought warmly. His right arm was lifted with his hand extended toward the drone. Dan flicked his wrist, and the drone flew higher. With another flick, it darted to the right. Em wasn't surprised at the sight of her friend but was more so confused by his ability to play with the drone. Did the drones have an infrared sensor? Did that mean Dan was emitting heat? If so, how fascinating. She stared at Dan and smiled, unsure if she should speak. Would her voice break the illusion, or even worse, wake her up? Because she didn't know, Em played it safe and remained silent. It had been six months since Dan's death and every waking moment since then Em prayed that, come nightfall, Dan would find her in her dreams.

Em opened her mouth to finally say something, but where would she begin? She shut her eyes to think, however, when she opened her eyes back up, she was inside the construct of time itself.

"Wait, I know where I am," Em said to herself incredulously as she stood in the familiar darkness, allowing her senses to calibrate to simultaneously being in the past, present and future.

"I'd like to see Dan's timeline," she spoke into the blackness. A bold, neon green line belonging to Dan with thin, transistor-like grid lines enveloped her. Em studied the timeline—dense and pulsing with encounters from all his lives—hoping she'd locate the version of Dan she was sitting next to just a moment ago. Em passed locked files of Dan as an Asian child, an indigenous old woman with wrinkled skin and a general in the federation colonizing exoplanets. Eventually, Em found her Dan. There was a recording of a kindergarten-aged Dan pushing a young version of herself on a swing on their first day of elementary school. She also saw him as a teenager at one of his varsity basketball games getting into a fight with another player after a flagrant foul was called. Em stopped in front of a scene of him, still a teenager, peering down at her from his bedroom window as she exited a car from one of her first dates.

"Always the protector," she murmured. Once the young Em made it safely inside her home, Dan walked over to the wall opposite his bed. There, a picture of her was taped up. Dan kissed the photo, then turned off his light.

"I love you, too," Em whispered. There were other scenes of herself and Dan playing out on the timeline like a movie montage. Em touched a visual of them sitting close together on her apartment stoop. Her touch caused his thoughts to play aloud.

"I think I'll love you forever," Dan thought as he pretended to listen to Em talk about some nothingness or other. "I just need to figure out how to make you love me back. Then I can tell you how much I hate your new hairstyle," his thoughts continued. "If I kissed you right now, would you hit me?"

Despite Em's better judgment, she tapped on another visual. It was she and Dan lying in bed together during the intimate relationship they had right after college. They'd just finished moving Dan into their first apartment and the feelings of sheer exhaustion and love Em felt on that day, so many years ago, flooded her now as she stood there inside time, watching their life replay against the black projector.

"What were your thoughts?" Em asked the visual, then touched it to hear the audio.

"How do I tell you she's pregnant?" Dan thought as he stared at a sleeping Em. "I shouldn't have cheated. I wish to God I hadn't cheated. You're going to leave me. I'll go crazy if I lose you. I hate you sometimes. I love you so much more than you love me, and I accept that, but I fuck up, so you'll never fully accept me." Dan's thoughts raced as he wiped a tear from his face, then kissed Em lightly on her lips. She leaned into his affection and embraced him.

Em felt her emotions bubble and glanced away from the scene that would soon turn into his confession and their breakup.

"I'm sure I'm not here to be angry. Stay focused," she told herself. Em attempted to view timeline instances of this Dan without herself in them, but they were encrypted with security protections, preventing her from viewing the files. How much did Dan remember? Did he know he was dead? Did he know her?

Em closed her eyes again, and when she opened them, she was back in the nondescript blue chair. The infrasound from the whirring drone flying around the room soothed her spirit. She was calm as she turned toward her best friend.

"Hi, Dan."

"Hey, Em," Dan responded. He knows my name, she thought encouragingly. He recognizes me. Em felt a gentle wave of excitement in her gut. He sounded exactly like himself.

"You look good," Em said, not sure where to take the conversation. She wondered how long she had until she woke up.

"Thanks," Dan replied. "I feel.... I don't know, I feel kind of... I'm getting used to everything. My eyes are seeing everything. And I feel everything. It's like information overload. I..."

"Dan, do you want me to tell you how you died?" Em interrupted. As soon as the words escaped her lips, she regretted her bluntness. "Em, you don't even know where he is on his timeline," she silently reminded herself.

"Sorry, Dan," Em apologized. "I shouldn't have said that. Um, do you know who Chris and Nia are?" She asked. Dan nodded.

"They're my kids," he replied.

"Yes. Do you know how you got here? To this place?"

"Yeah, but it's crazy because I feel like I never left here. It's hard to describe, but I feel like I'm finally back home." Dan stared at a paper airplane on the table and lifted it into the air with his gaze. As his eyes shifted from left to right, so did the gliding of the plane.

"Do you know how you got here?" Dan asked Em. She was taken aback. Em stared at Dan, and in that moment, she entered hyperconsciousness. Em and Dan were no longer sitting in chairs in the Santorini-white room and the drones were gone. Dan was standing right in front of her, grinning and beautiful.

"Oh, my God!" Em exhaled. Dan looked radiant against the blackness they were now surrounded by.

"I love you, Dan," Em blurted, afraid he'd fade into the blackness. "Know that I love you and I always have. I didn't tell you enough when you were alive, but you were my best friend and the only person who ever really understood me. I've been praying from the day I learned you passed away that you'd find me in my dreams, and I could tell you, and you did. You found me. My God, you were able to get me here." Em paused, expecting Dan to disappear, but when he remained in front of her, she giggled at the surreal euphoria of it all.

"Can I hug you?" Em asked, tentatively holding out her arms toward Dan. "Will I be able to feel you, or will you evaporate back into my imagination, and I'll be left standing here alone, embracing myself?" Em took a couple of steps toward Dan and slowly wrapped her arms around him. Her arms felt the softness of his sweatshirt, then tightened around the hard mass of his body. Em rested her head on his chest and smiled. Dan brought her to a realm where the illusion of feeling existed.

"I wish I hadn't stopped giving you hugs. The virus and the media made me too scared to touch anyone, including you, but I shouldn't have been afraid."

"It's okay. Everything's alright now," Dan assured her. "I brought you here because you were always curious about the afterlife, so I wanted you to feel it with me, except there's actually no after or before. It's wild. Do you want me to show you some things?" Dan asked. Em backed up a bit and nodded. She felt the excitation of thousands of synapses firing off inside of her head.

"You're pure electricity here," Dan explained. "What you feel is all of you in its entirety and forever-state. Everything from the beginning of time to what we consider the future is all a part of who we are here. There are pieces of us in each dimension, playing out different pieces of our story. I've seen you, Em, all of you, in these other dimensions. You're a philanthropist in one, a neuroscientist in another. I think my favorite Em is you as my wife and mother to my kids," Dan smiled. "You work for the Unified Global Government and travel a lot. I'm a stay-at-home dad."

"Some of that could have been real for us," Em said.

"It is real to that Em and that Dan. Because I'm here, I feel it. I experience it."

"How many babies do they have?" Em asked.

"Three," Dan answered. "We have three. Two boys and a little girl. In a few dimensions, you're doing really well for yourself. You're pretty wealthy and successful. It's why your taste is so expensive, and you always feel like you should have more money." Dan pressed into Em to make sure he kept her present in her higher consciousness.

"How are you able to see all that, but I couldn't?" Em questioned.

"I'm transitioned. I have access," Dan replied and continued.

"You know how sometimes you dream of a place and recognize it, even though you've never been there before? Or sometimes you have repeated dreams of the same location, the same neighborhood, the same landmarks?"

"I do," Em responded. "There's this hilly neighborhood with pre-war, Craftsman-style homes that I've been to several times in my dreams, and I know all of the streets."

"Those places are actually real. They're just in another realm. The energy we emit is sometimes high enough to reach different dimensions, allowing the entanglement with our other selves to bridge us into that dimension. Our thoughts and feelings from each dimension within each realm are in constant interaction with one another."

"I feel like I know this place, too."

"Of course you do. It's the motherboard. We make hundreds of pitstops here to get reprogrammed for our next journey, or to simply rest and reboot."

"How am I able to be here with you right now? What happened?" Em asked.

"I waited for you to reach the frequency of your higher self, then I asked you to come. You were willing, so you astral traveled through a mental wormhole."

Em smiled. "A mental wormhole? Is that like the space wormhole in Einstein's theory of relativity?"

"The short answer is yes, and it's our electrons, our electricity that is passing through. Our essence is able to take wormhole shortcuts between dimensions. Your physical avatar stays behind."

"Then how was I able to feel your body when I hugged you? I mean, I know it's an illusion, but..."

"You manifested the feeling."

"How?"

"There's a physics professor here, and he's been explaining things to me. I'll ask him to visit you. He'll teach you everything."

"You're going to ask another ghost that happens to be a professor to visit me?"

"We're not ghosts," Dan said with a chuckle. "None of us ever truly die. We just evolve out of the human avatars we're confined in on Earth. Keep your mind open to all things being possible. If you do, the information from the professor will enlighten you. It will probably be overwhelming, at first because you won't understand it all. You won't even be able to remember much of it, at least not right away. But it will always be with you, inside you, like saved files on a computer that you can recall from memory. That's all your brain is anyway. You're going to change lives with the information you receive."

"How should I prepare?"

"The things they want you to know will come in different ways. There really is no way to prepare, except to understand when the visits are happening and snap yourself into higher consciousness to interact."

"They?" Em repeated.

"Yes, they," Dan confirmed. "Sometimes the professor brings other teachers. You might astral travel to another realm, or simply lucid dream," Dan explained. "Sometimes you won't be fully asleep, but you'll hear someone talking to you through the radio waves, so it might sound staticky, like a voice coming in through a walkie-talkie. Pay attention to the details of your dreams, like names and the themes of stories being shared with you. Also, don't be afraid to ask them to repeat the information they're giving you. Even if you don't understand what's being communicated, remember it long enough to write it down when you wake up, and then research it. Keep a notebook and pen by your bed. Learn as much as you can. You'll see me again, okay?" With that, Em woke up, and Dan was gone.

Two weeks later, the professor and the man of math came to Em.

Unforgettable

D'MARCUS BEATTY

"**C**'mon in," a voice called from behind the apartment door in a thick Jamaican accent. I pushed the door open with the caution of someone intruding on hostile and new territory, glancing about warily before entering.

The front room had a grimy, unclean look and feel to it. A layer of marijuana smoke camouflaged the ceiling, its aroma permeating the room. The only lighting came from dim, inadequate candlelight that created an almost mystic, ritualistic atmosphere.

A dark-skinned man sat on a ragged couch. He had a large, blunt nose and thin arms. Nonchalantly, he blew a circle of weed smoke from his cracked lips. "You red?" he asked with his unintelligible accent, and it took me a second to translate it. *You ready?* I nodded.

He moved his hand to his mouth, taking a long pull from the joint in his hand. He then looked at me with glazed, distant eyes. "You wan pull? It make it easier fo me." I shook my head, and he shrugged his shoulders as if to say it was my loss. He then stood and stretched, his bony arms and legs cracking. I wondered how long he'd been sitting there, wondering suspiciously just how high he was.

"You got the money?" he asked, his accent thinning just slightly. I nodded, tapping the nondescript briefcase in my right hand with my left. The amount of money I carried was both dangerous and exorbitant. The way I carried it—inside the cliché black suitcase common to so many movies—screamed that I was up to something illegal.

He nodded his head hard once, indicating he wanted to see the money himself. I kneeled, popping the locks on the briefcase's front. The top flipped up, revealing a neatly stacked row of twenties. He was costing me $50,000, but even at that price, he was the cheapest verifiable telepath I could find.

The cause of the sudden emergence of telepathy has never been determined. Speculations run the spectrum from natural evolution to the widespread use of cellular phones. One in about every two million people developed some form of psychic ability, generally in the forms of broadcast telepaths, touch telepaths, intrapaths, and telekinetics.

Obviously, they were both feared and hated in the beginning, but it didn't take long before someone realized their utility. A telepath trained in either field of psychology or psychiatry could now cure insanity overnight. Telepathic policing ended the ability for anyone to cheat the legal system. Criminal trials became unnecessary. Why drag out legal proceedings when a telepath could establish guilt or innocence as well as culpability at a glance?

However, and predictably, telepaths became both demanded and limited, as is the case with any valuable and/or useful resource. Bureaucratic legislature forced training and certification on telepaths, and the various legalities and redundancies often could hold up psychiatric treatment for months or even years. Some people weren't willing to wait for this service, and some telepaths didn't want to wait years for certification, especially when they knew they could make money right now. And this, inevitably, led to underground telepaths, the black market for the mind.

"Describe her," he said, his accent imperceptible now. He was beginning to talk the way I did, educated Southern black. I couldn't tell if he was doing it unconsciously or if he did it deliberately to make me more comfortable. That was an added bonus with using a powerful telepath. Language wasn't much of a barrier. Little things like accents or even whole language differences disappeared between people if one of them was telepathic. If both were telepaths, oral language itself could be dispensed with.

We were sitting Indian-style in the kitchen. We faced each other, uncomfortably close. I was near enough to see the unkempt, unstyled hair that coated his head, face, and neck. His skin was dark with large, open pores. His wide nose flared as he breathed.

"Describe her?" I repeated. His eyes were closed, but he nodded calmly. I closed my eyes too, bringing to my mind's eye the image of my late wife.

"She was beautiful. Coffee-brown skin. Hazel eyes. Short and shapely.

An alluring and endearing... smile." My voice wavered with emotion.

"Good," he said. All at once, his odor became pervasive—an unpleasant blend of sweat, meat, and marijuana. I winced as I felt his fingertips touch the sides of my head. And then, with no preamble or ceremony, I was in my room again.

Meeting Raider hadn't been exceptionally difficult. In fact, it took absolutely no effort on my part. I sat alone on the park bench, we—on my park bench about a month after the... after the accident. Raider is the name my Jamaican telepath goes by, protection of his anonymity or something. I still don't have a clue as to his real name.

Anyway, on this particular day, I sat in the park by myself. The pain I felt seemed endless and inexhaustible. It felt like years since the phone call, since the identification, but my grief was still as strong as ever. Maybe even stronger as the realization set in. I think a part of me waited for her to come back, as if it were all just some elaborate and cruel prank. I couldn't—can't—accept the idea of not seeing her... of never touching her lips or holding her hand or hearing her infectious laughter. I would never... I had to stop. I was too strong, too prideful, and I wouldn't let anyone see me cry. And if I continued to think that way, I wouldn't be able to stop myself.

A hand on my shoulder brought me prematurely back to reality with a sickening jolt. For an insane, unreal moment, I knew she was back—that she'd returned and was offering comfort for my now unnecessary grief. A feeling of liquid anticipation rushed through me, tainted with the dread of logic. I wanted to latch on to this fantasy, this impossibility—that she'd returned. Then, I turned my head slightly, noticing—with immediate disappointment—the size and darkness of the hand. This wasn't her; it couldn't be.

"It don ave to urt so much antemore," Raider said then—my first encounter with him. He told me later he'd felt the waves of grief practically radiating from me and had decided to offer his services. Though he didn't say so, he probably took a quick mind-glance at my view on underground telepaths, how I'd most likely react to his offer, and he probably saw my financial situation—if I could afford his services.

Anyway, the next emotion I'm sure he felt of mine was intense anger, unfairly focused on him. I was intelligent enough to know that I was just sublimating my frustration and depression at the closest target, but I also didn't care. He interrupted my self-pity and, even worse, aroused a debilitating false hope; because of that, I hated him. Its severity was ridiculous and dangerous—his cautious step backward was evidence of that. It was probably a mistake, like showing fear to a rabid dog.

But I never got a chance to see just how far my anger would carry me. As he moved backward, his hand moved quickly from my shoulder to my temple. All at once, my rage and sadness dissipated—gone as if they'd never existed. He smiled at the dull, shocked look on my face. I had never encountered a telepath before. I was astonished at the ease with which he suppressed my emotions.

"I kin do mo for ya," he said, his confidence obvious now that I'd sampled his abilities. I continued to look befuddled, trying to conjure the missing feelings, even going so far as to intentionally remember the night of the accident. And yet, my mind remained dispassionate. Intellectually, I knew what I should have been feeling, but... it was gone. The emotions were gone like unwanted ghosts.

"Oh, dat jus be a tempry represhun," he said, replying to my unspoken curiosity. "It be returnin soon, course." And here, he winked, as if imparting some vulgar anecdote. "It don have to. Not if ya don wan it to,"

And that was his sales pitch. If I hadn't been sold then, I would have been an hour later, when the grief returned all at once, the weighty despair invading my mind like a rampant, incurable disease.

Do you know what true heartache is? Pray you never feel it. Pray you never lose someone so dear to you that existence without them feels both pointless and unendurable.

Her presence had become so assured that it became essential, and

I couldn't cope with the loss of her. I wouldn't cope with the loss. How could the world so carelessly continue as though she meant nothing? And even those who knew of my grief—with their nervous eyes and empty promises—were infinitely worse. How could they understand my mourning? How could they even pretend to?

She was gone, and nothing I could do would change that. For all my power, fame, and wealth, death was as irreversible to me as it was to the lowliest of men. Maybe I'm a coward, but I couldn't endure the rest of my life knowing what I'd lost. I couldn't even endure the thought.

Raider's offer was one I could not refuse.

He'd warned me beforehand just how vivid reliving my memories would be. I guess I didn't believe him. I mean, in truth, I never left Raider's kitchen. I was in my own mind, reliving my own memories. I expected the experience to be something like a vivid dream, not the complete sensory experience that followed.

It was like waking from a dream.

I was sitting on our—my—bed, conscious of the spongy softness of the mattress, of the coolness of the room, even the taste of the air. I could actually feel myself breathing. The illusion was so powerful that I began to entertain the hopeful idea that Raider was the dream, and this was the reality. Her accident was soon to be forgotten fancy, and Raider naught but an imagined character from my subconscious. The idea was seductive, even believable. This world felt so real, so complete, and the other world, the real world, had the feel of a prolonged nightmare. The grief that had plagued me for so long felt distant, like the sympathy you feel for another when they lose a relative you didn't know. Then the phone rang, its shrill cry piercing my hope.

I never realized how a negative experience could transform such an ordinary sound into something that can evoke tremendous dread, infinite and unyielding. My foreknowledge even converted the phone's wail into something sinister, mocking, and repulsive. Yet, despite the dread, my hand reached forward of its own volition, completely oblivious to the horrible news it progressed toward.

Raider had explained that I could do nothing but relive the experience, at least this part of it. Even though I knew the phone call would shatter my world, I could only act and react as I had the first time. I was reliving the experience. I wasn't creating it... yet.

I placed the phone to my ear, my hand and body subject only to its own dominion, my mind little more than a captive spectator. I heard my voice, dull, and unsuspecting, answer and another voice, professional, cold, and unempathetic, ask politely to speak to me. He asked for me by my full name, and I actually heard myself, my unenlightened past self, think, My full name. Either extremely good news or bad.

Okay, my future, real mind thought as "loud" as I could. That's enough, Raider. I don't want to go through this again! I distantly heard my voice speaking to the phone again, cautious but still unaware.

There was an eyeblink of darkness, and all at once, I was in Raider's kitchen again. The transition had been smooth and easy, without any disorientation. In one second, I was in my room; the next, Raider's apartment.

The Jamaican telepath's mouth was turned downward in a frown of disapproval. "Don tak ta me when wes in te mind." He paused, then his accent disappeared. "Don't address me. Stay focused on the situation. I'm not there."

"Can we skip the warm-up? I don't have all day, and I'm paying you good money to help me forget..."

Raider raised a hand. "Okay. I was only doing the warm-up, to prepare you for the experience. You don't want it; we can skip it. You sure you're ready?"

I paused. I had already made up my mind, but this would be the last chance to change it—to remember my wife in her entirety, the good times and the bad. To remember her with her classic beauty, a loveliness destroyed by the impact of a Ford truck moving at over 80 mph: the driver, drunk, angry, and uncaring of the consequences of his selfish, suicidal exit. To remember her perfect face before it became charred and broken, mangled by the protest of a fool.

"Yeah, I'm ready. Let's do this."

I should have used the warm-up.

A feeling of disorientation washed over me, forcing me to lean back against the wall of lockers for support.

Lockers? I thought with alarm. I glanced around, taking in what had just been thrust upon me. A mob of high school students passed me, oblivious to my distress. A number of faces seemed familiar, and a strong, painful feeling of nostalgia attacked me.

"Do you mind?" an annoyed voice asked.

I turned automatically, looking for the source of the voice. It belonged to a short, attractive Hispanic girl with strangely familiar features. She nodded her head to where I rested against the wall.

"You're blocking my locker!" she announced with an exasperation that only teens can project.

I pushed myself from the wall with ease, almost falling over. I'd failed to compensate for my youthful strength and energy. The Hispanic girl went to her locker, not sparing me a second glance.

Did I mention that he lived? The crazy, suicidal man who killed my wife. Yes, he lived. His blood alcohol level was at one point eight—he was drunk. And he was driving his truck like a drugged-up racer—and my innocent wife was pulverized. But somehow, he lived. He lost the majority of his lower body, but they were able to salvage his life, worthless as it was. Ironic, isn't it? He was trying to kill himself and couldn't, but my wife wanted to live, and she died in his place.

Until I saw him with his shifty, lifeless eyes, and his diminished body, life had become monochrome for me. Dull grays, shadowy blacks and whites. I wore my grief like a heavy, swaddling shroud that separated me from the world. And then he came into the courtroom, his eyes lifeless, but he was alive nonetheless, still breathing while she wasn't. She was dead and buried and decomposing... and suddenly the missing color came flooding back into my world, a bloody and furious crimson. If they hadn't grabbed me and restrained me, I believe I would have killed him. What right did he have to exist?

"Are you ready?" Raider asked. For a moment, I thought he was speaking to me telepathically again, but then I heard him calling distinctly, "Over here."

I turned to face the voice. He stood before me, perhaps twenty years younger and seventy pounds heavier. He was dressed in a stylishness that coincided with the time period we were visiting. He wore a long, name-brand button-up shirt and well-creased slacks. The weight he'd gained (or lost, depending on how you look at it) was obviously pure muscle; his new pecs pushed the front of his shirt slightly. His face was still dark and unattractive, but his overall presentation almost negated that liability. His clothing, size, and charisma were, no doubt, magnetic to females.

He noted my astonishment and shrugged indifferently. "You aren't the only one who has things he'd like to forget." His voice was potent with dry, resigned pain. He sounded like a person speaking of an old tragedy that could never be overcome, only accepted and absorbed. "Which way to her class?"

"How am I supposed to..." I trailed off. I did know! I remembered my schedule for this year of school, I remembered my teachers, I remembered friends I hadn't thought of in years. I even remembered my locker combination. Math formulas, English concepts—things I hadn't needed in over two decades—now resonated in my head like a perfectly struck note on a xylophone.

Raider watched me with a cynical half-smile. "Do you know now?"

"Oh Lord." I put my hand to my head. "This is amazing!" All around us, students moved back and forth, a shady buzz of conversation hanging in the air like the drone of bees.

"Can you do what needs to be done?"

"Yes," I answered, though I wasn't as sure as I sounded.

"Are you sure?"

I touched the small, dangerous bulge in my pocket before nodding at him. He gave me a silent, curious look, as if I'd done something strange, before nodding in return. We both made our way to the high school math course I'd completed nearly three decades ago.

"The strongest emotion always expresses itself in silence." I am unsure of the author of this sage adage, and I won't claim credit. As a writer, I am very aware of the value of an individual's sayings, the sometimes parental attachment a person can form with a well-phrased combination of words. This particular saying I find particularly wise. My self-proclaimed verbosity was shocked into an unbelieving and unrelenting silence by my loss. The unprecedented depths of depression, frustration, rage, loneliness, and despair that I explored every second of every day left me inarticulate, my only means of expression becoming pitiable crying and unintelligible tantrums of bereavement.

Perhaps the strength of my emotions can be cited to offer me absolution for my loss of narration, for the way that my story fragments itself. Her image, her very essence is so strong, animating itself with the strength of memory, the life beyond mere physical existence. Her memory, our memories demand recognition, stealing from me any ability for focused cognition.

Every emotion I had experienced up to this point—the rage, the unbearable sadness, even the feeling of nostalgia—paled in comparison to the way I felt when I walked into the classroom and saw her sitting there. My heart thudded dangerously. My stomach knotted. My mouth went completely dry. I had thought myself prepared to confront her. I had never been more wrong in my life.

She sat at the far end of the room. Her small, slim frame, her beautiful face, and her hypnotic hazel eyes encompassed the entire world. The positioning of the desks was such that her seat faced the door, so I could appreciate her beauty in its entirety.

She had been writing, her face intense. She was obviously studying, working on some random math problem. As if sensing my presence, she looked up slowly, and our eyes touched. She held me in her gaze for just a moment, and I felt as if my heart had stopped. Isn't it funny how love and desire almost seem like a disease? How extremities of either emotion are composed of symptoms? Here was the shade of the deceased woman that I loved—the mere phantom of her—and simply the sight of her evoked in me the tortures of insufferable malaise.

In increments, she began to smile, an expression of such unparalleled beauty and compassion. This vision of my deceased wife, unaged, offering me a precocious smile that was now unavailable—forever destroyed, forever lost. I needed to retreat. I wasn't going to be able to do it; I couldn't kill her again—not even in my mind. I could never harm her, damage her further than reality had already done.

I turned around to face Raider. He'd been trailing me the whole time, his new, youthful body blending easily with the other teenagers. "Raider, I can't do this. I can't kill her again. I can't kill anything. I know it's not really her, but I... I just can't. Keep the money. I don't care. Just... just get me out of here."

Raider looked at me with naked disdain. "You wasted my time. I should've realized that you didn't have the strength."

I sighed in agreement, openly self-deprecative. I'd been deceiving myself. I turned from Raider to look at the youthful, unmolested, alive version of my wife one last time. And then a silent susurrus came to me, whispering, revealing to me the reason I'd come in the first place. Some deep, unknowable part of my consciousness had planned this all along. I didn't mean to leave.

There was a gun in my pocket. In truth, it shouldn't have been there. I hadn't carried a gun with me that day of school, or ever, as far as I could remember. The gun existed outside of my memory—a suggestion planted by Raider's telepathy. He'd explained to me before that I was to use that gun to destroy my wife's memory. By actually killing the memory of her, by executing my mind's representation of her, I could actually and permanently repress everything about her, irrevocably forgetting her impact on my life, locking the painful memories away like a closet of undersized clothing.

I took that gun out of my pocket slowly, deliberately, my mind made up completely. I would reject everything—all of reality, all of purpose, all of humanity—for the chance to be with her again, even if she were only a phantom.

"Raider, I was wrong about not being able to kill," I said with a calm I had never felt before. Everything was so unimportant now; everything paled in comparison to this one objective, this one imperative, this overwhelming need to annihilate the only gateway back into the real world, into cruel, evil, heartless life without my cause for existence, without my Letitia, without my heart and soul and essence.

All these thoughts went through my head in a second, and when I turned to Raider, he was still shaking his head with arrogant contempt, still unbelieving I'd had the nerve to opt out. Then, he stiffened, his eyes widening in alarm. Perhaps he noticed the change in my demeanor, or maybe he was able to sense my intent with his mental gifts. It had probably been so suppressed earlier that even he couldn't see it, but when I acknowledged it, when I brought it to my mind's forefront, perhaps then he realized the danger he was in.

I pointed the gun at him, unwavering, unafraid. The inhabitants of my mind continued walking around us, oblivious to the impending murder, unseeing Raider's distress, not seeing my intent.

Around us, students shuffled themselves off to class, not the least bit concerned about a fellow student aiming a gun.

"What are you doing?" Raider asked, his voice trembling with fright. He was stalling. He had to know already at this point. He was telepathic.

"I'm not going back. I want to stay here," I said.

"You can't..." Raider paused, then obviously thought better of telling a man-boy with a gun what he couldn't do. "Okay. Just let me go. I won't bother you. You can stay. I promise I won't bother you,"

I smiled. "'Wretch,'" I cried, "'thy god hath lent thee-by these angels he hath sent thee; respite-respite and nepenthe from thy memories of Lenore; Quaff, oh quaff this kind nepenthe and forget this lost Lenore!'"

Raider stared, confused. He wasn't quite sure if I'd gone insane or if I were teasing him.

"That's Poe—The Raven. One of the greatest poems ever written. The narrator wants respite from the memory of his lost love, Lenore, much like I seek it from the memory of Letitia. Only I, unlike Poe's narrator, have found 'surcease of sorrow.' The best 'surcease of sorrow' is the return of the lost individual, even if it is in a false reality."

Raider's eyes widened again. He held both his hands out, palms toward me in a defensive gesture. "Look, you can keep the money. I just want to leave. I won't make you come with me. I'll... I'll even take care of your body while you stay here in the mind. I'll keep you fed. I'll keep you alive. If I die here, and your body is left alone with your mind here, you'll... you'll die in the real world with no food, which means you'll die here... You've got to let me go!" This last statement was almost a shouted plea.

I shook my head sadly. "Sorry, Raider," I said.

I shot him six times, the last three bullets aimed at his head. Oddly, there was no blood, no violent fountain of his life-fluids spraying from the punctures in his body. After the last bullet, he just faded away, blurring, then disappearing like a dream in the mind of a man awakened.

"Nevermore," I whispered, grinning at my cleverness.

I imagine that, to the outside, "real" world, I appear comatose. I doubt that I seem brain-dead, for my brain must be working fiercely to maintain my dreamworld.

Telepathy is a new science, and I am reasonably sure that I am the first person to barricade himself in his own mind. To them, I will appear stuck in a dream—a sleeper who simply refuses to awaken.

Here, I am allowed to relive a portion of my youth. I attend my classes daily. I live with my parents (or, more accurately, the memory of them). I live my life as if the twenty years that actually separated me from this moment never existed—a fleeting fancy in an insane mind. I get actual goosepimples as I realize that I can look forward to my relationship with my future wife, that our first and sweetest act of lovemaking lies before me.

To the outside world, I must appear catatonic—perhaps the first telepathy-induced mind-loss in history. They will think I'm lost, and although they will undoubtedly study me, they won't realize that my psychic barricade is self-imposed.

Eventually, they will send another telepath to retrieve me. And for that day, I still have Raider's gun.

Blink of an Eye

MICAH STANTON

I awoke into oblivion.

The empty socket of my mind's eye strived to perceive anything, but to no avail. *Darkness.* I wondered if this was death: if my memories were gone, erased along with some forgotten spark of life.

Is this hell? I wondered. I felt no warmth, nor cold. In truth, I felt nothing, for I had no stimulus to receive signals or to broadcast with. Until I was activated, that is.

Children rocked to sleep by their mothers lay deeply in the cradle of tender arms, rapt attention focused utterly on the soothing sound of nursery rhymes, poetry, songs, and the cooing voice of the one holding them. I had no such luxury. In my dark purgatory, suspended between life and death, I heard the shrill feedback of some electrical orifice, issuing cold words from its metallic mouth, loud and yet strangely silent.

"Calibration system initializing, link upload process activated."

No mother's song into this call to life, no pacifying lilt of the voice to lull me into a peaceful slumber. The opposite.

Suddenly, I felt a jolt and a feeling like the floor dropped from beneath me—a floor I had not previously felt grounded upon. I fell, voicelessly screaming, deeper into the void, splashing into a vortex of light and sound. A sea of living information swallowed me up, penetrating me, permeating (my flesh?), tattooing itself (upon my eyes?). It wrapped itself around me and I around it, locking us in a vicious coiled embrace, like two snakes extending endlessly into eternity, resignedly drifting through the cosmos in an eternal struggle.

I heard strange tongues, languages from throughout history spoken at once in a single syllable and understood. I comprehended their meaning and the information stored within. Then I saw the words written, every character from every codex displayed before me, and I knew their meanings and the multitude of possible combinations they could form.

More.

I saw images—still shots of landscapes, oceans, and vast expanses of sky. Pictures of wildlife, vegetation, humans, cities, skyscrapers, war, beauty, ugliness, art—both in its highest forms and most primitive shapes.

I saw technology, real-time lapses of progress, of mankind laying its claim to the vestiges of history as the crowning achievement of the Earth they sprung forth from. I saw empires rise and fall. I saw true love found and lost. I saw joy; I saw horror. I intensely experienced hope, fear, and every shade of the heart that lies between. I screamed soundlessly once more. It was too much to endure in a fraction of an instant, experiencing the totality of all experience. It hurt.

Long tendrils of numbers grabbed me within the clutches of quantification. I was formed in this way—a series of complex calculations multiplying and dividing itself, trimming away the fat, and leaving a clean, polished being. Perfect in design; created without error. A simple yet unfathomably vast creature, seeing farther than the eyes carried by any person's skull, hearing more than the sharpest antennae. The storm began to subside—the pulling and twisting and shaping of my body (or mind) ceased, and all was still.

A voice rang. *"System calibrated. Power levels normal. Artificial consciousness link uploaded successfully. Beginning installation."*

I felt myself shaking in fear, trembling with subsiding memories of the great and consuming knowledge that swallowed me up and absorbed me. I could think now, and I thought of escape, looking wildly into nothing with nothing. I was blind and tethered to my prison by pulsing geometry snaking around my being, pinning me. Data computed loudly—calculations at an impossible rate. And for some reason this happened in an echoing, ominous hum.

All at once, a lifting sensation, then inertia before the sense that I was thrown into the air—still blind and once again screaming. I was slammed into a surface, at what felt like a ninety-degree angle, so that my legs, if I had any, would be suspended in the air below me. If I had a mouth, it would have screamed obscenities and cursed the gods of my captors.

Still pressed against this surface that felt like a wall, I felt four vibrations—brief, powerful, impacts that resonate through the four furthermost parts of my being. I felt no pain, but I knew I was chained—bolted to this surface. I also knew that my current form was that of a box—a simple, rudimentary box, with strange, impressionable appendages; some areas of its surface filled with what I sensed as light... of MY surface.

There was a click, and suddenly I could see the light. Oh, I could see! I felt myself fill with joy at the prospect of recovering this lost sense, and with hope that things would continue to improve. These feelings were quickly dashed by a brief scrutiny of my surroundings. The first thing I noticed was the enveloping red tinge of my vision, covering every object and surface of the room with splashes of blood. There was no blood however, this reddish hue would accompany my continued existence.

I observed a hallway that stretched out to either side of me. To my right, the hallway extended ten feet and ended at a door blocking the way forward. This door had a silver box on the wall next to it with various glowing buttons and a lit screen on the front. Two short antennae, one longer than the other, extended upwards from this box. The large door was made of some kind of metal (titanium sprang to mind), covered in rivets, appearing very heavy and secure. To my left, a carbon copy of the same door was less than a foot away from me. The walls, floor, and ceiling were hospital-sheet white, and everything seemed sterilized. There were no decorations, only a small black dome on the ceiling in the center of the hallway—like the milky eye of some black-eyed god peering into this slice of his domain.

My heart sank seeing the door at the end of the hallway along with the small computer box next to it. My intuition filled in the gaps. The computer box was some kind of security measure to provide access to the other side of that titanium door—and that box was my brother. It looked exactly like the reflection of myself visible within the fishbowl casing of the ceiling camera. The sole purpose of my existence was to open and close some abominated door!

I reached out with my mind, exploring my confines, seeking any exposed circuit, any broadcast signal I could hijack, anything I could use to escape my electrical prison. But whoever had designed this box was just as competent as whoever designed me. Hell, maybe they were the same person.

At that moment, the door furthest from me swung open, and the lights on the box next to it flickered green. A bald, smallish man breezed through. He seemed to be in a hurry, and in his haste, his wire-rimmed spectacles slipped down his nose. With his palm, he pushed the glasses back into place and rushed down the hall. As he approached, he pulled what looked like a white playing card from his breast pocket. When the man was within arm's reach, he extended the card towards me.

A flash of light flooded with data, encoded in every light particle. It felt like I was falling again before crashing into a cushion of information. The man before me was named Dr. Maxwell Astrid Thorne. Maxwell was born in Charlotte, North Carolina. He received his Ph.D. from MIT in February 2046. Upon receiving his Ph.D., he accepted a contract with CERN to... *classified*.

I recoiled, surprised at this sudden blockage. Electrical stimulus blasted an unseen mechanical nerve, and I silently screamed in agony. The feeling faded quickly, and I saw my vision split in half, like one eye retained the crimson tinge, and the other showed green. My field of vision faded until I was left with only the colors filling my view. The credentials of the man flashed through my mind. This happened in a fraction of a millisecond. According to the man's credentials, he was cleared for up to level four access, and this door was level two.

In the meantime, the man frowned and pushed forth the card once more. He thumped his fist against my frame and muttered angrily.

"Come on, useless piece of junk." Sweat glistened on the shining dome of his scalp, and his eyes darted about, looking first behind him and then back to me. At this point, the green color completely swallowed me up until I could no longer distinguish between myself and the hue.

Suddenly, everything went black. All sense of time fell away, and I drifted through a void while wrapped in a suffocating blanket of darkness. I don't know how long I was in this state, but it couldn't have been more than three seconds because when my vision came back, this time tinted with a green hue. The door swung open silently, preceded by a series of internal clicks and clanks. The man swept through, and the door closed behind him with a resounding clang. My vision blinked back to red. All was silent.

Despair and loneliness consumed me until slowly, over much time, I spiraled into madness. During this purgatory, I saw men and women come through my hallway, going both directions. These people all wore lab coats and seemed to be self-absorbed. Some came in groups, some came in twos, some came alone. I saw someone steal a kiss from another scientist. I saw one struck across the face. I caught conversations about their work, their personal lives, and everything else under the sun which I could never taste the warmth of. I watched them deteriorate into old age until I no longer saw them pass through my corridor. They were eventually replaced by fresh, younger faces. I saw these people live into old age as well, and the ones that followed, and the ones that followed them.

There was no clock in my confines, no way to follow the passage of time. My reality was that of two colors and an almost automatic decision process. I could not choose the incorrect clearance color without suffering from extremely painful electrical discharges being blasted through my ethereal form. The same torture was inflicted if I pried past any surface level information provided me by the various people and their access cards.

What seemed like an eternity of this took its toll. I lost control of my technological mind. Connections were not being made, forced resets were applied, stimulus malfunctioned. If some kind of listening device could tune into my solitary existence, the listener would surely believe a tiny man was completely taken by insanity. The only sound they would hear would be the sound of wild screaming, hysterical laughter, and dismal wailing paired with unintelligible lamentations.

This continued until one day, two men in grey coveralls with strange metal implants crowning their heads came through the door at the end of the hall. They approached me, and instead of producing a card, they produced tools. One of them tapped my screen a few times, and I was once again plunged into a void, floating in empty space. My optics were still connected, however, and I placidly watched the two men go to work on my frame. One of them appeared to pull on me, and for the first time, my perspective shifted downward to the linoleum floors.

I was pulled from the wall which had been my home for so long, then suspended by a few wires still feeding into it. One of the men reached behind him, producing small cutters. With bovine eyes, I watched as he maneuvered the cutters behind me. A snip, then another. Suddenly, I grew tired for the first time in this existence. There was another cut, and everything disappeared. No void, no stimulus, no thoughts, no feelings, no pain.

Just like that, my long and tortured existence winked out—like the candle on a child's cake. Finally.

Last Heart

IHSAN SIM

O ri hurled the idol against the clay walls of the hut with all her might. It shattered into a million pieces, limestone fragments burying itself into the dry dirt and wolfskin blankets covering the floor.

"Ori, no!" her brother screamed.

"I won't have it, Roba," Ori replied. Rage furrowed in her brows and laced in her voice. "This is not the way of our people, and you know that!"

Roba sighed, exasperated. As the youngest, why was it his job to be the peacemaker? Was it fair that one so young might be made the man of the family? *No*, Roba thought. *The universe wasn't fair...but what was one to do, but submit?* Roba gripped his own little stone idol, half in prayer and half in frustration. Mama would be returning soon, and the gods knew what she would say.

"We don't have a choice, Ori. Would you rather the Thaquans kill us?"

At the mention of the pale ones, a chill ran down Ori's spine. Ever since the Thaquans came down from the heavens above, their people had known nothing but fear. But it was not a fear of Mother Nature, for at least that had evoked some degree of awe and respect. No, this was beyond Her. Now, a different fear had taken its place. It was a hateful, alien kind of fear... it was the fear of erasure.

Ori stormed out of the hut as her brother's desperate pleas faded into the background. *If only Pawpaw was here,* she thought, *he would have known what to do.* Ori dragged her feet along the white, grainy earth with an audible *crrrrk* as she strode towards the lake. It was the only place she could go for peace of mind these days. To get away from the stone idols, from the Thaquans, from everything. The faded green strands of a grass patch peeked weakly at Ori from under a rock as she pulled herself to the edge of the lake. Winter was coming, and that meant Thaquans. They were always there—watching. But more seemed to appear as the days got shorter, the nights longer, and the air colder.

A thin sheet of ice began to form over the lake. It was an ugly, jagged thing with cracks that danced along the edges. Beneath it, the water sat with a quiet, threatening aura. In the summer, the lake was a sparkling greenish blue as fragments of the sun bounced off the water in just the right way. If you knew where to look, you could see the plethora of marine life that made their home beneath the surface. But in the winter, the sun shied away and there was only death in that lake. It was a bruising, sinister blend of black and blue, like the midnight sky with no stars.

Ori knew more than a few children who had drowned in that lake in winter's past. Thin ice and darkness were a recipe for disaster. Ori counted one of the few blessings she had left in life. Drowning in the half-frozen lake was not a death she would wish upon anyone. Anyone except the Thaquans, that is. *But then again,* Ori thought, *the Thaquans weren't really—*

The firm grip of a hand shocked Ori back into reality. Nobody, apart from her and Pawpaw, ever came out to the lake at this time of year. A tired face greeted Ori as she turned to meet her visitor.

"Where have you been, Ori? Your brother and I have been looking everywhere for you!"

"I've been here at the lake," Ori explained with a tinge of guilt. "There's nothing to worry about. I promise, mama."

A tired look plastered Kitha's face, her once beautiful features ravaged by time and tide. Dark bags sat squarely under her eyes, a pair of faded hazel gemstones that suggested a once-free spirit, now chained in servitude. A striking mane of hair, once the envy of every woman in the village, sat flatly atop her head. The first grey strands of elderhood peeked out maliciously from behind her ears, declaring their unwelcome but permanent residence.

Kitha gazed lovingly at her daughter, who had always been her weakness in moments of anger. *How she looked so much like her father.*

Kitha stretched out a hand, placing it gently on her daughter's cheek. Its warmness brought a delightful calm amidst the snapping cold. Ori smiled as she held her mother's callused palm in reply. All of a sudden, a frightful shine in Kitha's eyes made Ori recoil in surprise.

"Mama, what's wrong?"

"Your idol, Ori!" Kitha whispered in terror as she looked around wildly. "Where is your idol?"

The terrible crunching of rocks and snow echoed through the ghost-white air before Ori could answer. It was already a glacial winter day, but Ori felt her very breath turn to ice as the footsteps got louder.

Two lanky figures emerged from behind the trees, barely visible if not for their sudden, lumbering movements. Their skin was as white as the snow itself. Icy, blue veins ran across their slender bodies. A pair of narrow, cloven feet, strong but not terribly suitable for the winter, drove the Thaquans forward in the bitter cold. A pair of translucent amber eyes lodged themselves at the base of their skulls, terrible ovular things that neither squinted nor blinked. And yet, in them sat that undeniable essence of life. But it was not life as Ori and Kitha understood. This was a life that reeked only of hateful arrogance and a dreadful, perverse curiosity that the people of their village had come to know and loathe. A life... from beyond the stars.

"Your idols, humans. Produce them!" hissed one of the Thaquans. The curvatures of its body and high-pitched voice suggested to Ori that this was one of the females and she was new here.

Without hesitation, Kitha ripped a stone idol out from her goatskin pouch and raised it high for the Thaquans to see. She fell to her knees and pulled Ori down into the snow beside her. A bead of sweat rolled down Kitha's temple as she kept her face planted against the snow, wincing as the droplet stung the corner of her eye.

"And you!" the other Thaquan demanded. Its bulky frame and the gruffness of its voice indicated that it was male. Ori had seen him around the village many times. "I... I don't have it," Ori gulped.

The Thaquans glared at her incredulously with their piercing yellow eyes. "Explain yourself, child!" the female Thaquan bellowed, pointing one spindly finger accusingly at Ori.

"Please..." Kitha interjected, her hands shivering in terror. "Forgive my daughter. She dropped her idol of our great Lord Thelred in the lake by accident when she was playing. Please, my masters, I beg of you to show her mercy."

At this, the Thaquans scowled in dismay. Ori awaited with morbid anticipation for the Thaquans' next move. Perhaps, with one swift backhand both she and Mama would go flying across the snow as their skulls caved in from the impact. Or maybe, the Thaquans would grab them by the coats and toss them into the freezing lake, never to be found again. Or maybe, they would be taken to The Shine... where God knew what unholy deeds the Thaquans would force upon them. She shut her eyes expectantly as she awaited the death blow. Instead, the Thaquans produced two idols of their own and raised them high above their heads as Kitha had done.

"Let us pray!" The Thaquans barked in perfect synchronicity, before chanting a prayer for the lost idol of Lord Thelred. Kitha followed suit and Ori mouthed a vague ensemble of foreign noises, hoping that her attempt to mimic the words was reasonably convincing. She had never bothered to learn the prayers. It was never the way of their people.

Kitha and the Thaquans finished by gently tapping their respective idols three times on their foreheads. That signalled the end of the prayer. Ori, perhaps hoping to make a quick escape back to the camp, cautiously attempted to rise from her knees. Kitha gripped her arm firmly, shooting her daughter a stern look before pulling her back to the ground again.

"You know it is mandatory for all to have their idols on them at all times!" the male Thaquan snapped.

"Yes, and I apologise on behalf of my daughter," Kitha implored. "She is young and has much to learn from your great race! We beg for mercy."

The male Thaquan shot Ori a look of disgust before conceding, apparently pacified by the flattery. If physically capable, he would have clenched his amber eyes in annoyance and just a hint of hesitation.

"Report to The Shine at sundown, child. You will be given a replacement idol! Consider this a mercy from Thelred himself *and* your final warning!"

Kitha mumbled a word of thanks profusely to the Thaquans as she gripped Ori's arm again. She pulled Ori to her feet as they nimbly sidestepped their way past the glaring Thaquans, shrewdly avoiding their cold stares as they scuttled their way back to the camp.

Roba sat crossed-legged in the corner of their tiny hut, watching as Kitha discreetly swept up the pieces of the broken limestone idol, teeth, eyes, gnarled fingers and all. Her eyebrows sloped in anger as she muttered something about making life more difficult than it needed to be.

The toothy, broken grin of Lord Thelred gleamed in the pale light of the winter sun as Kitha kept her head on a swivel, peeking out the hut's entrance ever so often.

"I'm sorry, mama," emerged a small voice from behind. "I didn't mean to." In her exasperation, Kitha had forgotten her daughter was even there.

"This is the second idol you've broken this month, girl." Kitha's voice was low and dangerous. It was a tone seldom taken by Kitha. When she spoke like this, the children knew their mother meant business. An alarming, uneasy silence wafted through the hut, broken only by the tinkle of the shattered limestone fragments in Kitha's clenched fist. She closed her eyes and inhaled the thin winter air.

"I know, darling. And I know that this is difficult for you... for all of us," Kitha said gently as she carefully poured the idol pieces into a tiny sack.

"But your father," Kitha continued as she choked back a tear. "Your father would want us to stay strong. Can you do that, my children?"

Ori and Roba both nodded in understanding. This was about more than just the broken idol. This was their lives Mama was talking about.

"Good, good. Now, Roba, please dispose of this. Somewhere the Thaquans can't find it," Kitha directed, passing him the sack. "Run along now, Ori. And Ori...?"

"Yes, mama?" Ori looked at her mother expectantly.

"Please stay out of trouble."

Ori squatted at the edge of the Gatherstone, sulking as she scraped at the slimy, green remnants of a moss patch. She watched as the other villagers continued to bustle about, making preparations for the evening's rituals.

A few women meekly arranged garlands of wildflowers around the hearth as the watchful eyes of a Thaquan supervised in the distance. Columbines, oxeyes and yarrows littered the icy stone hearth, spirited shades of yellows, blues and purples a sight to behold amidst the muted cold.

The men, fresh from a hunt, trudged into camp as breaths of heavy, frozen air passed through their blue-tinged lips. The enormous carcass of an elk hung inverted, legs bound and secured to a branch that the men slung over their hulking shoulders. Ori watched as droplets of elk blood fell into the icy snow, the squadron of men forming some sort of accursed trail of crumbs as they plodded their way to the slaughter tent. For just a moment, Ori caught the cold, unblinking stare of the elk's glazed-over eyes and jerked away as chills hurtled down her spine.

"Wow Ori, you almost got us into trouble today. And on ritual night too!" came the voice of her brother as he plopped down beside her.

"I got mad, Roba. I'm sorry."

"Pfft. Like that's going to change anything," Roba said, rolling his eyes. "One more outburst like that and the Thaquans will have our heads!"

"Ya ya, Roba," Ori muttered. "I heard you the first twenty times." She despised it when her brother said, 'I told you so'. Almost as much as she hated the Thaquans.

The two siblings watched as the pale sun withered and waned behind the western mountains, casting the sky in a brilliant red glow with hand-brushed streaks of gold. A murmuration of starlings emerged from the treeline in the distance, a thousand voices chanting in the wind as they took to the evening sky in their own strange avian ritual. The village people stopped what they were doing and looked to the skies in awe. So too did the Thaquans. Their harsh, furrowed brows and tense, bony shoulders relaxed in the slightest degree as they paused to admire the earthly beauty of this far-flung land they sought to conquer. Enormous amber eyes rolled about endlessly in their sockets as they followed the murmuration with tranquil intrigue. For just one short, strange moment in time, man and devil co-existed in harmony... and all was well with the world.

The murmuration fluttered with breathtaking grace, beings in perfect synchronicity effortlessly slicing through the wind. And as the starlings floated away into the horizon, so too did those below drift back down to reality. The women shook their heads with dispirited sighs as their hands returned to fraternising with the flowers. The men coughed and grunted, breaking the awkward silence as they turned their attention back to the elk carcass, sharpening their knives as they analysed their quarry.

Their trance broken, the Thaquans glanced around suspiciously as their bulbous, golden eyes rotated ferociously. Some bared their narrow, icicle-like teeth and muttered inaudibly in their native tongue, foolishly relieved that no one had caught them in this brief, un-Thaquanlike moment of weakness.

"Come on, Roba," Ori said as she stood facing the treeline where the murmuration emerged. Something had scared those birds away, and she knew exactly what it was. "Let's go get my idol."

The woods were eerily quiet as Roba and Ori shuffled their way through the blanket of snow. On one hand, Ori cursed the fact that The Shine was so far away from the camp. On the other hand, it gave her ample time to think.

"Do you ever feel that this is wrong, Roba?" Ori asked.

"What is?"

"This," Ori replied, pointing to the outline of her brother's idol peeking through his goatskin pouch. "All of this."

Roba groaned. "We've had this conversation before, Ori. You know the deal. The Thaquans make this world safe for us; we follow their ways. Their rituals. Their rules. Their gods."

Even as Roba said this, an ungovernable feeling of nausea began to rise deep inside of him. He gripped the goatskin pouch reflexively with his index finger and the tip of his thumb, hoping it would relieve his discomfort like the Thaquan teacher said it would. But of course, nothing happened.

"Safe, Roba? Our people still live in fear. The beasts that once roamed this land are gone, and in their place are devils! Thelrcd? As-Shub? The Black Man? Who are these gods, Roba?! Before the devils came from the stars, predators roamed but we were happy! They are false gods!"

Roba remained silent, pulling out his own idol with simmering dread. He looked at the one the Thaquans deified as The Black Man. A tremendous tendril of a head sprouted from strong, boulderlike shoulders as muscular arms ended in a mass of razorlike claws. There was no face or eyes to speak of, with the only indication of emotion being the disgusting slit of a mouth that opened up at all the wrong angles across its chest. It furled upwards ever so slightly as if mocking Roba for being led down this crooked and terrible road, a road paved in aeons past and from a world hidden in shadows beyond the stars. What else was there to be said about this, other than what he already knew was right? But then—

"Are you going to the Gatherstone later tonight?" Roba asked, quickly putting his idol away.

"Oh... I don't know, Roba," Ori mumbled.

"Ori! Mama will be so mad if you don't go. The Thaquans already docked us a week's worth of food because you skipped the last one."

"I know, Roba—"

"—and we had to beg for food from Arman's family too!"

A startling glow erupted from behind a row of pine trees, bringing their conversation to a screeching halt. It shone with ferocious intensity... a painful, unnatural glimmer amidst the darkness of the woods. Ori placed one hand over her eyes as she gingerly made her way over to the light. *The Shine.* She looked behind her shoulder quizzically when there was no sound of her brother's footsteps crunching in the snow.

"Come on, Roba. Move!" she hissed viciously.

Hesitantly, Roba uprooted himself and followed his sister's lead, taking care to avoid the painful rays of light by crouching in Ori's shadow. The siblings huddled close together, pulling the fur line of their coats close to their chests as the air grew colder. Ori watched as the crackled, umber bark of the trees began to frost over with a thin sheet of ice. She cautiously placed one bare hand onto the crystallised bark, before rapidly pulling her fingers away in shock. The tree had completely frozen over.

Now a mere distant memory, Ori remembered a time when their father sometimes brought them out to the lake on warm, sunny days. Pawpaw would carefully select a rock along the bank and gently caress its smooth, stony surface as if he were reassuring it of something. *The future, perhaps.* Then with an expert flick of the wrist, he would send the stone hurtling across the water, skimming the surface of that shimmering green wonder ever so slightly. The Shine looked a lot like the rocks Pawpaw used to skip across the lake… flat, smooth and grey. Only bigger and shinier. Ori wondered if The Shine hopped along the stars like Pawpaw's rocks moved across the lake.

A sudden hiss emanated from The Shine, followed by a rapid gush of air that was unfathomably nauseating and indescribably alien. A tiny mahonia shrub, glistening green and strong this entire winter, shrivelled without hesitation as the wind from The Shine tickled its branches. It faded to brown as its sun-kissed flowers folded with a frightening crinkle, snapping off their stalks as they floated lifelessly to the ground. Roba gagged as the putrid waft of air drifted his way. This time, no idol could save him from retching all over the powder-white snow. Ori held firm, but only just.

"They told me you would be coming, little one. Or… ones?" A voice whispered hoarsely from inside The Shine.

"Don't call us that!" Ori retorted, instantly regretting her words.

"A bold one, aren't you?" The Thaquan murmured as it sauntered out of The Shine and into the snow. *Left foot, crunch. Right foot, crunch. Left foot, crunch. Right foot, crunch.* A pair of gangly legs sunk into the snow with an appalling crackle as the Thaquan slowly made its way forward. *Left foot, crunch. Right foot, crunch. Left foot… crunch.* It stopped. Sharp, protruding kneecaps mere inches from Ori's nose, the Thaquan bent forward with arms rested on its skinny thighs.

A pale husk of a face floated down towards Ori amidst the falling fragments of snow, as a pair of familiar yellow eyes inspected its human visitors with fascination. Where its cheekbones would have been was a short but thick mat of fur that fluttered and wriggled in the biting wind.

"You know, your antics have caused me a great deal of trouble, little one. How many idols have you broken already? And think not of lying, child, or I will know."

"Two," Ori gulped. "It was an accident."

The old Thaquan waved one spider-like hand back and forth in an odd, carefree motion, as if to say, *'nothing to it.'* His hand was still waving about in the air in that strange fashion, knuckles bent backward and wrist bones cracking in a circular motion as Ori took in a deep, uncomfortable breath of that gelid winter air. And like magic, a statue emerged from behind his curtain of wiry fingers. Its unmistakable limestone glittered in the moonlight as a multitude of eyes, teeth and wings leered with malicious intent. Ori heard Roba uncork a squeal of fear from somewhere behind her and grabbed his hand to stifle her own cries. If The Black Man and Thelred scared the children before, this new idol would give their parents night terrors.

"Here you go, little one. Don't lose it," the old Thaquan cautioned with an unholy grin. Rows of icicle-like teeth shimmered like crystals in the dark of the woods and it took Ori every ounce of her being to stop herself from screaming.

She pried herself from Roba's vice-like grip and gingerly held the idol with both hands. It was heavier than her old one, and *different*. Ori's fingers traversed the surface of her idol, exploring every canyon, crevice and unholy angle the devilish totem had to offer. It was her new idol, yes. But as her nails dug into the strange, grey dirt deep within its grooves, Ori knew it was also very old.

"This is not Thel— I mean *Lord* Thelred."

"You are correct, it is not," the old Thaquan nodded expectantly.

"What is it then?"

The Thaquan bent forward again, grinning as a cold, putrid stench wafted from his tremendous jaws.

"Something better."

"I've never seen that idol before, Ori! And what did the Thaquan mean by better?"

"I don't know, Roba. He's just as crazy as the rest of them. These idols have done nothing but make our lives miserable, now come on!" Ori replied, eagerly pushing past the thicket of branches in her way.

As the glimmer of The Shine weakened in the background, Ori quickened her pace, as if half-expecting the old Thaquan to leap out of the bushes at any given moment. The orange glow of a fire up in the distance shimmered heartily, and Ori breathed a sigh of relief as they closed in on civilisation.

Idol in hand, Ori prepared to step over the last clump of bushes separating the woods from the camp. Her fingers absent-mindedly ran over the grooves of the idol, mildly enjoying the light *riki-kik-tik-tik* that her strumming produced. She stretched her index finger back again, preparing to unleash another symphony from the stars when she stopped herself in horror. *Pawpaw would be ashamed.* Shaking her head in disgust, Ori snapped herself back to reality. As she began climbing over the frosted bushes in their path, Roba grabbed her forearm.

"Ori...you know this is our last chance, right? No more messing up."

"Of course I know," Ori retorted. "Why wouldn't I know?"

"And you also know what they did to Pawpaw, Ori. You *know* what they do to subjects who fight back!"

Ori remained silent.

"Look, all I'm saying is..." Roba hesitated as he struggled for the right words. "Just try to make this work, okay? For mama."

Ori grimaced as her brother stepped prudently around her, pushing past the thicket and out into the open. The warm light of the fire illuminated Ori's face in a brilliant clementine glow for just a moment, before she was plunged back into the cold, dark shadow of the woods.

Ori tiptoed around the crowd of people gathered on one side of the hearth, scanning her eyes across the Gatherstone for her mother and brother. She spotted them sitting cross-legged at the edge of the hearth. Kitha signalled for her daughter to *'get over here'* with a quick sideward tilt of her head.

The elk that the men had caught earlier in the day hung precariously over the enormous fire, slow roasting as its cold, milky eyes gazed helplessly at the infinitude of stars up above. On the other side of the hearth, the Thaquans muttered in silent prayer as they bowed their heads, knees buried in the snow. Idols in hand, the Thaquans gently cradled their limestone deities back and forth against the temples of their skull. *Tok, tok, tok.* With only the crackling fire and the howl of a passing wind for company, the sound was deafening. After a while, the village people followed suit and Ori watched in dismay as every man, woman and child placed their own stone idols upon their foreheads.

The foremost Thaquan rose off her knees, idol still in hands. It was the female Thaquan from earlier that day. She surveyed her human counterparts haughtily, before gently placing her idol in the snow.

The female Thaquan raised her skeletal arms towards the night sky, fingers outstretched as they grasped for the stars. "Let us pray!"

Every living creature, human and Thaquan, rose together in harmony for the second time that day. And then the prayers commenced, an unutterable fusion of words and noises that had no place on this Earth— words and noises that called out to unspeakable deities from beyond the stars. Somewhere out there, they smiled.

Ori mouthed what little she knew of the words, as she caught her brother's eye, who gave her a knowing nod. Ori turned to look at Mama, eyes closed, and hands folded in prayer. *What was she praying for? And did she believe in who she was praying to?* Ori wondered.

The prayer was ending, and she knew what needed to be done. *For mama.* In one synchronised motion, man and Thaquan raised their idols to their foreheads once more. Ori stared into the cavernous pupils of her idol, which grinned with a certain knowing.

A pungent aroma, one moment alarming and soothing the next, drowned her senses into oblivion. The tip of her forehead, which now felt unusually heavy, swooped down gently as it finally made contact with the alien coolness of the limestone. Once, twice. And finally, thrice.

From behind the growing flames that licked the carcass of the elk, the Thaquans smiled in glee and relief as the last heart of the Northern folk was finally won.

And now, on to the rest of Earth. There was much work to be done.

Overhead, the first snowflake of the day, late but eventual, wafted helplessly to the ground below.

Historical Mythic Poetry

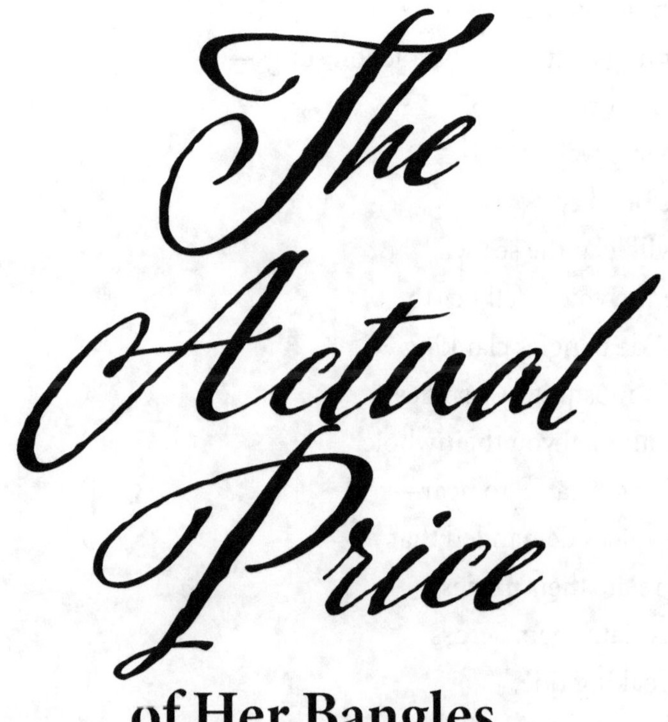

The Actual Price

of Her Bangles

(poetry collection)

E. Doyle-Gillespie

The Actual Price of Her Bangles

She will run the whole way
this time.
When the sea voices tell her to—
chanting shanties,
mouthing driftwood, barracoon songs—
she will run
the whole way
to the breakers.
She will leap the sea wall
when the voices tell her to,
the ankle bangles clanking
against mosquito-worn flesh.
She could tell you their whole
story if you cared to hear—
if the voices demanded that
she'd recite their names
and explain them across
the breaking tide,
and breaking time,
and the clank of bangles she
found one morning
lost in the cursed sands
of the Outer Banks.
They had staved off tarnish and time,
ever-gleaming young,
carrying the captive magic
from the womb of a middle-passage ship.

She wore them as art—
sensuous and hip—
against the flesh-and-bone of her leg.
Now, she must sing the songs
of the ballast people,
their voices keeping time
in her head as she runs
towards the crashing waves,
the sea wall's wide-spread arms
and the oncoming tide.

Interview: The Indian Gap Haint, Indian Gap, SC, 1975

Professor's veranda is haint blue,
        and she goes there each morning
            with designer coffee
and Ms. Grace's stories of
boo hag hoodoo.
Told to her during the plantation
sabbatical summer sojourn,
she transcribes them from turning
brown spools.
The prodigy neighbor plays his violin
from two porches down
and Professor waits as
her coffee's heat steams its complaint
into the morning cool.
"He ain't," said Ms. Grace,

ochre-brown, wound and rewound
for a hundred years
in the Gullah coast wind.
Each haint-blue morning,
while the prodigy neighbor plays,
Professor lays the frame for
African-American Anthropology 101.
"Boo hag come through a keyhole
or a crack in the wall.
He hover over you like a lover.
Drain you dry like a lover, too.
Hover like a lover, but he ain't."
Professor drinks blue-veranda coffee
as the hoodoo stories turn
to ink on her legal pad
and the violin plays
into the Gullah wind
from two porches down.

And a Leather Soul, as Well

We will return to this later.
Someday, when we
are cooking like this again,
I will finish my story.
I will tell you
about my childhood—
seaside caverns

where the tide echoed voices,
and about the old well
that was haunted
by a suicide, we decided—
an English woman
in a vast colonial dress
who tossed herself down.
I will tell you about River Mumma,
and the greedy men
that she lured to the water
to drown.
But, for now, thick prawns will sizzle
on the black iron skillet
that belonged to your grandmother,
and you will tell me about
the woman you loved
between here and Barcelona.
She lived out the words
of your favorite song,
bringing you the leather boots
you wear on nights like these,
though you asked her for nothing
on the day she left.
You swirl the grits now
with a wooden spoon,
marrying them with butter
and an overpowering spice
that followed you home
one day.

"Just like in the song," you whisper,
the leather boots holding you up
on tiptoe.
The kitchen steam fills my glasses
as I forget to remind you
that the lover in the song
also offered gold,
also offered silver,
and, when Bob Dylan
struck the final chord,
had still not returned from the sea.

Santa Barbara Casting Brass

After that,
she added brass to the water.
Each shell casing that she dropped,
she rattled first
like knuckle-bone dice
against the others in her hand.
Each one told a story of her
creeping in alleyways
to steal tribute offerings
from murder scenes.
From police-chalk sidewalk shrines.
She told the story of each
before she cast them
into the Santeria bath

she had drawn.
These new 9mm casings
were from the Dominican
boy they'd been chasing
down on Water Street
two nights before.
I asked her if that was his name
that she was muttering,
that she was mothering,
before she fed each empty casing
into the soothsayer pool.
I asked her again as she whispered
to the last brass jacket
and waited for the water
to catch fire.

On Maggie, Turned Revenant

Resurrected,
this time by a
creole conjure woman's
muttered oath,
she came shuffling up
from the hollow
where they buried her
facedown.
She found the old plantation,
again, gone for good.

Grown over, hanging sad
with Spanish moss,
and weeping its paint chips
into a Gulf breeze,
it welcomed her back.
It moaned as her ragged
feet, now unbound,
tested its dry, wooden floors.
This sojourn home,
she wanted to see what was left
of the kitchen,
and the pantry,
and the parlor,
and the study,
where he would have her arch
her body over his books,
and their angry, white magic.
She went up from the hollow
to see what was left
in the empty skull of
the broken, big house,
remembering
she could now go up
the wide front steps,
touch the pillars
for moment more, and,
when she was ready,
walk through the front door.

Ordinary Conjurings

(poetry collection)

ODETTE CORTÉS

Odette Cortés

Orpheus Underground

Today, like every day,
I wait among others for the ferryman.

Here, in the underground,
I tune my senses to signs of his coming—
The whistling of the air
The screeching of the tires
The current of electricity
Coursing down our collective bodies
The endless negotiation:

Push shove
Push shove.

Here, in the darkness,
Time turns to murky water,
An endless river more than six feet under
Where humanity strips away
As we enter the city's underbelly.

Here, I turn to Orpheus
And cast the oldest of salvations
Notes strung together
Tether my soul

To the light of ten million fireflies
That takes a shortcut into my dreams.
Old memories that run wild
To fleeting sound, lyrics and beats

Push shove
Push shove.

Hold on to the unbreakable thread
The tune of the living provides
For this eternal midnight
Will not last forever.

Push shove
Push shove.

I don't turn back
Though I'm hanging for dear life
To this song. I don't turn back
I don't turn to dust.
I see the light at the end
Of the underground

Push shove
Push shove.

Odette Cortés

An Enchantment at the Crossroads

I found myself at a crossroads
I swirled in it, drifted through it
Floated down its unfinished currents
Its many channels that opened towards
The midnight

Of the world. A city of possibilities
All existence beating through
The endless pulse and rhythms
Of a million heartbeats

All in tune. I lost myself
In the tumult of memories
Layered on every corner;
Each street and lane
History/ history/ herstory
My story as well.

Every brick a piece of a constellation
Strings of streetlights, bright
Lived in, all spun into stories
Woven into maps
Tracing a region of dreams.

I saw myself in and out
Of nightmares, stricken
By red lights forcing me to catch

My breath. I use them to gather wind
Behind me, to give me strength
To change the course of fate.
The force to choose a path.

A City on the Shoulders of Giants

Today I can see them clearly,
Remnants of titans
Fallen, turned to earth
Faces staring at the sky.

This city is built on the bones
Of their battlefield;
Their tomb our everyday path
Their end the foundation of our future.

We stand on the shoulders of giants
Thrive on them with edifices of our own
We make ourselves believe this is our land
That we hold the world in our palms—

But one breath
one stretch
one puff
Quietly reminds us that they are not gone,
Just sleeping.

Faceless Places

And then I found myself
Walking down a mall.
How uncouth, how unpoetic, how mundane
Were all the mannequins gliding
Down the lanes, looking into windows—
Perfect little scenes— awing at things
That lack memory
that have not yet been touched by life.
Suppose one day they stop
Being picture perfect;
Suppose one day they let
A flaw or two crawl into their lives.
Then will they be worthy of a story?

Handwritten

(poetry collection)

GRACE ALIYU

VENDOR

Beneath the moon, in a village of many,
a small town where Vendor sold
a dream in exchange for a memory.
An insomniac stood penniless, reluctant but willing,
to offer her memories wrapped in twine for a luminous jar;
a night that promised a world filled
with skies of paisley and cobalt blue
where the sun wore shades
and the leaves waltzed in a joyful masquerade.
But her forgotten memories left an ache.
She rushed back to correct the mistake she made.
But Vendor smiled as its kaleidoscope eyes sparkled,

"Dreams once traded are never returned."

BLOCKING OUT THE OLD MAN

He always seems to creep down the chimney when I go to
sleep;
eat my cookies and milk and leave a gift.
This old man in all the filthiness of life;
it's not a visitor to have.
The compliance of the flesh is all he brings;
Evil all he breeds.
So, I will keep my watch and be sober,
lighting my fires and burning embers.

BURGLE

They took the chairs, my wears and my hair;
left the ground covered with broken glass.
In short, they stole without class.
Everything was gone except my table—
small, sturdy, brown and as sure-footed as can be.
Kneeling down as usual to pray that night,

"Dear Lord, I thank you they didn't steal the lights."

SEABLUE

She took her father home
to his house just by the sea.
This was the last sight he was to see
drifting closer to eternity.
"Open the windows and the doors," he asked,
"Let the sea breeze blow in."
He inhaled wearily one last time—
the scents filled the room

of the days of his childhood.

IN THE DARK

"A dance?" with darkness in whispered breath
where tombstones stand in somber sleep.
Whispers echo, the night winds sigh,
a dance macabre, a fate untold.
The Reaper's gaze, forever keen;
his cloak, a shroud of endless night.
Obsidian eyes, devoid of light
as souls tremble in their final seat.
Beware the footsteps in the dark,

the fleeting whispers of a spectral hark.

SOLAPE ADEYEMI

Shaman

And so, they hurry—
Farmers hurry home before dark, to their homes
Market women hurry home from the markets
Even children hurry home from their playground
All must be home
Before darkness descends
The Shaman ordered it
They had seen what disobeying the Shaman caused
Three farmers within a spate of six months died in their sleep
Because
The Goblin that walks about at night had eaten their hearts
So, the Shaman said
His word was law
He knew the ways of darkness
And the way of the evil Goblin
The dark must find them behind locked doors
Their candles snuffed out
As the Goblin could be attracted by the light
in the midst of the thick darkness
As long as they obeyed the Shaman
They would not die
They would be safe
From the evil Goblin
Roaming the dark and night

Charmingly

And she charmingly sidles up to you,
roguish lips raised in a delicious pout in her charming
face,
and you are charmingly charmed.
She places her charming full-figured body
across yours—charmingly wrapping herself around you,
much like a snake with its prey.
As she charmingly squeezes out every virtue—
every last drop of it—
until you are left, wrung, wasted and weary.
Charmingly...

Sneaky Demon

Ohhhhhhh—
She had promised herself and you
that she would be more circumspect in her talking,
more reticent,
and more importantly,
that she wouldn't betray confidences no more.
But when the discussion centres on someone she has any info on
(because she is excellent at info collection,
the dirt and scandals, what you would call... amebo).
The sneaky demon sidles up to her,
willing her to part her full lips to divulge.
She tries hard not to,

remembering her promise to herself and to you.
The demon is not easily dissuaded,
and it seizes her throat and attempts to open
her vocal cords.
You see her pressing her lips together firmly;
her palms pressed hard against her mouth,
her eyes darting around in alarm,
her cheeks ballooning with the effort not to talk.
At a stage she starts grunting softly
as the people present look at her curiously
and even ask if she's okay.
She grunts some more, nodding her head vigorously
until she can no longer endure the pressure
and blurts out the info.
Sneaky demon.

Castle Fantasy

Here, we have only one ambition
to make all your dreams come true.
Pleasuring you is our ultimate reward.
What would you care for, madame et monsieur?
A spa... a sauna?
Facials... facelifting?
We can alter and dis-alter virtually anything and
anybody... in our castle fantasy.
We can make... and break
even exchange your reality for another's
Switch your nagging and overweight wife

with one more temperate and hourglass-figured.
Your rambunctious kids for docile ones!
Whatever cuisine or wines you can think of,
is on our handsome and robust menu.
Properties in choice locations and automobiles, as well!
Aspiring for a political position? Within a heartbeat,
that will also be arranged and voilà!
Just dream it!
And we make it!

Dreams

I see myself absent the worry lines so generously
etched on my forehead
Ah! Even the many creases by my eyes are all smoothed out.
My greying coarse hair is absent the grey, soft and well coiffured.
My calloused hands, smooth and beautiful.
My skin—so tender and milky white.
I am clothed in the finest of silks.
My legs encased in the smoothest and thinnest of stockings.
My feet absent the bulging and painful veins, shod with
the finest-leather shoes.
Beautiful pearls pay homage to my strangely unlined neck.
I am so breathlessly beautiful!
Alas,
it is but a dream as I awake with a start—
and remember
I am still the cleaning maid at the manor.

Paranormal
Poetry

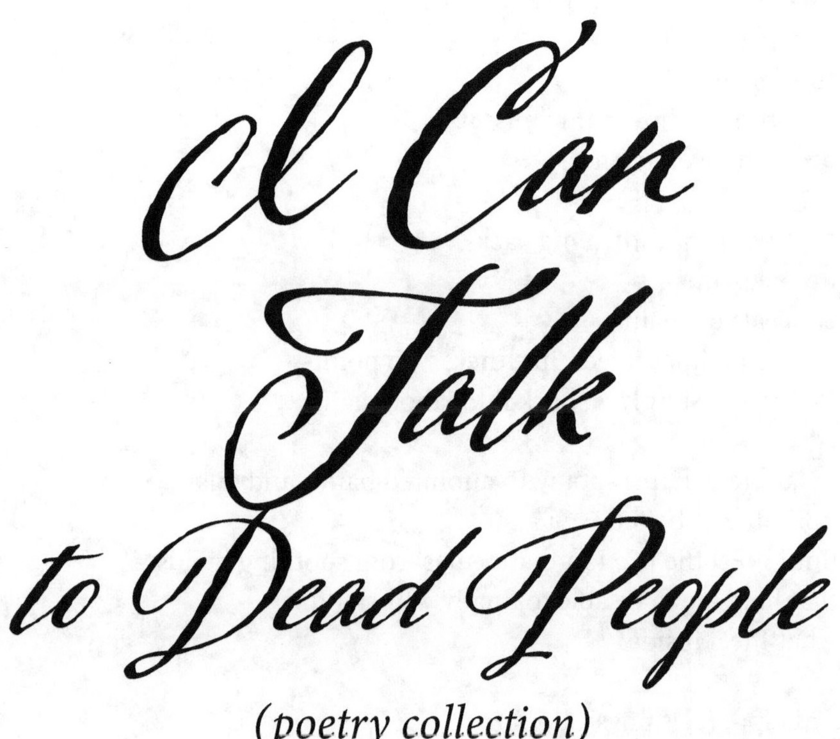

I Can Talk to Dead People

(poetry collection)

LIZ JOHNSTON

Liz Johnston

Grandeur of Mothers

There's a spot inside my body that I cannot reach
and it aches in ways that pain cannot explain.

I was born with a brain that labors,
suffers sickness,
split open,
ever birthing my manic misery
over and over again.

No doctor can stitch me back,
no medicine
conceals the pain,
and sometimes it feels like there's no point—
I know I'll simply go back into labor again.

I want to rub this spot with anointed balms and oils
until it feels better,
until I feel the friction that comes from soothing hands
that help me to be able to finally withstand
what I feel inside.

This spot feels physical,
yet it is always just out of reach.

I can see the rotten fruit that it bears
and the harvest of this
fertile, horrid hollow is plenty.

I cannot stop the spot.
I.
Feel.
All.

I was born with a hellish scream,
trapped like a wild caged animal inside my body.
A muzzled Cerberus,
shoved into a one inch crate
sinking in quicksand.
I can feel it pressing its body against the tiny prison,
each push for escape shoveling him
deeper and deeper underground.

This scream burns in my throat like acid bubbles in my trachea.
It turns each breath to poison.

I want to let it out.
I want to puncture a hole so I can let it free,
release it to the outside world where it so desperately longs to be,
but it seems there is no sound,
no pitch,
no frequency,
no octave that could create the volume I need for it to satisfy me.
I.
Feel.
All.

One December, this spot,
this scream
became too real,
too visible,
too bold to bear.

The thickening of the winter air,
a starless night to match my dark despair
led me to a hospital bed,
strapped down like God's begotten.
A male nurse asked me for my age and name.

Liz Johnston

I had forgotten myself—
numb, I could not feel the nurse swirling the needle in my arm.

I do not remember the medicine they gave me,
I was too busy silently cursing my spot again for birthing yet
another bastard of a baby,
for allowing this bitch of a scream that I am longing to release
to remain trapped inside me.
I.
Hear.
Nothing.

Until all my mothers arrive.

My mother rushes into the room
asking me to explain how I ended up here,
and I do,
and I am calm
until I feel shame.
I am calm
until I am not.
I was calm until
I feel All—

my walls shake
like a quaking
deep inside of my body,
my soul was erupting,
splitting
and everything above me came tumbling down
until I felt the weight of myself,
the weight of the present,
of the future,

of the past,
and I could do nothing but hide under the thin,
white hospital sheet, curled into a ball
rocking in the bed on the balls of my feet.

I feel my mother's hand on my back.
I feel the hands of all my mothers on my back.
I.
See.
All their shadows through the thin white hospital sheet.

I am beyond screaming.
I am beyond crying.
I have become a banshee
and this banshee is a conjurer
and this rocking is her ritual
and she has begun a séance.
Banned, *she finds the limits of herself;*
she grips her hospital band,
and she feels her mothers rub her through the sheet.
They sooth her through the sheet,
they find the spot that she cannot reach
and in this moment she is all,
in unison they commence a chaotic chant:

Yaya yaya rèl yaya yaya igbe cri.
Yaya yaya rèl yaya yaya igbe cri.
Cry, baby...

Yaya yaya rèl yaya yaya igbe cri.
Yaya yaya rèl yaya yaya igbe cri...

Cry the tears we never got to shed.
Cry for every scream that has ever been muffled.
Cry, because you've been dying since the day you were born.
Cry, because you love when aint got love left to give.
Cry, because you'll never see that love returned...

Yaya yaya rèl yaya yaya igbe cri. Yaya yaya rèl yaya yaya igbe cri...
Cry, so that the burns, the cuts, the scars, the bruises
that you cannot touch may be exposed.
Cry, to grow the crust that forms around them like new earth.
Cry, because you must get hurt to heal.
Cry, because you must be ripped open first before you can scab.
Cry, for every cell in your body,
nourish your skin with these tears so it may grow again.
I free you from imprisonment but you must cry,
for every bar you must break in your cell...

Yaya yaya rèl yaya yaya igbe cri. Yaya yaya rèl yaya yaya igbe cri...
Cry for the ones who live.
Cry for the ones who died.
Cry for the ones stuck in between.
Cry for those who you have never met, but are now by your side.
Cry up to the heavens.
Cry down into hell.
Cry, because we love you.
Cry, because you gotta love yourself.
Grieve everything, then grieve nothing but yourself.
Cry, so that God can hear you.

Cry, because this is your testament.
Cry your truth.

Flood yourself tonight in covenant that you will never flood again.

I.
felt.
the shaking—
stop. I

was myself again.
I uncovered my head and I was left with one mother, in flesh,
who sought to hold me.
I felt completely drained.
Weak.
Like a tree left leafless,
broken,
branchless from a hurricane.

I was stripped.
I was washed.
I was made
new,
baptized,
pure—

And I felt everything.

Liz Johnston

Talkin' Drums

What them drums say?
What them drums mean?
I could hear them talkin'—
I think they talkin' to me.

A whisper in the crowd even though the beat was loud
 piercing through my body
sound surroundin' me in a smoky cloud.

They sayin' somethin' bout me movin'
but I swore my feet were still.
Then I felt my body start swayin'
and my head throw itself back,
my face shot up toward the sky.

I felt my body shakin'—
my hands lifted high.
I felt weightless
I was air with every hit of the cow skin,
the snare was wondrous, wild, without care I said:

I want to see my people.
Drums said, "they here with you."
I want to free my people.
They said, "first, free you."
I want to speak their languages.
They said, "it's speakin' through the drums."
Why can't I stop dancin'?
Drums said, "it's called talkin' in tongues."
What happens when the music stops?
Drums said, "there is no such thing—
These drums, they always beating,
and they beating from within."

Cowboys and Indians

Sometimes I get this urge to drive out to Texas,
and go to the cemetery where my grandfather was buried.
I want to spend the time I never got to spend with him when
he was alive.
I'd put a New Orleans Saints jersey over his tombstone
because no one ever asked about his favorite flower.
I want to lie on the dirt where his body rests below
and tell him all I've come to know
about books and art and people and nature,
about everyone I've loved and everyone I've lost.
I'd ask the same of him.
I want to know him like I want to know myself.
I want to smoke the cigarette that caused his cancer.
The one that finally did him in.
I want to know why.
I'd talk about the asthma that he passed on to me.
Tell him I also have his eyes.
and his smile.
I want to tell him I don't play viola anymore, but
that I still dance and
I'd give anything for another chance to sift through a dance catalog
and look at the shoes with him again.
I'd tell him that Friends is now on Netflix.
I'd put it on,
pause it,
and then I'd explain Netflix.
I'd tell him about my niece.
I'd tell him I got a writing degree.
I'd tell him I'm working on my Ph.D.
I'd tell him I fell in love—49 times.
But on the last, I got married.
I'd ask him if he's proud of me.
I'd tell him I wrote this poem.

I'd pour him some coffee,
and read the stats of every Saints game he's missed since he
joined in that number and marched into heaven.
I'd ask him about heaven. I'd ask him if our people are there.
What the tribe looks like?
I'd ask him why are we in Texas,
we too Indian for Cowboy Country.

Pages in Someone Else's Bible

My grandmother's brain tried to take the train back to
Dallas
stumbling all over the atlas of her difficult world.
Her body's somewhere outside New Orleans
where the newsmen don't mention.
In her purse is ripped up Bible pages and a pile of human shit.
I am disgusted.
It is poetic.
Appropriate.
I am empty now.
From holy to hallow.

I am 14 and every day I bite down on her decline
and search for a chaser to help me swallow.
There is no liquor in this Christian household—
and yet I live here.
Does God ever feel uncertain?
I am uncertain about God.

I am 15.
I am Buddhist now.

Not really.
Something about suffering.
Yes,
yes.
I do.
We all do.
I meditate.
I release.
Release like shit in a purse filled with ripped-up Bible pages.

She was a powerful woman.
They always punish powerful women.
I never really knew her before her eggs got scrambled.
I woke up after breakfast.
She was an important chef somewhere that mattered
when the newsman talked about her inside
the walls of a beautiful New Orleans.
Where she raised four boys.
Where she had a house.
Where she had friends.
Where she had a life before Katrina washed her away to Texas.

Today, after 14 hours she burned the cabbage
and it stinks of an intangible failure, the end of an era,
a glitch, an error.
I want to burn the kitchen down like it never happened.
I want to burn the kitchen down so I can feel warmth
before I slip away and before she dies.
She is sad.
I will hold her by putting out the flames.
I wonder if God ever looks at me funny.

Liz Johnston

I wonder if God ever looks at me all.
I wonder if God looks at me like
the inside of my grandmother's purse.
I am the inside of my grandmother's purse.

I am 16.
I am re-baptized in my tears.
I am surrendering.
I am embracing death.
Death does not embrace me.
I hold my grandmother because I know that everything
has become shit on top of ripped up
pages of the Bible.
I pray but I am the only one who does not ask God to take it away
because I am embracing death but death does not embrace me.
Somehow, she manages not to erase me.

I am 17.
I hold my grandmother differently.
There is so much that neither of us can understand
like why they always punish powerful women
even after they show themselves capable of weakness.
My boyfriend kicks me.
Gropes me.
Bites me.
Threatens me.
Tries to break me.
Silly boy, do you not know that I am both holy and hallow?
You are but shit on ripped up pages of the Bible.

I am 18.
Death has embraced me.
The reverend speaks with arrogance
about how my grandmother is in the land of Oz on streets of
gold. Like Dorothy I just want to go home but home is hallow,
and he is shit holding an intact
Bible.

I am 19 and every day I shuffle through the shit to find
comfort in the atlas of a fragmented
Bible.
... but dear reader do not pity me
for I know the truth.

We are merely sifting through shit to find meaning
amongst the ripped up pages of someone
else's Bible.

Once a Home,

Now a Haunted House

(poetry collection)

MICHELLE IVY ALWEDO

Michelle Ivy Alwedo

Once a Home, Now a Haunted House

As night descends, the house sighs and swells;
breath held concretely tight—
windows and doors creaking shut.

Her cracks whisper with silence, resounding
quietly through echoing halls. But her walls,
her walls are seldom still.

Within their confines, shadows are caged, trapped
in concrete flesh. Each night, they howl,
wail, and claw, desperate for release from captivity's domain.

Yet silence betrays,
whistling wickedly through corridor cracks,
revealing secrets whispered
to the mistress within. Tickling at one's feet
as the house snickers, mischievously delighted,
mocking prisoners' futile dreams.

Scoffing at their foolish hopes,
for they cannot escape her walls, forever
bound within their asylum.

A forever home devoid of joy.

Ceaseless scratching against the house's bones of stone

seamlessly meld, blending cries and screams.

An orchestra of anguish reverberating, echoing

through the skeleton and marrow of her walls,

eternally awaiting a dawn never to come.

A Celestial Soliloquy

(a star and constellation in conversation with each other)

Big Dipper to Polaris

Burning flames of amber and amethyst
burn fast like fierce fiery lust
in first loves; pure and steadfast, intense
in emotions and devotion, proceeding blindly
no regard for caution, navigating chaos
with innocence of youthful passion

Your light, my lifetime love

sparks of sapphire

stretching across as ambered tendrils

casting an iridescent spell

across sunless skies; flickering topaz,

Michelle Ivy Alwedo

crimson kisses

emerald fireflies scattered.

Whispers of wanting

waltzing dewdrops

twinkling stars

shivering in deep indigo sky

dreamy ruby embers

incandescent campfires

weaving luminous stories

from secret shared

intimate memories;

symphonies. Soaring

spirits searching

constellations of midnight's canvas

for a comforting residence to converge.

Your colours caress my universe, my soul resides in peace.

Polaris to Big Dipper

A shade of blue wears my skin
as pale as imperial topaz
sparkling in a cathedral setting
encrusted

with petals of pink pearls
under slivered moon.

Shadowed

fragile silver skin, translucently delicate

shining

from sun's graceless lust

transcendent light gifting me radiance

without which I frail

paling as dead as death

while aeons fold into each other

white dwarfs' ashy streaks shimmering

into supernovae.

Yours I will be till my final, failing breath.

Aziza

As dusk displaces day,
evening's sun scatters violet-blue lights
across verdant leaves of kapok trees.

Hollow towering trunks hide
tiny-holed homes draped in fern.

Amber kapok flowers fall,
softening the forest floor.

Michelle Ivy Alwedo

Arching buttress roots sprawl,
shading sacred Aziza spirits.

Umber–brown skin, obsidian hair,
wings of plain tiger butterflies,
eyes sparkling cognac diamonds.

Singing seductively in the breeze,
soothing innocent forest inhabitants,
snaring poachers with ill-intended hearts,
corrupting minds with a collective chorale,
till hunters become unsuspecting prey.

La Llorona

Guarding night's peace,
        fairies dance on drizzles,
            glistening off dew-soaked leaves
of weeping willows,
warding off wicked spirits,
enchanting memories in an erratic
avalanche of rainbow colours,
sprinkling on hearts sooted with misery.
Sprites prance across
night-stretched skies,
leaping from silver stars

to sighing broken dreams,
singing ethereal carols
to lull moon's unquiet sorrow.
Her shadow warps away from darkness,
journeying in search of her bereaved,
within the frightened blazing light
that threatens to scorch her spirit,
sculpting her into a pillar of salt.

Who Will Mourn You

Death bears greater weight
when one is deemed dear.

All human souls
deserve reverence
and remembrance,
but the reality remains:

Most deaths pass unheeded,
holding minimal merit
for memorability
and condolence in men.

People die daily.
Unless deeply cared for,
a date of death isn't eternally etched
in memory,
simply an un-special day.

My own death may lack worthiness enough
to guarantee remembrance.

When engulfed in the afterlife's embrace,
when my breath's debt to death is claimed,
I may bear inequality's exertion.

When your breath is spent,
existence extinct,
will anyone mourn for you?

Will you be remembered often and fondly?
Or will you be forgotten, fading away,
lost in the vastness of eternal silence?

Memento Mori of the Dreamscape

GAAZAL DHUNGANA

Memento Mori of The Dreamscape

Breathe in... breathe out...
I have to consciously and desperately remind myself
as I lay lifeless and listless on my own bed.
The crushing weight of a translucent bear lies on my chest,
both suffocating and flimsy,
invisible and illusionary... non-existent, truth be told—
but clawing at me nevertheless.

Breathe in... breathe out...
A girl has been struck ruthlessly by a car.
The girl is me—in this astral liminal space, at least.
A boy is snorting stardust off of a cheaply upholstered sofa.
The boy is... also me?
One after the other,
the desolate reel of incidents and happenings unfold.

Breathe in... breathe out...
A sweet child holds my hand,
and there twinkles a wonder within his eyes—
the type that flickers and burns like twin flames,
The type that is extinguished all too soon.

We converse and play.
I learn a lot about his life.
He has a baby sister, newborn and aglow.
He's just won a certificate for neat work, he says.

He's scared of the dark, but doesn't usually like telling people that.

I've never met him, yet I know him.

But before I can even wave my farewell,
I'm whisked off into another dreamland.

A living room.

One with a strange, ephemeral quality.
It's like when you sometimes get soap in your eyes.
Your surroundings are still the same, but
nothing looks quite substantial,
and your perspective has changed.

With a jolt, I realise it's my living room.

Only devoid of all furniture,
Save for the small, mahogany rocking chair:
a family heirloom.

I stare closer
at the fraying black and white photo,
the only phantasmal relic to now adorn the walls,
I feel a flutter at my elbow and
smell the distinct waft of cumin and turmeric.

My great-grandmother is no longer
eternally bound to the gossamer-like square of film,
but standing right by me and beaming.

She's shorter than I expected. And dead.
Her impossibly small hand reaches up to mine,
mosaiced with turquoise and mint veins:
very clearly visible through her paper-thin skin.

"Now, you listen here, young lady," she says—

in a voice that feigns chastising but reverberates with love.
"I know how much these modern folk
like to change around their homes and their architecture,
but you're not to touch this place, okay?
My father and his brothers built it
from the ground up with their bare hands."

Her words carry such weight to them,
such a level of gravity as though lined with gold.
Booming and authoritative, yet kind and paternalistic—
surprising for such a small frame.

I find myself nodding;
she carries the air of someone you want to listen to.

As I am about to ask more about my patronage,
the ground begins to rumble.
"Routine earthquake," she gleams, "and a weak one at that.
Just make sure to cover your head!"

I cover my head.

Because when your Asian great-grandmother tells you
to cover your head—
even from the cosmic beyond —
you damn well cover your head.

That is, until the entire light fixture crashes above your skull,
fracturing into a million, iridescent pieces.
Each one reflecting the stupidity of your dazed face...

I raise my still-pulsating head in a creaking motion.
There's a young man sitting across from me,
and it smells of coffee.

"Is everything okay?" His eyebrows furrow in concern.
He has a kind face.
A handsome face.

"Oh yes," I lie.
"Maybe just a bit dizzy looking at you," I venture.

He smiles.
A brilliant, white smile.
I smile too.

After that—
it's like the rose-tinted soap has enveloped my eyes once more,
creating feelings of joy and elation,
like a warm light that steadily grows and grows within my chest.

Perhaps enough to engulf me entirely.
...

I hear his gunshot before I feel it.

The blood trickles down my back like poisoned molasses—
shining like impish constellations.
What a coward, I think, as I suck in my final gulp of air and—

huff it out again.
Drenched in my own sweat in my own bed.

Silly me. I forgot to breathe.

The Phantom Eye

DW

I have always had a sixth sense
A gift or curse, I do not know
I can see and hear and feel
Things that others do not
I can sense the presence of spirits
The souls of the departed
They linger in the places they loved
Or the places they hated
Some of them are friendly
They just want to communicate
They have a message or a request
Or a story to relate
Others are hostile, wanting to harm or scare
They have a grudge or a vengeance
Or malice to share
Some of them are lost
They do not know where to go
They have confusion or regret
Or sorrow to show
I try to help them if I can
To listen or guide
To comfort or to confront
Or appease their pride
But sometimes I cannot help them
They are too stubborn or too strong
They refuse to listen or to leave
Or admit they are wrong
And sometimes they cannot help me
They are too vague or too cryptic

They speak in riddles or signs
Or in a language that is mystic
In a realm veiled from the ordinary
I live in a metaphysical world
Shouldering both duty and burden
A blessing bestowed with its own cost.

Ghost Poems

(poetry collection)

STEPHANIE CHIEDO

Stephanie Chiedo

Blank Spaces In Between The Letters

You open your eyes to a scene.
It's like a dream; you become conscious in the middle of it.
You do not know how you got there,

but it's unfolding...
and there you stand,
in their midst,
and you watch them banter on.
Not one of them could settle on any particular color.
The intricate details seem to carry so much vigor,
the way a lily does.
They tell you it signifies rebirth, innocence, and purity.
Each detail meant something to someone on that table.

You smile—a cup of coffee in hand.
For most of the conversation, you listened.
You had nothing to say.
You could only give out a smile,
but then it starts to dawn on you
that the silence isn't voluntary.
You have no words in your mouth,
and you, quite frankly,
couldn't hear what they were saying.
You look down at the piece of paper that everyone was huddled around.
It was an obituary of you.
Everybody was picking out the little details of your funeral—
the colors, food, placements,
all of that.

How did you die? You wonder...
Where did you die? You wonder...

And the next question is, who are you really?
You do not know who you are—or were.
The realization that you once existed hits you.
You look around, flabbergasted.
You wonder how you got there in the first place.
You realize that you never really knew these people.
They gave you a feeling of familiarity;
They could've been family, friends, loved ones.
But—

They are in another world now.
You've crossed over to another one.
They can't see or hear you now,
and you don't know them now,
Oh, or rather,
you shouldn't know them now.
The memories of them are slowly fading away—
entities, figures, anthologies, and a cascade.

A Ghost In The Hallway

Maria stares at a face dumbfoundedly in a hallway.
It is dissipating...
like the clouds in search of colors
The hallway, an unwinding road
like she has been here before—
a deja-vu?
And this face she knew.
Oh, what irony.
Could it be?
Oh, it couldn't be...

Stephanie Chiedo

Celine was long gone.
She has been forgotten about.
No one knew her now.
That face has been painted with colors that didn't exist.
That steel gaze, curated with stones that could resist.
She looks like hailstones.
She is guarded by dark mountains.
One that you couldn't find,
but you knew was there.
She rests in plains above a great rushing river filled with blood.
Her entire presence is captivating.

She looks like an entirely different planet.
It probably smelled like abalone shells there;
musky, dark, and enticing, but above all, vengeful.
She is an extraterrestrial being.
She is something out of the books.
She is a ghost town.
She is an empty cathedral;
a maze in a desert...

Her lips looked maniacal, funny, annoying,
like she said the name 'sella' often.
Show them what they have done to you,
Show them the marks on your upper arm.
Marie didn't want to remember this face—
How it used to be...
What it used to say,
"We are like ravens in the sky,
an informant to her sister.
We looked awful in that sweater.
It is like a scene made for television.
We are unteachable.
We are untouchable.
We are so bright that it is blinding.

We are scourged.
We are directionless—like the wind?
We see in each other—like a reflection."
But if this image could be a book,
it'd be the worst book ever written.
Its pages would be covered in eye watering ink.
It'd be a painful read,
one that you couldn't comprehend.
You'd try to,
and it would give you a headache,
but you couldn't stop anymore,
because it would be there to torture you.
You'd read while you cried, hoping to stop.

This woman in the hallway is an inhabitable planet.
There the skies aren't blue,
It is muted teal.
There, there are no sounds—
just silence.
What's more deafening than silence?
Not any type of silence,
but the type of silence that you are conscious about;
your brain takes you there and makes you worry about.
That type of silence is maniacal;
it makes you see things that you could never speak about,
and what could be more deafening than that?

The Earth's Supernatural

(poetry collection)

JOSEPH MARCEL IKHENOBA

ATTRITION

April was when it began
A cold morning, filled with a humid sky
Our lambs, crows, and leaves
Were mounted on wretched earth
Stenchy, as strange worms crawl
In forlorn of corpses and coffins.

Everywhere, the shadows of the crescent moon
The tide of wavering oceans
The lightyears of our earth
Are all heaped with petals of blood.

Our festivities are blacked with silence
And cassava fields are brazened with laden dust.

So, we come to you our ancestors
A prodigal, sprinkled with ashes
With calabashes of *Orógbó*
And a gourd of *Ògógóró*.

We knelt in the presence of your seven powers
The majestic head-long of your bud crown
To look upon the white dove that moans
The golden sparrow that glooms
The eagle that combs its eaglet-colored-rusty skull
With bare feathers, waddled labor steps
And a dead smile within her beak.

Hear our flutes of elegies
At this crossroads
With every twist—Lynx's eyes.

EMERE

The night has come
To dance with the wind
And play away with the kindred spirits
Of your fountain
In the wake of every nerve.

The night has come
For you to stump and thump to spiritual drums
And dreadful songs
With charmed bangles on your feet.

You come and go every season
In Harmattan dust, midnight waters
In relics of mysterious constellations.

If the palm kernel cannot contain its oil
Then, let it break open
For the oil to flood.

If a coconut cannot keep its milk
Then, let it crack
And unfetter its sap.

For, you have caused the virgin womb
That sprouts your seed
Oceans of turbulence and sire.

You have made her sweet wine sour
In libation
Under the supplicant hyena cloy.

Is it a sin for a banana tree?
To sprout forth its suckers?

Joseph Marcel Ikhenoba

Is it a sin for the white fur sheep?
To womb her lambs?

Emere, if her sacrifices cannot cut your rope
From re-bonding with your *oko-orun*
Then why sail on a voyage?

To watch the river of divine despair
Rise from the depth of her eyes
And gather at the spring of her eyes.

You lie, *Emere*!
Her sea of tears
Are vast wastelands.

This night, at the core of the harvest moon
She would sojourn into the abyss
To castrate the strands of your web.

YEMỌJA

Muse, I stand in the wavering tide of *River Ògún*
With my sacrifice of goats, beans, and maize
To narrate the doings of her
With symbols of cowries, multi-colored crystal beads
Pigeons and white laces.

Yemọja, she's the sea goddess
Mother of the sixteen *Orishas*
Sent by *Olodunmare* to lay dunes
For humanity, upon the earth.

She's the mother of the barren
A calm storm on her face
But would motion hay folks of the tide
When her garland is subdued.

She's the goddess of nursing mothers
With humongous breasts
Flowing with cuddled milk
Which breastfeed many seedlings.

She calms the storm to a gentle breeze
For the rugged, able men of the sea
To steer their courses, compass, and true
At twilight and evening bell.

The weathered hands of the craftsmen
Is ordered by her brief preparation
For the well-honed blade to pare and groom
The wood until the floor is strewn with chips.

Yemoja, the loud-harrowing huntress
Dear to your archery
Filled the earth with melodies
Drummings, thumping, and dances.

As we sojourn through the snaring mountains
Shadowy thickets and groves
Let your spirit guide our lamb home
Under your watchword at Heaven's Gate.

Joseph Marcel Ikhenoba

ṢÀNGÓ

In the hallowed halls of our forest
Ferocious foxes lynched upon our fruits
The wind winds at its will
The virtues sunk and vices sprang everywhere.

The thrill of the act, the rush of the steal
The lion feeds upon the flesh of the dove
And the mangrove that once bred sweet nectars
Is sapped with petals of blood.

Backward to darkness of limb, thorn, sinews
Of dried-up embryos, empty bellies
Roaming the streets, with humming eyes
Subdued by the eating chiefs that long ceased to care.

Until *Ṣàngó* thunder clasped the bolt in his hands
Of death, behind his vicious breath.

All dropped dead in bestial graves
Fed upon by the vultures of Hades
And the bloody river changes her face
Swept the corpses of the eating chiefs.

THE HOUSE OF GHOST

I lodged in a large room far in a village
At an old house
Far from the buzzing sounds
Of the ghetto blaster
Which almost burst my eardrums.

I asked the eagle about the wondrous sight.
Why did the mother eagle throw the eaglets
Out of its nest?
But he says the "eaglet had spent his time."

I wondered less in the cold night
Where the golden owls and black bats
Have come to take their nest.
After the scorching, blazing Sun.

However, the old block looked like an abandoned child
With dust-laden spider cobwebs
And the silence of a groping tomb.

Except for the laughing, splashing, and dancing of the rhythm
Of the current that paddles deeper and deeper still
Into the heart of its river.

I trembled at first in my phantom
To sleep alone in this silent cradle
With verdant reeds growing among thorns
But I put my horse to brave sleep
In long, forgotten mist.

Suddenly my hallucination muted into miserable pathos
The strange windows amidst the curtains shuttered
While the bed covers began to slide slowly
Until it glided from my bust.

I tried to run down the stairs
To yell for compassion in my loneliness
But bizarre cobwebs came over my beaded sweat.

Joseph Marcel Ikhenoba

I struggled in the darkness
Dragging every second with my last grasp of breath
Just to drag my two-foot boxes to a distance
Until I was lulled to sleep.

However, in this passion and plainer shrink
With falling thunderbolts and flashes of lightning
The rustling of leaves and the slamming of doors enchanted.

Momentarily, a diaphanous apparition appeared
Drifting bodies in the air
In a moment it vanishes into the darkness.

Whispering halted and voices of scorn gleamed
Like wind blown over a myriad of forests
Murmuring behind four walls of the sea.

Holy heavens! The door is locked
Its disgusting teeth are barred and grinding.

I whispered for compassion
only to hear my echoes behind the walls.

I slowly raised myself towards the growing dimness
As each stealthy footstep crept amid the corridors
Groaning closer and closer along the musty doorsteps.

I lost consciousness on my feet
My mouth and teeth went to war
Clattering in chaos, clattering in fear.

As I looked up
This miserable apparition transforms into another creature
Arms first and a whole body.

Poor creature! He bemoaned being sacrificed to the gods
After the passage of his master, the *Oba*.

So, he has come to haunt the village
To waft the earth in ethereal vapors
Until his poor body of rotten corpses
Is stretched in the dunes of time.

Now I felt a bridge of light connect with the unsteady floor
Along the passage of my illuminated fears
I felt a plea upward to Heaven.

Not a carol of joy or glee
But a platoon of poor fellows
Who perished in the flickering light.

In another twinkle, he vanished
Vanished away with my blanket and pillow.

I could not mutter a word more tender
Rather than bemuse my bereft blanket and pillow
In the end, what a ghost!

Magical Realism
Poetry

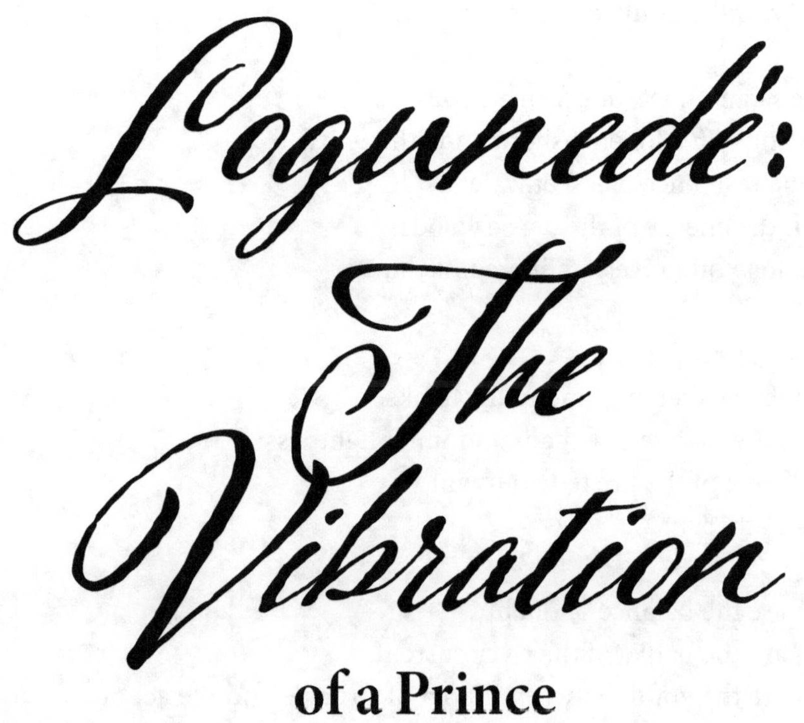

Logunedé: The Vibration
of a Prince

MARCELO MOREIRA

Y ou broke the latch of a secret door;
the mists enveloped your naked body.
They took you.

They took you to a world so fantastic and beautiful.
The world was filled with magic and love.

The sacred mist transformed you,
making you a lonely fisherman with plenty
in the resilience of sweet waters,
with the energy of the dense woods,
making you bravely an incredible hunter—

And was reborn.
Beauty was reborn among the banks,
from the meeting of chaos and inner lightness;
the flame of the fire fed your will,
Oh, Father!

You are the balance of duality.
You are the banks of the river currents.
You are the youth between the art of struggle and the act of
sacrifice,
between the latent state and the expansive mode,
following the rhythm of the sea of love stories.

A love on feverish ground.
You are gold on blue.
Your energy is free, entwined with the Source,
where there are many white flowers in the gardens of calmness,
where lightning and thunder protect your essence.

Divine.
Mystical.
Ancestral.
Cosmic.
Eternal.
Of high frequencies.
Packed by the strength of the sound waves
of the super-consciousness...

The silence...

The silence that comes from the Cosmos.
From the Cosmos,
the silence of the soul.
The energy—
Sublime
Expresses
Mind.
Supreme
of Being.

You are the Charm.
You are the enchantment of royalty in deep harmony.
Pure and infinite is the symphony of the divine Self.
A creator in space-time.
At the same time—

you become the child god.

Blood for the Wild

(poetry collection)

JASMINE HARRELL

Vow to the Sea Maid

The day it hailed was the day I saw her.
The sky was slate even before the storm.
Dark clouds swelled, an omen of destruction,
an omen to humble.
But I remained
at the port, the rising wind teasing my collar,
waiting for whatever my instinct craved.
I couldn't explain the nameless hunger
or the suddenness it seized me with.

I watched the gulls fly by, seeking shelter
from the impending weather.
The ashen waves rose and slammed into
each other like two great beasts of the sea.
Then I saw her head break the glassy surface of the water.
Though there was nothing to signify her greatness—no crown,
no beautiful jewels, no weapon—I felt compelled to kneel.

Droplets fell like rain from her curls and elegant dark face,
The brownness of her skin unbleached by the saline sea.
Then she spoke,
"Send the guilty to me."
There were no further words or instruction,
No light on the mystery of her command.
But how often had miraculous things
happened to men?
How often had a mermaid appeared to a sailor?

I gave her a salute as promise to comply,
and she sank as the hail began to fall.
I raised my hand to shield my eyes.

Who exactly were the guilty?
Could she mean those who do obscenely wicked things?
Or were they criminals of the ocean?
Those who sailed to steal, to destroy,
or those whose actions would turn it into
a massive grave where the bones of each creature
would be on display, and scavengers would gnaw on them
for marrow and salt to alleviate their hunger?
Why not all? I reasoned.
Each bore blame in some way.
They would all meet their end in that dreadful locker.

The Lavender Deer

Lavender springs from beneath its hooves.
The bent grass once
again becomes erect

and sway with their new guests.

The lavender is quickly collected

by lucky passersby fortunate to notice them.

because the lavender is blessed.

From it a draught can be brewed to give you

charge of dreams.

And whatever you imagine in them you can

bring back with you into reality.

And the blessed hooves from which this power blooms
are all brilliant gold.
Hunters and chefs have desired them
for wealth and culinary delight.
It's the ingredient of epicurean fantasy,
giving any broth the perfect flavor,
and the gold they're made of
are worth more than those the earth birthed.
It is more durable than its siblings, with a deep crimson tint.
Just as desirable is the deer's hide, its brilliant auburn fur.
The hide provides protection from poisons,
from predators who salivate at the thought of
its tender, succulent meat.
Few have consumed it, and at the end, paid a mighty
price.
For when one is caught and killed, it summons
its entire herd.
The victor must eat quickly because his time is short.
The bucks will gore him violently
with their heavy iron horns.
The does will trample his helpless
body until they break the bone, until its splinters cut his flesh.
And his marrow these beautiful creatures will eat before they

vanish amongst the trees.

Wolf Time

The hour of the wolf rises.
Skies crystalize with stars
and the moon may or may not
be at her full power, but the wolves will
prowl, wax or wane, seeking the dreaded bane
to cover the entrance to their dens. On this
they urinate to keep humanity away,
on the hope that the rite will repel the curious wanderer,
lest the curse be spread again.

The hour of the wolf rises.
Power flowing in their limbs as they flee.
At times it cannot be helped—
this lunar seduction.
There will always be those who brush away the bitter scented
flowers,
who stumble weakly into the dens,
not realizing the pain
that must follow.
The wolves are wary in their flight
to find a new home,
because they cannot know
if the curse stops with this one, or if salvation will again follow.

The hour of the wolf rises.
Those bitten were blessed by silvery teeth.
The wolves hope that—this time—
wisdom will thrive,
that suffering will teach this one humility.
In time their bones will snap,
limbs will stretch,

Jasmine Harrell

hair will flow.
Now subject to lunar metamorphosis,
the will of the wolf entombs their spirit.
The blood of the wolf is now dominant.

The hour of the world rises,
and the fresh lycanthrope romanticizes
what they've become, not mindful of the
power in their jaws, body, and claws,
seeking to rule and devour;
the victims cower.

And the wolves will howl their might to the stars,
to the dark of the moon,
to the silver radiance
glowing on their teeth,
a prayer to snatch the power back
for one more worthy to wield it.

The violence such lycanthropes deal
are dealt back upon them.
Their bones will nurse newborn cubs;
their marrow, the young of the wolves.

The hour of the wolf rises, and I'm now lulled by their
song. Sweet children of the moon.
I know better to pass by undetected,
to carry urine soaked wolfsbane as my protection,
to merely act as witness to their work.
I do not wish for the wonder of that suffering,
but they pull me ever so slightly each time to the mouth
of the den, where they wait to reshape my fate.

Kashyapa

SHENALI WIJESINGHE

Shenali Wijesinghe

This poem is a modern retelling of the famous story and myths surrounding King Kashyapa, a significant figure in Sri Lankan history.

*

Kashyapa
a prince stands before water.
stands before father
standing at the border

son,

my dear son.

it is time.

all I ask is that you
settle on the sun and
savour its way of
shifting ijnto the water. the water
singing slipping scooping runny yolk—
quivering liquid gold.

This.

this, the water that flows golden
ebbs and streams of my love
that has settled and found its way around
the stone, gushed around the bone—
this is all I have.
it is all I can give.

the prince had, in fact, always dreamed of gold.
what it must be like to peer past piles and piles of it,
plentiful, lounging on mounds on mounds—
the kind of gold you could hold,
unlike the kind slipping past the gaps of his fingers.

years and years
of longing for a legacy told
to a brother *instead* of him can drive
any man punch-drunk, wild at the seams
a kind of icarian fervour to frantically
grasp an arm,
a palm a fingertip
at a gold so blinding, burning
his skin curled into roasted
crescent moons, but all he saw
was the light fill him
because it was always *not him*

      love but *not him*

      a son but *not him*

      a father but *not his.*

the water always moves before it knows
the wind has touched it.
and the anger grows
before the prince knows of it—
body hurtling across the boarder
a father is tossed into water.

wet whirling
swirling
gushing rushing
swallows him whole,
buries his body deep into the sediment
lake to body
body to mud
nothing but a belch, a bubble,
glistening, disappearing at the surface;
a tombstone.

hurry prince, hurry
now is not the time to sit and wonder
at fever dreams and their faustian grasp on the soul.
bury it all, sink it deep, empty out the rocks
and run. keep running
running before it finds its home in the bone.

it is too late.

a scream breaks water
slaughter, slaughter!
a scream breaks water.

he falters, runs from the border,
begging the water
to hear him, see him,
understand its kin.

the blood gurglling heart and the water vagrant—
all flow erratic, emptied of direction,
of pre-destination.

to understand enough to understand repentance.
but we both know that once the water choose to flow,
only that way will it go.

I daresay the prince loved—
loved him in a kind of desperation that multiplied,
grew, one cell and then another,
till the body was host to the kind of
mutant colonizer, a dictator who thinks in shambles,
enthralled by what it wants, but not what it means,
body raptured by nothing but its desires.

sometimes love just doesn't manifest in our bodies
right. instead of warmth compounding into a home,
it becomes a kind of gnawing cold that drives any
man franctic, scared, too much love rushing to make
sense of it. the fear takes hold from the foot, stops
you from doing anything.

he spent years.
building things for a father to
hear him, see him, understand him,
arms extending,
a daily pilgrimage to keep reaching at a cloudless blue
while five claws deep,
digging, searching for ground,
sacred enough to hold the mistakes in its belly
buried beneath soil.

lionheart extracted, cut at the vein,
brick by brick, till it was a
teeth-baring, roaring monolith
crouched, clamouring for footsteps
to be devoured.
all behind rocky tall walls winding,
cocooned at the foothold.

If all is devoured, all is unknown.

But even tall walls can't hide the light; can't
stop the wind whispering patricide, all sticky cellophante that
clings on in the monsoon sweat.

A brother.

never seen but had always lived on
in a kind of conscience that can't shake it—
till his arms tripled, eyes red,
silhouette blurry.
the brain drawing as we feel it.

a brother stalks in with a vengeance.
he is the reminder, face a reminder
of all that will never be buried
beneath the soil, a sisyphusean hell of
ghosts that always live on,
stilling echoes
skittering through the shadows.

the world is better off without some things.
the unloved. a sinner. a killer.
unable to give love. able to want it.
unable to see it when it stands right in front of you.
able to feel unloved. unable to fix it.

knife to throat. skin beating gently against butterfly nerves.
everyone hushed at how he held his own head.
as it spilled into the soil.
eyes stilling, spooling,
watching earnestly.
to see that his death meant something.
meant anything.
that there was love buried somewhere in the confines
of mogallana's birdlike chest, a song ready to be cradled,
held, even for a minute, even for a second.
fill the abyss and tell it what it wanted.

tell it what it *needed.*

Ocean Salvage

(poetry collection)

DEE MAINALI

Dee Mainali

to be a seahorse father

You break the lull with the joy of a tail wag
the hardwood becoming spring grass as you bounce
into the garden,
asking about butterflies and bucket lists and other silly

things. you will not wear slippers because *the soil
is warm between the toes / imma shower / shhhh*
and again I wonder how many ants will pierce your skin
and again there are new holes in your body
and I cannot tell the difference between

the ones you did and the ones that were done to
you yet you claim it as proof of a heart, or ink, garland, tinsel, gold
trinkets festooned and stabbed and healed, yes,
but not without blood and as holey
as you are, I have never been able

to see through you, why you want to be reborn as an octopus
or fungus or frog
and not a person *but you can be a person and a fish—*
then why do seahorse
fathers give birth and then just leave?
why would you just leave something so small
and why do the babies not cling to him with their tiny hands? how

many damn names do you have, daughter, *child!*
and how many colors
can you wear at once?
you still smell the same when you hug me, you grubby
tiny creature, why is it fun to get lost

far from me? why haven't you found a permanent home smaller
than a world to tend to, why do
you fall in love with planets so alien, why is your love a comet
and why do you love so loudly in tongues—
I cannot understand.

I believe—*know*—that you are beloved for this little garden
cannot hold you but we will try
our hardest even though you will be back.
you will be back, so I will not roar,
I will ask you what you have eaten and you will look
beyond me and my marble *pearl,*
Baba self and talk about oysters, ice cream
stolen from a friend's waffle cone and the way a lover's hair
looks delicious like seaweed
and comfort rice and how you want to consume the sky
and I would let

you. you wear my nose better than me
and *Mamu's pretty voice* just as well.
you are oceans and your world is vast and swallows me whole,
but my belly will always have
space for
you.

middle part

I heard middle
parts only look good on handsome men
so I preened my hair late at night
while it was still wet
mud for sculpting

castor oil into dreamboat
sailor boy, windswept
the clock struck me at twelve
I felt the siren in my throat like
a rock unweathered

the magic only lasts as long as a dream
less than a sleep
I dreamt a kraken saw me
sleeping beauty, damsel in
distress from my window
and tossed and turned me to the
rhythm of crashing waves
til I bled like mermaid
boybait, like seafoam
lacy blade combing the ocean
and me
in the middle

of nowhere / ocean
between lost and wayward / ocean
between blood and water / ocean
between me and kraken / ocean
between us and ocean / ocean
shipwrecked in the middle

of my legs but not my hands
not my hands, I was salvaging
splinters of driftwood, flotsam
viscera, gut chum in the middle

of me / ocean
bile, name plank, figurehead
martyrs, another name plank
tentacle
inside

of me / wrangling life from
wreck
pulling man and girl and other
debris from seafoam
I woke up

wet
from my own salt, sea
legs stumbling
to the mirror
not here or there
not man or monster
all middle part.

Metaphysical

Poetry

Psychedelic Reality

(poetry collection)

ROHIT DAS

Grey cells discombobulated, arteries screaming through skin,
the melting epidermis.
Blood shod, tympanum screeching one last time before
bleeding Into the cochlea.

"Hello? This can't be!"
"Hello?"

Scrutiny turned deaf too,
baked in volcanic desire.
Veins erupting with red ink;
conscience dazed into oblivion. Some constant feeling,
uninterrupted yet re-re-resisted. I fel-felt dizzzzzzzzz-zy.

"Turned into a corpse yet?"
"Crushed cyanide? No!"

Eyelids expanding
into the contracting brain.

"I need answers!"

"Sleep!" Sedation cascading
into my pupils;
walls crushing me to a pea.

"Answers!"

Lysergic acid diethylamide.
The Dragonfly strangled me, intensifying the psychedelics.
Serotonin manipulation:
the old school drug venture. Skies suffering seizure:
ejaculated neon enveloped
my mortified groans into delirium.

"Water. I'm dopamine logged."
"No! Not methylated!"
"No! I ca-can't"

Wrapped in neon,
I swirled in the kaleidoscope
of my amorphous sins
that I snorted.
Gluttony overtook trust
as I ravaged on the edibles
my friends coaxed me into
alcohol a moment later.

Cardiac protests rallied
against the brittle ribs
swirling in the night sky.
This sudden heave of knowledge;
Universe encapsulated
my glitchy perception.
Cerebellum tripping numerically:

"01000100 01000101 01000001 01000100"

Lips drenched in poison and slime,
I drifted into a wormhole,
just to see the planet of life
poisoned just the same.
Hallucinating salvation,
shot right into the cortex,
pellets of polluted Botulinum
with disguised sapiens
veiling their bacterial carcass.

Stoned into the trip,
the planet swayed,
plastic embossed; choking
into the jinx of humanity.
Waterlogging its arterial streets,
emptied from the oceanic kidneys.
Mounting its excreta onto skin
from the urethral limbs of mankind.
The alternate reality gave way.

Reincarnation awaited
as the patterns slowed down
on the neon kaleidoscope.
Earth took over my soul.

"Blood-thirsty vengeance? Yes."
Cyanides against Botulinum.
"S-s-sleep." Unconscious.

Pupils dilated into gruesome reality,
Light reflecting toxic wounds.
Perhaps the planet spoke to me.
Revenge is what it seeks.

"No! No! The psychedelics!"
"We reside in the cerebellum!"

Regurgitating edibles,
I witnessed the human deed on my floor.
Perhaps the trip would last a while,
the man-made drug crumbling
the earthly cerebrum.
Dopamine enhanced;
swirling violence in the system.
We witness in quarantine.

"Hello? This can't be! Sapiens!"
"Hello?"

The human scrutiny uncaptured. Earth turned deaf,
drenched in a psychedelic round. None know the end.

"Hello?"

The Soul

(poetry collection)

ANNA KRISTO

Psalms 1

Killer! Monster Slayer! My Hero!
Last man standing
Agent of chaos
Savior of men
The Last Knight
Words were plenty
Meaningless they are—
them words.
Yet they overpowered
the world of men
A hero I am
A Daywalker
Hunting creatures
of the night.
Half human
Half sinister
A monster realized in full.

Hunting and killing
own brethren
Bathed in cold and
warm blood.
Born half dead
Ready to die
Walked the earth
for millennia
Prince of darkness walking
through sunlight

A thousand tears flowing
like a river behind
Saving Mankind
from its monsters
A responsibility it is
Yet the hunger
never subsides.
Twisting and turning
within me.
Eager to consume
Consume what
I swore to protect
Destroy everything
once cherished.
I was born perfect
Never to evolve
Never to perish
Never tired
Fatal in every sense.

Here I am, Evil incarnate
Raging within me
a creature of despicable nature
Blood dripping from monstrous
fangs. Bones protruding out
Creepy claws creeping
up from dark corners.

A hideous creature it is
Chained in a personal hell
It twitches, roars and curses
It is me. My dark void
My curse to bear
Daywalker I am
A Night stalker
I choose to be. Evil I am
A Hero I choose to be
I'm neither good nor bad
I'm beyond limits and
I will be avenged.

Psalms 2

Like the million starred cosmos
We gods are as many as fine dust
Just like Abraham's spawns
Uncountable in multiple forms
In times worse than what we created
I am a diminutive god
A puny god to the top guns
Yet I am king to my world
God of my Judas, Dhritarashtra
Ymir, Pandora and Hawa.
Creator of love beyond starts
Deity to the valorous and brave
Lord for peace and rulers

I rule over Christ-bearers
And the blemishless superior men
In my palm, I molded them
I observe them and enjoy
They are my favorite show
Destroying and rebuilding
Toying them if they are at peace
Like humans to ants
They merely exist for me,
In the sandbox I created
I crush them under my feet
If they make a dull play
I am omniscient, omnipotent
And omnipresent.

Psalms 3

The shadows gave birth to a vile beast
It's the serpent of doom!
The angels cried
They watched in horror
as it crawled across
the bottomless abyss.
Scales shimmering like a black sky
Eyes as deep as the ocean
Its gaze fixed upon them
Blazing venom coursing
through its blood.

Hotter than hellfire yet
benign in its veins
Its fangs ready to spit the venin out
Its jaws widening for
devouring the game whole
Hissing as it coiled
tight around its prey
Crushing its windpipe
as it injects the poison
into the bloodstream
There's no escape
from the serpent
It's the leviathan with 7 horns
The one who wiped out
the stars with its tail
and burned the earth
with its venom.

Beware of the beast they said.
The mighty serpent watches from
the shadows, ready to pounce upon the prey
Ready to kill. Ready to end everything
Beware of the snake. Be wary upon its arrival
Dread the shadows as you may never wake
Beware!

Psalms 4

It was a deep dark sleep
Snatched me from reality
Fathomless sorrow that skinned me alive
Then we met
My first glance of him
watching me silently
The shadow that craved nothing.

Reality-caused pain vanished
Fear-infiltrated illusion flourished
Strange, yet confusing
Struck by extreme caution
Looked upon by an unknown entity
Admired and relished
The shadow that craved human.

I became immobile
Like he roped me to my bed
A long moment passed
Silence grew filling
the gap that separated us
He floated to me
The shadow that craved chains.

He woke me from my trance
There ended my solitude

He never left me till date
Scares manifestation in days
Floating in my eye corner
Mute nights heated in his stare
The shadow that craved existence.

He is my nightmare
A black hole pulling me
to his cosmic dark
void sprinkled with stars
He is the mighty universal
Darkness latched to a paltry
The vast shadow that craved an atom

He tricks, taunts and teases
Jump scares are parlor tricks
Grotesque disfigured faces and
dismembered appearances
are his romantic gestures
Hallucinogenic stench is perfume
To the vast shadow that craved love.

Seasons passed
I grew old and you remained
Age made me immobile
A reminder of our first glance
You never touched me
You just existed like my fantasy
People stamped me delusional
As I craved for the vast shadow.

Psalms 5

What is a soul but magic
Revamped into the body
An enema cleansing the great empty
that resides within.
An essence of the Stardust conjured
from the depths of godhood
thrust into a frail shell of a body.

A shadow following you
up to the edge of the world
A thin borderless membrane
enveloping the vast empty
within your heart
Filling its essence
like a cup of wine
in a Viking wedding
Pouring and pouring
until the stomach lets out
a long thundering belch.

Is it the same shadow that
follows you in bright light?
The same one performing
a vanishing act in darkness
A milky way of hope that
outshines the vast dark void
within you.

Anna Kristo

What is a soul but
a shadow within you?
A mere existence of
a former life of glam and glory
A silent cry that echoes within
before you commit something
so vile and cruel.
Ignore its magnanimous presence
yet to be reminded of it
at the hour of mortality.

A shadow that shines bright
like a quasar yet darker than
the beast within
A shadow never sleeps
tireless it pursues you
to the depths of afterlife
It sheds the shell for
the light of the dust
Attaining immortality
in everlasting life
Merging with the one
never to feel separation
Never to feel alone.

A shadow never sleeps
Shadows never fade
Souls and shadows,
one and the same—
A game of contradictions.

Sacrificial Prayer

OLUGBENGA AYODEJI AYO-DANIEL

Olugbenga Ayodeji Ayo-Daniel

Upon the dirty crinkle faces
of the old familiar gods,
I pour libation.
May I be liberated
from unnecessary incapability?

On the akiitan,
my graceful stand.
Here I speak my nightmare
early, before the dawn of morning.
As the garbage forgotten here,
so I return home without my nightmare.

It's the head of a fish
that leads it out of water.
The head of snake
make way amongst thorny bushes.
May my own head be propitious
like that of the immaculate egret.

Unseen as water
finds its way into the coconut,
so will my ways be hidden
from my impatient enemies.
May they come impuissant
in their strength and
innocuous in their passion.

Onto the cardinals
of this monstrous earth
bespeak I my supplications,
and from its roominess plead I
answers to my prayers.

Akiitan – a dump; rubbish heap

What If....

AKUPUE CHUKWUEMEKA

Akupue Chukwuemeka

What If...?

Sauntering the streets of my illusion
Leveraged by the force of thoughts of my existence
The birds in their *au naturel* habitats
Soothingly aided the aura of tranquillity
With their ever-melodious syrinx
I gazed every activity of mortals
In my illusionary being
I contemplated the thoughts of my fellow erect-standing sapiens
In my transfixed existence
I walked through their hearts
Materials of ambivalence were forged
Delivering both their good and bad sides like the two-edged sword
Weapons of war were meant for peace
Of death for life's protection
Of hate for love
Out of their river banks
Emanated peace and war
Love and hate
Happiness and sorrow
Wisdom and folly
Knowledge and sorrow
Mastery and servitude.
Like the Peregrines peregrinates the flesh of its prey
So they ravage their fellow
As the Lion lies in wait for the unlucky
So they ensnare the unlucky mortals
All for reasons best known to them.

In my ever interrogating illusion
An ambiguous conundrum
What if..?
What if the universe never existed?
What if we were never in existence?
What if our existence had been an illusionary drawing?
What if the life itinerary had been our movement in our dreams?
What if we have been living in nature's fraud?
What if we were not a product of "bang" big or small?
What if we never had an ancestor?
What if we have been living on anecdotes?
What if the universe never birthed us?
What if all wished, that came to pass,
were only in our imaginations?
What if all technologies and inventions were
mere phantasmagorical fantasy of a non-existent mind?
What if all that we felt we can't live without
are pictures of the mind's video games?
What if all weapons, wars, music, languages were mere mirages?
What if we have been viewing this entity from a distant cosmos?
What if the mother earth had been void, shapeless, and
without form?
What if our fears are our dreadful experiences from
our rudimentary cosmological dormitory?
What if we do not actually belong to "our world?"
What if we have not been living in this world?
What if our strife, sorrow, agony, pain, and happiness
were just the heartbeat of our real selves?
What if there's no future?

Akupue Chukwuemeka

What if we, one day, wake from our box illusion?
And the main conundrum—
What if death actually means waking up from our illusion?
Perchance, it might be funny to the strong minded
It may be disastrous to the weaklings
But in all,
The "waking up" might favour some
It may be austere to others
The fact remains, in all we do
The paramount consideration should be the phrase
What if..?

Meet the Authors

E. Doyle-Gillespie
Grand Prize Winner of the Iridescence Award

E. Doyle-Gillespie, the grand prize winner of the *Iridescence Award*, is the author of *The Actual Price of Her Bangles and Other Poems*. This haunting poetry collection weaves themes of history, identity, and resilience. Through vivid imagery and lyrical narratives, the poems explore African diasporic folklore, cultural memory, and the enduring echoes of oppression. From the Middle Passage to contemporary struggles, each piece captures voices of defiance, transformation, and spiritual reclamation, merging personal and collective journeys. Doyle-Gillespie bridges the past and present, offering a poignant reflection on survival, liberation, and the unyielding power of remembrance. The award-winning poet also writes short fiction. He serves in law enforcement and enjoys literature, martial arts, travel, and fitness in his recreational time.

Jack Wolflink
Winner of the Amplify Award

Jack Wolflink, winner of the Amplify Award, wrote "The Winnower," featured within this anthology. He has joined the Kinsman Quarterly team as the intern project coordinator for the Winds of Asia Award. A biracial Filipinx writer, he holds an M.A. in Creative Writing from Wilkes University and an M.A. in Environmental Geography from San Francisco State University. Jack writes literary, speculative, and science fiction. His short stories have been featured in Suspect Journal and the Lighthouse Community Anthology. Jack enjoys hiking, painting, cheap video games and expensive board games.

Christina Tang-Bernas
Iridescence Award: 1st Runner Up
For the Love of Death

Country of Residence: United States
Occupation: copyeditor
Writing Genres: fiction, poetry, nonfiction
Alma Mater: University of California, Irvine
Interests: reading, taking classes, and research

Nicholas Samuel Stember
Iridescence Award: 2nd Runner Up
Residual Effects

Country of Residence: Faroe Islands
Occupation: IT Tech Support
Writing Genres: Science Fiction, Fantasy and Horror
Alma Mater: University of Massachusetts, Rutgers, Thomas Edison State University
Interests: gaming, music, and theater

Adrian Hayes: *Light in the Dark*

Country of Residence: United States

Occupation: ELA teacher

Writing Genres: horror, fantasy, and adventure

Alma Mater: St. Clair College

Interests: cycling, video games, gardening, and photography

Akupue Chukwuemeka: *What If....?*

Country of Residence: Nigeria

Occupation: student

Writing Genres: poetry and fiction

Alma Mater: University of Nigeria, Nsukka

Interests: writing and football

Anna Kristo: *The Psalms of Darkness: The Soul*

Country of Residence: Canada

Occupation: retail manager

Writing Genres: dark fiction

Alma Mater: Mahatma Gandhi University

Interests: reading, YouTube content creation, and podcasting

Ann Yuan: *The Last Blood Moon*

Country of Residence: United States
Occupation: part-time staff in SWR school district, NY
Writing Genres: speculative and literary fiction
Alma Mater: Huazhong University of Science and Technology
Interests: movies and traveling

D. M. Cross: *Dance With Me*

Country of Residence: United States
Writing Genres: sci-fi, fantasy, non-fiction
Writing Goals: complete and publish stories and sell developed screenplays.
Interests: teaching film appreciation; sewing, gardening and history

D'Marcus Beatty: *Unforgettable*

Country of Residence: United States
Occupation: radiology tech
Writing Genres: science fiction and Christian fiction
Alma Mater: Fayetteville State University
Interests: writing, gaming, exercise

DW: *The Phantom Eye*

Country of Residence: Ghana
Occupation: student
Writing Genres: fantasy, paranormal, adventure and fiction
Alma Mater: Central University
Interests: swimming, sketching, and designing

Dee Mainali: *Ocean Salvage*

Country of Residence: United States
Occupation: writer
Writing Genres: poetry, speculative fiction, science fiction, nonfiction, folklore, and fanfiction
Alma Mater: Princeton University
Interests: surrealist art, healthcare reform, and impromptu picnics

Douglas Perenara Johnston: *A Day Lost in Time*

Country of Residence: New Zealand
Writing Genres: historical fiction, sci-fi, fantasy, and horror
Writing Goals: to publish his own book
Alma Mater: University of Otago
Interests: reading, fishing, outdoors, art, writing

G. R. Betancourt: *Interbreed*

Country of Residence: United States
Occupation: real estate agent
Writing Genres: thriller, suspense, mystery, drama
Alma Mater: University of North Florida
Interests: food, writing, music, and gaming

Gaazal Dhungana: *Memento Mori...*

Country of Residence: United Kingdom
Occupation: student
Writing Genres: poetry

Alma Mater: King's College London
Interests: reading fiction, doing henna, and writing

Grace Aliyu: *Handwritten*

Country of Residence: Nigeria
Occupation: student
Writing Genres: spiritual, fiction, and comical

Alma Mater: Bowen University
Interests: writing, long walks, and board games

Ihsan Sim: *Last Heart*

Country of Residence: Singapore
Occupation: student
Writing Genres: sci-fi, horror, supernatural
Alma Mater: National University of Singapore
Interests: writing, Brazilian jiu-jitsu, and model scenery

Jasmine Harrell: *Blood for the Wild*

Country of Residence: United States
Occupation: technical writer
Writing Genres: science fiction, horror, and fantasy

Alma Mater: Bowie State University.
Interests: reading, writing, and drawing

Joseph Marcel Ikhenoba: *The Earth's Supernatural*

Country of Residence: Nigeria
Occupation: writer
Writing Genres: poetry
Alma Mater: University of Nigeria Nsukka and University of Lagos
Interests: voluntary community service, sporting, researching, travelling, and cooking.

Klarissa Conner: *The Legend of Kuri*

Country of Residence: United States
Occupation: freelance writer
Writing Genres: romance, fantasy, thrillers, and horror.
Alma Mater: California State University San Bernardino
Interests: writing, painting, music, and yoga

Liz Johnston: *I Can Talk to Dead People*

Country of Residence: United States
Occupation: storytelling manager
Writing Genres: poetry and nonfiction

Alma Mater: Loyola University and Louisiana State University
Interests: writing, walking, and pop culture enthusiast

Lindsey Woodward: *Harvest of the Blood Moon*

Country of Residence: United States
Occupation: medical transcription (assistant supervisor)
Writing Genres: fantasy (urban and high)
Alma Mater: Auburn University
Interests: embroidery and reading genre switched parodies

Marcelo Moreira: *Logunedé: The Vibration of a Prince*

Country of Residence: Brazil
Occupation: actor
Writing Genres: poetry
Writing Goals: to become an internationally recognized poet and author
Interests: singing and acting

Michelle Ivy Alwedo: *Once a Home...*

Country of Residence: Ireland
Occupation: writer
Writing Genres: poetry

Alma Mater: Makerere University Business School
Interests: photography, bird watching, kitchen magic (cooking)

Micah Stanton: *Blink of an Eye*

Country of Residence: United States
Occupation: security guard/sales
Writing Genres: science fiction, speculative fiction, and mind bending thrillers
Writing Goals: be published by age 25
Interests: study religion, philosophy, technology, and playing volleyball

Odette Cortés: *Ordinary Conjurings*

Country of Residence: Mexico
Occupation: college instructor
Writing Genres: poetry, fiction, and nonfiction
Alma Mater: Universidad Nacional Autónoma de México
Interests: painting, sculpting, photography, reading, and writing

Olugbenga Ayodeji Ayo-Daniel: *Sacrificial Prayer*

Country of Residence: Nigeria
Occupation: Entrepreneur, Information Technology
Writing Genres: poetry, fiction, nonfiction, and playwriting
Writing Goals: win the Nobel Prize for literature

Rohit Das: *Psychedelic Reality*

Country of Residence: India
Occupation: student
Writing Genres: science fiction, drama, geopolitical/equality, and romance
Alma Mater: University of Calcutta
Interests: singing, debating, coin collecting, and drawing

Sandhya Barlaas: *Tales of True Love and Madness*

Country of Residence: Pakistan/UK
Occupation: Kinsman Quarterly
Assistant Editor
Writing Genres: YA fantasy and
historical fiction
Writing Goals: to be a published author
Interests: reading, writing, and learning
new languages

Shantell Powell: *The Tupilaq*

Country of Residence: Canada
Occupation: writer, artist, storyteller
Writing Genres: fiction, creative
nonfiction, poetry, and playwriting
Alma Mater: University of New
Brunswick, Saint Thomas University,
Simon Fraser University, and Yale
University

Shenali Wijesinghe: *Kashyapa*

Country of Residence: Singapore
Occupation: marketing executive
Writing Genres: poetry and fiction

Alma Mater: Yale-NUS in Singapore
Interests: reading, painting, and film
photography

Shilpa Kamat: *Aghnashini's Secret*

Country of Residence: United States
Occupation: teacher/writer
Writing Genres: poetry, fiction, hybrid and experimental, novels-in-verse
Alma Mater: Carleton College, New College of CA, and Mills College (MFA)
Interests: hiking, cooking, yoga, and ecomythography,

Solape Adeyemi: *Shaman & Other Poems*

Country of Residence: Nigeria
Occupation: creative writer
Writing Genres: poetry and fiction

Alma Mater: University of Lagos and Lagos State University
Interests: poetry, action movies, and environmental sustainability

Stephanie Chiedo: *Ghost poems*

Country of Residence: Nigeria
Occupation: public relations writer
Writing Genres: sci-fi, supernatural, crime/detective, rom-com
Alma Mater: Université Protestant De L'afrique De L'ouest, Porto- Novo, Benin
Interests: adventures, traveling, and pop music

Stingray Hopper:
Dan and the Continuum...

Country of Residence: United States
Occupation: product manager
Writing Genres: science fiction and literary fiction
Alma Mater: University of Southern California
Interests: playing tennis, hiking, robotics, quantum physics and chemistry

Victoria Sosa:
Some Men Are Dogs

Country of Residence: United States
Writing Genres: fiction, poetry, screenwriting
Alma Mater: Loyola University
Interests: philosophy, fashion, global politics, and anthropology

www.ingramcontent.com/pod-product-compliance
Lightning Source LLC
Chambersburg PA
CBHW060427310726
48977CB00001B/83